How to Be an American Housewife

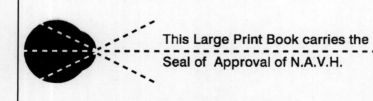

This Large Print Book carries the Seal of Approval of N.A.V.H.

How to Be an American Housewife

Margaret Dilloway

THORNDIKE PRESS
A part of Gale, Cengage Learning

Detroit • New York • San Francisco • New Haven, Conn • Waterville, Maine • London

30.99

GALE
CENGAGE Learning™

Thorndike Press® Large Print Basic.
The text of this Large Print edition is unabridged.
Other aspects of the book may vary from the original edition.
Set in 16 pt. Plantin.

LIBRARY OF CONGRESS CATALOGING-IN-PUBLICATION DATA

Dilloway, Margaret.
   How to be an American housewife / by Margaret Dilloway.
      p. cm. — (Thorndike Press large print basic)
      ISBN-13: 978-1-4104-3276-6
      ISBN-10: 1-4104-3276-9
      1. Mothers and daughters—Fiction. 2. Large type books. I.
Title.
PS3604.I4627H68 2010b
813'.6—dc22   2010033727

Published in 2010 by arrangement with G. P. Putnam's Sons, a member of Penguin Group (USA) Inc.

Printed in the United States of America
1 2 3 4 5 6 7 14 13 12 11 10

FOR MY MOTHER, SUIKO O'BRIEN,
1932–1994

PART ONE:
JACARANDA STREET

Once you leave Japan, it is extremely unlikely that you will return, unless your husband is stationed there again or becomes wealthy.

Take a few reminders of Japan with you, if you have room. Or make arrangements to write to a caring relative who is willing to send you letters or items from your homeland. This can ease homesickness.

And be sure to tell your family, "Sayonara."

— from the chapter "Turning American," in TAMIKO KELLY AND JUN TANAKA, *How to Be an American Housewife* (1955)

ONE

I had always been a disobedient girl.

When I was four, we lived in a grand house with a courtyard and a koi fishpond. My father worked as a lawyer and we were still rich, rich enough to have beautiful silk dresses and for me to have dolls with real hair and porcelain faces, not the corn-husk dolls I played with later.

We even had a nanny to help my mother. One day, Nanny told me she was taking my baby brother and me on a picnic. We walked for what seemed like miles, until my small feet were blistered. In those days, people expected more from a four-year-old than they do now.

"Where are we going?" I asked Nanny.

"To rest from the heat," she said. "By a pond."

I did not like Nanny. I didn't trust how she eyed my brother, Taro, like he was the last bowl of rice. She always hugged him

9

tight, so tight he wailed, like she wanted to absorb him into her body. She had never had a son of her own, only daughters. Sometimes she called Taro "my little peach," like he was the peach boy out of the old fairy tale, granted as a wish to the old woman.

I told my mother that Nanny made me uncomfortable. She dismissed it as the whining of a spoiled child. "You don't like Nanny because she makes you behave," Mother said. "Now go with her. I have business in town, and your father is busy, too."

Nanny was old and had a crippled leg; she moved slowly. We stopped by a tree-shaded pond to play and have lunch. Afterward, in the high-noon heat, she took us under a willow tree to nap. Day turned to night. I awoke with a start to see the moon rising above the fields. "Where are we?" I asked.

"Shush," Nanny said soothingly, smoothing my bangs back. "We're going on a trip to my hometown." She looked down the road as though waiting for someone, or something. Her eyes glittered black onyx in the dim light. Taro began wailing and Nanny stuck a bottle into his mouth. "Go back to sleep, Shoko-chan."

Something was not right. We had missed

supper. Mother didn't allow us to stay outside past dark. I stood. "You take us home right now!" I screamed.

"Sit down, sit down," Nanny said, trying to push on my shoulders. "You bad girl, listen to Nanny."

"No!" I kicked her in the shin as hard as I could, then pushed Taro's pram back up the road. I knew the way home, even though it was far.

Nanny's hand grabbed my arm and she lifted me up. Now she looked like a terrible witch, her wiry white hair free of her scarf, her jagged teeth bared like a wolf. "We're going on a trip. You must listen to Nanny!"

I bit her hand, bearing down hard in desperation. She yowled and dropped me. I stood up and pushed Taro away again.

This time she didn't follow. I looked back once and saw her standing in the middle of the road, holding her hand. Taro wailed.

Mother and Father were outside the wall of our house, looking left and right. They'd sent servants out looking for us. When they heard Taro, they ran to meet us. "Where have you been?" Mother cried, sweeping me up. Father cradled Taro to his face. Taro quieted.

"I told you she was no good!" I said, and recounted what had happened.

Some mothers would have not believed their child, but mine did. Mother said she had tried to steal us. Or, at the very least, steal my brother. Who knows what she would have done with me. "If it weren't for Shoko," Mother would retell visitors, shaking her head, *"Ai!"*

I was a hero. All because I wouldn't listen.

Within a year or so after that, Father tired of dealing with bad people in his business. "Too much cheating," he told my mother. "All anyone cares about is money. Money is God."

He was always so busy. Perhaps he felt guilty that a nanny had almost made off with his children. He decided to sell the house and his practice and become a priest in the Konkokyo, the Konko Church.

In 1859, there was a Japanese village where people feared a god called Konjin, who brought misfortune. One farmer named Kawate Bunji had a streak of bad luck. Once when Bunji fell very ill, he was visited by the god Konjin, who told him that people shouldn't fear him, that he was good, and that his real name was Tenchi Kane no Kami, "One True God of Heaven and Earth." When Bunji became well, word of his visit from Konjin spread. People came to the farmer Bunji for help, and Tenchi Kane no Kami would speak through him. Bunji's name became Konkokyo Daijin, and he became a god, too. The Konko Church was born.

Mother never made a word of complaint when Father became a priest. Instead, she sold the house and all of our fine possessions, bargaining a more than fair price — "It goes to the church and brings you honor, what more could you wish?" she told the buyer. She let me keep one doll, my Shirley Temple with curly hair Father had bought in Tokyo, the one that melted later when I left it too close to the fireplace.

We moved to a tiny house with dirt floors covered by tatami mats. It was near the church in Ueki where my father would serve as priest. My sister, Suki, who was born that year, never knew a different life. I think that was why she was such a happy person. Or maybe it was because our parents never acted differently, rich or poor. Mother always made arrangements of flowers to brighten the room. We celebrated the festivals, with a little less feasting. Only I, with my memories of dolls and dresses, felt resentment.

Taro and I always played together. We were good friends until it began to bother

Taro that I could hit a ball farther than he could, or climb a higher tree, or beat him in every race.

When Father decided I was too old to be a tomboy, around age thirteen, he made me take dance lessons, like all young ladies did. I did what my father told me to do. I was disobedient, not foolish. I learned how to flip open a fan with a flick of my wrist, peering over it at the audience. I also learned the shamisen, which was a little harp. The teacher said I was a beauty, and very talented. I didn't quite believe her until I saw how the men watched me at our talent show.

I came onstage in my beautiful silk kimono and red lips as my teacher played her shamisen. The bulbs shone in my eyes, but I would not squint. I lowered my gaze and snapped open my fan as I launched into the dance.

I heard an intake of breath from the men. I looked up and saw their admiring gazes fixed on me. I blushed, and kept on, knowing that wherever I went onstage their stares would follow. The other girls became invisible. I had more power in dance than I did at baseball.

I understood then that my skills in school or in sports would not make my life come about in the way I wished. I took my bows

14

at that recital, vowing I would learn what I needed and make the best marriage possible.

The war had changed my life's direction from East to West. I heard about Pearl Harbor from my father. I was in third grade. Father, a priest in a religion that believed in peace, was worried. "America is so big," he fretted. "They will destroy us."

Mother reassured him. "If the Emperor says we will win, it will be fine. Japan is mighty."

Father seemed to be the only one around who questioned the Emperor. Everyone else thought we would triumph easily and show the West how strong we were. Even Father dared not bad-mouth the Emperor in public. The Emperor was supposed to be a god, and to say anything to the contrary could land you in prison.

At first, the war stayed far away, something we knew only from the radio. Then we began having blackouts and sirens. We built shelters in the hillsides to hide in when the planes came.

"Why would they bother with a country-side village, with no targets except chickens?" Father said.

But they did. One night, the alarms went

off and we blacked out our windows so the planes wouldn't have easy targets. "It's just a drill," Father told us. We didn't bother to go out to the shelters.

But then we heard a great roar, the bombers overhead.

A blast rumbled the house. Something had been destroyed. At first light, I went outside. Our neighbor, Mrs. Miyama, and her little boy had been using their outhouse, and the light had been a beacon. Just like that, they were gone.

Another time, Taro, Suki, and I were walking to school. It was fall, the air just turning cold, the sky still gray. We had on our navy-blue-and-white school uniforms, our nice shoes that we could wear only to school. I remember that Taro's hair was slicked down as flat as Mother could get it.

Our road went through farmland, a country road with country people, nothing of any significance. Nothing that the Americans should bother with. Suddenly we heard the roar again. It was deafening. Suki stopped and clapped her hands over her ears. Father had told me what to do.

"Drop!" I ordered, pulling my sister to the ground and falling on top of her. Taro fell, too.

There were popping noises and the brown

dirt in front of us lifted. We were being shot at. Three little children. I put my head down and prayed that we would be all right. The plane flew past and I started to get up.

The noise returned as the plane turned around. "It's coming back!" Taro yelled. He grabbed my arm, I grabbed Suki's arm, and we jumped over an embankment into an irrigation ditch at the side of the road. I looked up and saw the pilot and the plane as it came low. It had a star on its side, a skull and crossbones on the tail, and a half-naked woman painted near the front. The pilot saw me and laughed. He had been playing with us, scaring us. If he had wanted to, he could have killed us. That was the first time I ever saw an American.

Suki's face and body were muddy, and she was wailing. I took a chunk of mud out of her pigtails. Taro stood up and kicked at the dirt embankment, causing a slew of pebbles to fall down. He shook his fist toward the plane. "We will kill you all!" he shouted. "American fiends!"

I had not thought of this story for years.

I sat up on the couch in my San Diego living room, where I had been napping. Bright morning light made the room uncomfortably warm.

When I had told this story to my daughter, Sue, when she was still young enough to ask for stories, she had looked at me as if I were telling a grim fairy tale. "Why would they do that?" she had whispered, her eyes big.

"Those stories scare her," my husband, Charlie, had said. "The past is past."

He was right. And so I hardly talked about my past at all to my daughter. It was a lifetime ago. I had grown tired of my own stories, even of my old dreams. What good did dreams do me now? When you are young, dreams are the reason you pray for a new year and better luck.

Except for this. This one small dream of mine.

Taro and I together again.

I got a piece of tissue-thin airmail stationery and my husband's fountain pen out of the desk drawer. Sitting down on the floor at the coffee table, I put the pen to my lips, thinking. From the garage, Charlie sang as he put laundry in the washer. One of my adult son Mike's cats meowed at the screen door. I began my letter to Taro.

Many American husbands enjoy traditional aspects of Japanese culture, including the o-furo and the massage.

American husbands expect their Wives to be well-versed in massage as a Japanese tradition. Many men find that a small Japanese wife is an asset when she walks on his back after a long, tiring day.

Often when a Japanese person begins consuming Western foods, they become fat. Do not overindulge. It is important to keep oneself at a light enough weight so that the husband's back is uninjured.

The o-furo may also be enjoyed by your husband. Offering to scrub his back as you would with a Japanese spouse is likely to be welcomed. It is a small piece of service you may offer to him.

— from the chapter "A Map to Husbands,"
How to Be an American Housewife

Two

I carried the letter into my bedroom, pushing the door shut with my shoulder. We had lived here for over thirty years, and still this bedroom door was not fixed. I looked about for a place to hide the letter. Not that my husband, Charlie, was nosy, but he always thought of reasons to say no to me.

I stuck the note into my underwear drawer in the dresser. I met the eyes of the two Japanese samurai dolls in their glass case on top of the bureau. The man had a sword, and the girl had a tiny metal knife tucked into her kimono sleeve. A secret weapon no one saw. Underneath their case I had a secret of my own.

I opened the little glass door and lifted out the dolls, then lifted up a hidden compartment. Inside that was my *hesokuri,* my secret money. I'd been pinching pennies all these years. Stealing out of Charlie's change jar, saving bits of our tax refunds and

Charlie's Navy retirement checks. Now I had a lot. Enough to go to Japan. I touched the cash and smiled.

Then I opened my closet to decide what to wear to see my cardiologist, Dr. Cunningham. Lately, I had been seeing him too much, getting tests and medications. My heart was giving out, and other things along with it. Last summer, I'd gotten Bell's palsy, paralyzing my face's right side for a week. I got a patch, like a pirate, so my eye wouldn't dry out. People crossed the street when they saw me coming. Once, they would have crossed the street to look at me.

"I ugly now," I said to Charlie more than once, just to hear him tell me I was beautiful.

He didn't disappoint. "You're beautiful still, Shoko."

"Why this happen?" I asked.

"No one knows," he said. "Only God."

Only God. I prayed to *kamisama,* not God, as my parents had raised me. I sighed and took out a pair of slacks I had worn the previous week, wondering if Dr. Cunningham would recognize them.

Unlike many of the new doctors at Balboa Naval Medical Center, where the doctors who just graduated from medical school go for training, Dr. Cunningham seemed to

21

know what was going on.

I liked Dr. Cunningham. He looked just like Tyrone Power, a movie star I had loved when I was young. And he was single! If I had been young and single, I could have gotten him for sure. When I was in my teens, I'd been the prettiest girl around. High defined cheekbones, Cupid's bow of a full mouth, shiny blue-black hair, and pale white skin, like a baby's. I had an hourglass shape even with no girdle — a full bust, tiny waist (twenty-two inches), and womanly bottom. Men chased me from the time I turned twelve. And I enjoyed it, though being a nice girl, I shouldn't have.

My own daughter was as enchanting, if not more so. She didn't have short Japanese legs like I did. Her limbs were long and lean, her neck and fingers graceful. Eurasians were exotic, and men liked that, too. Sue could have had anyone, if she'd only waited for college before finding a husband, instead of marrying the first boy who came along. Which did not last, as I knew it would not.

I said to Dr. Cunningham, "My daughter could marry anyone, you know. Rich businessman love her."

And then Dr. Cunningham said, "If she's half as lovely as you, Mrs. Morgan, I'm

22

missing out." He was so nice!

I picked up the phone by the bed now and dialed Sue's cell phone, hoping she wouldn't see my number and let it go to voice mail. I held my breath, waiting. She picked up. "What's up, Mom?" She sounded artificially cheerful. I imagined her sitting at her desk, twirling her dark brown hair around one finger, her pale face greenish in the light from her computer screen.

"Suiko-chan. You wanna take me doctor today?" I asked. "Got appointment after lunchtime."

I heard her carefully repressed sigh. "Is Dad busy?"

"Don't know. Maybe so." I couldn't tell her that Charlie had taken me yesterday and the day before that. I didn't want to worry her.

"I have a meeting, Mom." Sue was a manager at a financial services firm. Her voice turned brisk. "Are you still trying to get me to meet your doctor?"

I was glad she couldn't see the surprise on my face. If I could have, I would have chosen a husband for Sue. Sue needed someone already established, who had done all the hard work already. She needed someone to take care of her, so the dark circles under her eyes would go away.

Dr. Cunningham would be perfect. But in America, they find husbands themselves. I had found Charlie myself, almost American-style, and maybe I would have done things differently if I could go back.

"He's not interested, Mom," Sue said, her voice so flat it made my heart ache even more. "He's being polite. What's he supposed to say? Don't bother the man."

"But you need *see* this guy. If I you, I grab him up! Single doctor won't last long." I tried to keep my voice light, but my daughter didn't understand. A single doctor really wouldn't last long.

Sue snorted. "Mom, please. I can find my own man."

But she couldn't.

I heard what she was saying. *Stay out of my life.* I sat for a moment in silence. *I am writing a letter to your uncle now,* I wanted to tell her. *I am going to Japan. Don't you want to know?* I wanted to tell her so much more.

Dr. Cunningham had told me my heart was getting flabby, which meant it wasn't working well. He wanted me to have surgery with a specialist. They would cut a wedge out and make it smaller. "It's risky, but not as risky as a transplant," he had said.

"Fine," I had said. It took them months to schedule anything. I'd be to Japan and back before the first pre-op appointment.

"Is there something else, Mom?" Sue was trying to sound patient but not succeeding.

I tried to think quickly of something that would make her want to come with me. My daughter was too sensitive, too fast to hear criticism. Perhaps it was partially my fault.

I did not have the knack of subtlety. When she was a college sophomore, Sue had come to me while I was in my bedroom one afternoon. She squeaked the door closed, her face so pale, even in the golden light coming in from the west, that I thought she was ill. She sat on my side of the bed, next to the photo of my parents. "What's a matter you, Suiko-chan?" I asked her.

"Craig and I are going to move in together," she whispered.

I was shocked. I shouted at her. "You do that," I said, "and we no pay college no more! You bring shame on us." In my town, my family would never have been able to show their faces again if I had done something so scandalous.

Sue had looked around. "Shame from whom? We don't have any family here. The neighbors don't care." The afternoon sun made her hair glint red. "Besides, you're hardly paying anything. I have a ton of loans."

"I no can hold my head up." I was really hoping this would make her ditch Craig.

She had sighed. Nineteen years old, she was at the peak of her beauty. She thought her beauty would go on forever. The way I thought mine would. She needed to find someone better while she still could. "Then it's Plan B. We're getting married."

"Marry?" I closed my eyes and changed my tactics. My lovely daughter could not marry this person, the first boy she'd ever kissed. I had told her that you should only kiss if you were going to get married, but that was to keep her from being a slut. I never thought she'd take it so seriously. "Why you gonna marry same guy you drag around high school? That's why we send college. Find good man marry."

"There's nothing wrong with Craig." Sue's voice rose in anger.

She was right. There was nothing wrong with him. Except he would make a lousy husband. Too flighty, too artistic. High-maintenance. Maybe in twenty years he'd be ready. "Sue," I pleaded.

"Don't worry. I'll be out of your hair in a week," she spat, leaving the house. "I won't shame you anymore." The next weekend, she was in Vegas. Too young to drink but

26

old enough to get married. And to have a baby.

I never said a bad word about Craig again, no matter what he did or how he acted.

Sue thought differently than I did, and I didn't understand her. Sometimes I thought I had chased her out of the house too soon, been too hard on her the way I had been too easy on her brother. It seemed both parenting methods had failed.

On the line with my daughter, I heard another beep. "Mom, my boss is calling me," Sue said. "Is there anything else you needed?"

It wasn't the right time to tell her everything. Not on the phone. "Go, then." I hung up. I suspected her boss wasn't on the phone, that she was simply tired of listening to her old mother. But she couldn't keep the honcho waiting.

I got dressed. In my bedroom, I had crammed pieces of Japan everywhere, all covered up. There was a hand-painted folding screen by the closet, wrapped in black trash bags. Scrolls and fans were in boxes in the closet. I didn't want anything to be ruined by the light, not until I could take them out again. When the kids took their junk out of the other bedrooms, I would make a Japanese room.

These things used to be displayed, treasured. When Charlie first brought me from Japan to Norfolk, I decorated our home to the best of my ability, with my Japanese furniture that Charlie and I had taken equal delight in picking out and that the Navy had shipped over: the Japanese screen painted with a waterfall and peacocks; ink-painted scrolls; statues of badgers and lions; and silk satin floor cushions I'd made. We had a sofa, too, but no one used it. With Mike a baby, the floor was more convenient.

Once a week, I'd go to the park and clip whatever foliage and flowers I could find, arranging them in the Japanese way on the sideboard. A tall piece, a medium-size piece, and a small, all designed to suggest nature.

We had lived in a small two-bedroom town house with floors so crooked, you could roll a Coke can from one end to the other. Charlie was getting ready to ship out for at least a year, and it would be just me and the baby.

Charlie's relatives lived in Maryland, and they came to visit a few times. His mother, Millie, a stout woman who had borne eight children in ten years, was so encouraging that I thought all Americans would be like her. "Don't you marry her and then get rid of her like everybody else," she took Charlie aside and warned. Many Japanese women who married servicemen got abandoned when they got to the States and they found out how hard it was to live in a biracial marriage. Even more got left back in Japan, pregnant and unmarried.

"Don't worry," Charlie said.

"You call if you need anything, and I'll get someone to take me here," his mother said every time she left.

"Yes, Mother." I knew I would never bother her.

When she visited, she would bring me practical things, like boxes of tissue or a frying pan. I was grateful, but not when she looked around our small apartment.

It was different from her house, where nobody took off their shoes and they would rather use bricks and boards for shelving than spend money on furniture, and the only decorations were pictures of Jesus. If she had flowers, she stuck them all in a vase so big you couldn't see the other person at the table.

"This is all so fancy," Millie said every time she visited, trying to understand but not succeeding.

This way of living was the only way I knew. I couldn't live in a space without having something lovely to look at. Even when my parents were poor, they could still trim a pine bush outside into a bonsai. I imagined Millie went home and talked about how Charlie's wife spent all his money on unimportant clutter.

Charlie enjoyed Japanese art, though. I tried to teach him *sumi-e* brush painting, but no matter how much he practiced, his paintings looked like rudimentary stick figures. "How you get a few strokes to look like a deer — you're a genius," he said to me.

I only knew what a "genius" was from his awed tone. "Try again."

"There's only room for one genius here." He had three of my paintings matted and framed, and they hung in a trio on the wall.

Adjusting to the U.S. was difficult in other ways for me, especially in the beginning. If I borrowed an egg from a neighbor, I returned two, the Japanese way. They didn't understand; why did I give them two? It made them angry, like I was insulting them. When you "borrowed" an egg or a cup of sugar in America, you never actually returned it. Charlie had to explain: "It's her tradition."

"Never heard of a tradition like that," our neighbors said.

When Charlie wasn't home to explain my odd ways to people, I went to the store alone, with Mike bundled up in a thousand layers in his stroller. I made sure to dress up. My favorite outfit was a pencil skirt, button-up black blouse with white pipe trim, and heels. It wasn't the most comfortable thing to take care of a child in, but I was young and didn't care. I wanted to look presentable, not like a maid or a Jap with buckteeth and wild hair, but an American girl.

As I walked the two blocks from housing to the store, people stopped and stared, whispering, "There goes that Jap wife!" I smiled and waved, even when mothers held their children against them. A few of them stopped me, said hello, wanted to touch my hair, so much coarser than theirs. "Like horsehair!" they exclaimed.

I reminded myself that the Japanese had done the same thing with Charlie and his fire-red hair. "There goes the demon!" they had whispered. Certainly I could take it.

I kept my head high and said, "Hello!" I had practiced my *l* sounds in the mirror before I ever left Japan. It didn't matter whether people said hello back or not. I was holding up my end. What they did was their own business.

I swung my legs up onto the bed and massaged my ankle, wishing I could run for miles, like Sue could. I remembered how it felt not to get winded. When I was a kid, I had been a real tomboy. "Stay inside, Shoko," Father had said to me. "Your skin will get dark."

But I loved to play baseball, and I hit the ball better than the boys. I still loved baseball today. I watched every game I could on television, making Charlie grumble. He hated sports. I hated being indoors, but now allergies and the sun bothered me too much to spend time outside.

Once, when I was little, I sneaked out to the field where my brother played ball with his friends. "Go home and do the laundry, Shoko," Taro yelled at me when he saw me. His friends laughed and Taro drew himself up taller than he was, which was still half a head shorter than me. His black hair poked out crazily from under his ball cap; Taro had an unfortunate double-helix cowlick on the crown of his head. "We don't want girls messing up our game."

I couldn't let my little brother speak that way to me, especially in front of his older friend, Tetsuo, who always looked at me in a sly way and winked. I squared my shoulders. "I bet you your *manju* that I hit a home run." Our mother was making the steamed sweet bean cakes. Treats were getting fewer these days, so this was a bet of the utmost seriousness.

Of course I did hit a homer. Tetsuo and the other boys hooted and hollered. And Taro ran home and told our father, who beat me with a willow stick. "For being better than a boy?" I had shouted at him as he did it.

"For disobedience," Father had said, giving me an extra whack for talking back. Father, a tall and skinny scholar with glasses falling down his nose, hardly had the heart to give me a good beating. He did it only because it was the right thing for a father to do when a daughter ran wild.

Worst of all, he gave Taro my *manju.* But that night, after everyone had gone to sleep, I'd been awakened by a soft prodding on my cheek and the smell of sweet beans at my nose. "Here, Shoko-chan," Taro had whispered. "I'm sorry." He had given me two, his and mine.

"You better be sorry," I had responded, stuffing both into my cheeks. "I'll really fix you next time." I punched his arm. Taro giggled, and we drifted to sleep, the *manju* beans making my lips sticky.

Was Taro even still alive?

If you are lucky enough to become a mother to a son, do not attempt to raise him in the American way. Raise him in the Japanese way and he will become a fine young man in the Japanese tradition.

This means treating him better than you treat your husband. Prepare all your son's favorite meals, buy him toys when he desires them, try to accommodate all his desires before he can voice them. In this way, you will gain his respect and appreciation.

— from the chapter
"American Family Habits,"
How to Be an American Housewife

THREE

Charlie interrupted my memories by coming in and patting my shin. "You want me to bring you Sanka in here?"

I sat up, then lay back down. How idiotic that the simple act of getting dressed had tired me out. Some days were better than others. "Please."

"Okay." He got up and left before I could mention my letter.

I stretched, thinking about how I would run after I got my heart fixed, then got up and applied my makeup. I only wore it to the store or to the doctor's, really the only places we ever went anymore.

Loud TV came out of my son's room, which was across from ours. I smelled cigarettes. My chest tightened. I went out and pounded on his door. "No smoke in house, Mike!"

He cracked the door open, his nearly black eyes rimmed with red. There were so many papers and trash and clothes on the floor you couldn't see the carpet. At the foot of his bed was a big-screen TV, up too loud. "What?" he said, like when he was sixteen, me trying to get him to come out for dinner, when he'd rather eat in his room alone. This was Mike's way.

Mike looked much more Japanese than Sue. He had sharp high cheekbones, eyes that turned up at the corners. His nose had a flat bridge like my brother's, but was long like his father's. Ever since he was little, wherever we went, people had stared at his Asian eyes, his sharp cheekbones, and his coarse black hair. He looked like the star of an old samurai movie, out of place in this time. I told him to stick his tongue out at them.

Maybe that was why he preferred the company of animals. Everywhere we moved, he had fish and a lizard. I wouldn't let him have cats and dogs until after we were done with our overseas tours, so we wouldn't have to give them up.

Moving so much for the Navy had been hard for Mike. It took him about two and a half years to make a good friend, and three years was how long each duty station lasted. When we left Washington state, Mike was six. He had sat down in the doorway of our old Craftsman bungalow and held on to the doorjamb, rocking himself back and forth while the movers hauled off our belongings, while his little friend Jimmy came to say good-bye, and his father and I packed the car. Five hours total. Nothing would budge him. "I'm staying. I like it."

I tried to pick him up. "Come on. We miss plane."

His fingernails left grooves in the wood, and he screeched. It sounded like a bald eagle getting shot down. He banged his head on the doorjamb.

"You hurt self! Stop!" I tried to block him and he gave me a tremendous slap on the arm. I backed off.

"Cut it out, Mike." Charlie put the last piece of luggage in the car and turned around, his face reddening in anger. "Get over here right now."

"I'll run away." Mike looked up at me. His face was sweaty and tear-stained. A bright red gash and a purple bruise were starting to appear. I bent to touch it and he jerked away.

I looked at my husband. Charlie wiped his brow, then sat down next to him and put his arm around him. "Mike, Daddy's getting time off after we move. I'll take you fishing in Guam. You won't believe the fish they have there. And the water's so warm. You can swim every day." Charlie always made the most of his leave time, taking Mike camping and fishing and giving me a break to be alone.

"But Jimmy's not there."

"You can write."

He glared at his father. "I don't know how."

Charlie ignored that. "Listen. This is how life is, Mike, and you have to adjust." Charlie stood up. "Get in the car."

He held on to the doorjamb. "No."

Charlie looked at Mike, then at me. "Fine. Get in the car, Shoko."

I did.

Charlie turned the ignition on and drove away quickly.

"What you doing?" I cried, looking back at my son. Mike's mouth was open in a wail.

"Teaching him a lesson for throwing a tantrum."

I turned, wondering if Mike would run to the neighbor's, if he would run down the driveway after us. Mike was still holding on to the house.

We drove to the end of the block, then turned around. Mike was still on the doorstep, his hands now in his lap, his face covered by new tears.

"I thought you left me," he said, hiccuping.

"We never leave you." I tried to put my arms around him. He pushed me off.

He stared. I saw that he did not believe me.

"You ready now?" Charlie asked him.

He went silently to the car, his head hanging down. Mike was too easily broken. What other children shrugged off, Mike could not. I shook my head at Charlie and got in the backseat next to my son. Charlie drove us silently to the airport.

Mike never complained about moving again. Instead he would sit in a corner, a blanket pulled over his head, shutting out us and the rest of the world, until I took him by the hand and led him to the car.

I stared at him now, an adult leaning against his doorjamb, seeing the little boy. "The smoke hurt my heart."

"What's the problem? I've got the window open." He cleared his throat. I hoped he wouldn't get lung cancer.

A black cat ran into the hallway. "Shoot." Mike had just gotten a notice to get out of his old place. Over the years, Mike had moved out and back more times than I could count. This time, he moved back in with four cats. They peed all over the living room. I put my foot down. Now he kept them in his room, taking out the window screen so they could come in and out as they liked. But we were near a mountain, and coyotes had eaten two in the last week.

Mike slammed his door shut, chasing the cat. I leaned against the wall. He caught it in the living room and brought it back, cradled in his arms like a baby.

I crossed my arms. "You pay Daddy first month rent?"

Mike shrugged, pushing back his long hair with one hand. He went in his room and returned with a hundred-dollar bill, handing it to me without a word.

"How work going?" Mike had begun a new job at a pet store.

He shrugged again, and his eyes flicked back toward his closed door like he was missing his favorite show. "Fine."

"Maybe you go back school, be a vet? You like that. Never too late." I would go back to school, if I could. Grossmont Community College was only a mile away.

"Maybe. Yeah."

I knew he only said that to make me shut up. "No more smoke room. Outside only."

"Fine." He was barely listening, his head cocked toward the television dialogue.

I wanted to tell him more: that he needed

to clean the filthy bathroom he used; that he should rinse out his dishes; that he should keep his room neat. It was no use. If he cleaned the bathroom, first I'd have to nag, and then he'd do a halfway bad job at it, so I would have to redo it anyway. It was easier for me or Charlie to do, even with our ailments.

"You have dinner with us?" I asked him.

He shrugged.

"What mean? Say yes, say no. No shrug."

"No, then." He shuffled his feet.

"Got work?"

"Yeah." The cat in his arms purred. He put his nose to its nose.

"You not watch so much TV. Make brain Jell-O. Read book." I scratched the cat's neck. It licked my hand, sandpapery wet.

"Okay." Mike opened his door and disappeared inside.

I wondered if we should keep letting him move back in. After all, he was fifty. But he still hadn't married. And who would ever marry him?

I raised him like my mother had raised my brother. By doing everything for him. I knew no better. I had hoped he would still grow up to be a hard worker. Japanese boys turn out fine raised like this, but apparently not Americans. Or not my son.

41

When Mike was a toddler and we lived in Virginia, I'd take him to the park and try to meet other children for playmates. For both of us.

Children that young — Mike was a year and a half — didn't care what a child looked like. Their mothers did. "He doesn't look the least bit American," one mother remarked to me as our sons dug sand near each other. "He really takes after you."

The mothers varied from polite to downright cold. I couldn't blame them. Some had lost their fathers in the war with Japan. But I felt they could afford to be a little forgiving, seeing as how we lost in the end. Especially the manner in which we lost.

Time did not make our way smoother. When Mike was twelve and playing Little League in Oakland, all the mothers had to make treats for their end-of-season party. Mike had told me about it as I sat on the bleachers watching the game, by myself, on the top row. "It's tomorrow," he said, throwing the ball into his mitt and not looking at me.

The other mothers sat a few rows down or clumped in groups of two or three. They wore button-down shirts in pastel colors and capri pants, like a secret uniform. "Why they no tell me?" I asked.

He shrugged and asked for snack money. I gave him a quarter and moved two benches down to Jackie, the team mother. Jackie had dark hair and a flip just like Jackie O, whom she resembled. She wore a giant floppy straw hat.

Jackie smiled politely and I back at her. "Hi, Shoko, how are you?"

"Very well, thank you." I used my softest, most pleasant voice. "Jackie. I bring popacor-nu barus to party."

"What's that?" Jackie said, not moving her lips from the smile.

"Popacor-nu barus."

She blinked. "I'm sorry. One more time?"

"Popacor-nu. Barus." I made the shape with my hands.

Jackie was silent, her head cocked to the side, the smile fading. The other mothers watched. Did they not understand, either?

Mike had come back and was standing in the dirt by the bleachers, watching. "It's popcorn balls!" he shouted. "What the hell is so hard to understand? You people are stupid. This team is stupid." He threw his hat down.

I never went to another game. But neither did I cry about it. Mike did not, either, or if he did, he did not let us know.

I sorrowed for Mike. He had not changed

much from the little boy on the front stoop. Less fussy, yes. But still easily broken. No one had ever been able to understand him. Always, he was moody, a loner, smart as a whip but lazy. Often he was in his own world, amusing himself. Today, Charlie said Mike might have been called "mildly autistic," but not when he was growing up. Back then, he was just different, and we had done the best we could.

I only hoped that Charlie would let Mike keep staying here after I was gone. He had nowhere else to go.

Charlie came down the hall, a mug of Sanka in his hands. "You want to have spaghetti tonight?"

"No, no," I murmured. "We out of noodle." I considered telling Charlie about the letter right then. Perhaps he would have advice. *Our dear Suki has passed on,* I had written thus far. *Perhaps it is time for us to make amends . . .* Only last week, my sister's husband had sent word that Suki had passed on months ago, from the same condition I had. Her heart. There was no explanation for why he had waited so long to tell me. I was out here in the West, as forgotten as a ghost.

"I'll fry us some steaks. Better take them

44

out of the freezer." Charlie hummed as he went into the bedroom and began putting away laundry.

"I cook tonight. Your steak dry."

He laughed. "I'll make yours bloody." He folded and sang.

Charlie had taken over most of the cooking. On days when I was tired, he pan-fried meat and made rice with microwaved frozen vegetables. Nothing like what I could make. I was just glad to have someone cook for me. Otherwise, we'd be eating cold cereal.

I hadn't always been a good cook. I had made spaghetti for Charlie for the first time in 1955, in that Norfolk house.

The spaghetti recipe was in the new American cookbook that Charlie gave me, *How to Be an American Housewife.* Written in Japanese and in English, it also taught the American way of housekeeping. I had never imagined that I would need such a book, since my mother and my high school had prepared me for being an excellent wife, but I had to admit, American ways were different. I took the book very seriously and made the spaghetti exactly as it said.

The spaghetti recipe had worked. I cooked all day long, using tomatoes I grew in our little garden. The tomatoes were huge that year — our cat Miki used the garden as a litterbox, and I also composted bits and pieces of kitchen scraps.

With Mike wrapped up on my back in a long bolt of material, I used all the strange ingredients we didn't have in Japan — sugar, bay leaf, basil, oregano, sage. "Everything in Japan tastes fishy," Charlie once told me, "even the spaghetti."

"Then why like sushi?" I asked.

"That's not fishy," he said.

That made no sense, so I threw my hands up.

I made certain not to use any fish sauce or soy sauce in this dish, though either would have made it taste a lot better. Then I let it simmer all day, just like it said to, wondering when my new husband would get home. The Navy mostly kept him on a regular schedule when he was ashore, but you never knew for sure. A military wife knew her husband doesn't truly belong to her.

When I heard Charlie singing up the walkway, I put the plate on the table and waited. I hadn't even eaten myself, though it was nearly seven o'clock. Mike was already asleep in the dresser drawer we had pulled out and padded as a temporary crib, swaddled in a receiving blanket I had knitted myself.

"Tadaima!" Charlie sang out the traditional Japanese greeting. I'm home.

"Okaeri!" I responded. Welcome back.

"Boy, it's too quiet in here." He hung his sailor hat by the door, his curly red hair popping up, and left his shiny black shoes next to my pumps. Then he turned on the television. "I'm going to look at Mike for a minute." Charlie headed for the bedroom. He loved that boy; he'd wake him up to hear his voice coo.

"No. You crazy? Never go back sleep." I blocked the doorway. "Eat."

He kissed me with a laugh, spinning me around so the collar on his dark sailor's uniform flew out. "Yes, madame." He scraped the metal chair out from the table and swung his leg over it, cowboy style. Then he tasted the spaghetti. I held my breath. He made a face. "Too sweet."

I sat down, trying to think of the English words. I shook my head and raised my hands. "What mean?"

"It's not like my mother's." He pushed the plate away. "I don't like the onion chunks."

His mother's sauce had most certainly been watered-down tomato paste and sugar, with no spices because they were poor. I stood up so quickly that the little wooden

47

table slid away from me. "No eat, I throw!" I pointed at his head.

"What?" His lips twitched, trying not to smile.

"I throw." I picked up the plate. I saw that on television once. That was how I spent most of my time in America, watching television and learning English. On one show, the wife threw the dinner at the husband's face. "This from book." I shook my head. "No throw out." I would never really throw food at Charlie. I only wanted his attention. I never wasted food. In Japan, we never wasted a grain of rice or a speck of salt.

Charlie's eyes were big. I thought about our wedding day, when I wore a tall headdress. Some people said it was to cover up the woman's horns that showed up after marriage. That's what my father told Charlie, who had laughed. I wondered if Charlie was thinking about that, too, thinking that my horns were showing.

"All right, already," he said, putting a forkful into his mouth. He stared at the TV, like he always did. He used to watch it until two or three every night, even when there was nothing good on. And then he ate the entire plate, with seconds. As he should have. It was delicious, worth all my effort.

I had spent most of the previous day searching for the spices in the Commissary, the discount grocery store on the base where we bought our food. It was a marvel unlike anything else I'd seen in America so far, including the Statue of Liberty. There were gleaming aisles of every type of food you could dream of. In Japan, especially during the war, the storekeepers only had a few bags of rice. Salt. Some roots. Here, I wanted to buy everything and nothing. I didn't know how to cook the big juicy steaks Charlie loved; mine turned out leather dry. I had no idea how to make soup without miso or fish stock. I used water instead, and it tasted awful.

Day after day, I experimented with American foods from the Commissary, learning how to cook all over again. Fry up a piece of meat, boil potatoes, carefully reading the recipes in my book over and over. It was hard learning recipes from a book, all alone, with new ingredients. Sometimes I misread them, mixing up "baking powder" and "baking soda" more than once.

My own mother had taught me how to cook by observation. No formal measurements. Learning how to cook was like learning a language. You picked it up. All I had to do was be around her while she made rice or *manju* or fish stock, and just like that, I knew how to make these things, too.

From the time I first had memories, my mother had been teaching me how to be a good housewife. I helped her do the chores every day, cooking and cleaning and sewing. As we worked, she would sing. Usually she sang *isobushi*, meaning "rocky-beach melody," in her high, thin voice. It was one of the oldest folk songs, the same song fishermen and Noh actors had performed. It sounded like wailing, a lament.

Mother was tough; she came from farming peasant stock. She had a long torso, short powerful legs, and wide feet. The type of person who could squat in a field like a salaryman sat at a desk. Her hair had been half gray since I could remember. Her kimonos were darker colors, solid blues and reds flecked with white.

"Shoko-chan," she would say, "take this for me." I would take over stirring the pot of vegetables while she shifted my little sister Suki from her back to her front to nurse. In those days, children got nursed for a long time, until age two or three or even older. Sometimes that was all of the nourishment they got. It certainly was for my sister.

I watched my mother, her weariness

etched on her face though her voice soared, her breasts two sad sacks of rice, and her song seemed more like a warning to me.

When I had my own daughter, I had tried to teach her how to cook, but Sue was a clumsy child. Nervous.

Once, at age seven or so, she made cookies with me. "Measure flour. Make flat with knife," I said to her. She spilled the flour all over immediately, then the sugar on the floor, then stuck a finger up her nose as she stood there, almost crying. I couldn't believe it. When I was seven, I was cooking and going to the shops alone, and my child couldn't even measure flour or tie a shoe.

"You watch, okay? Sit watch."

She had sat with a sad face on the chair.

"When old, no spill, you can help, okay?" I felt bad for her, but I did not have the time or energy to redo what she had done.

Now I realized I was too impatient. I should have taught her how to clean up. I should have shown her what to do as my mother had for me. Maybe that was why Sue could not learn my own *isobushi,* hear my own warning.

Getting used to American negativity can be difficult. Americans do not politely defer or help you save face; they simply say, "No," loudly and emphatically. Being aware of this phenomenon will help prevent shock.

Japanese say "No" when they mean "Perhaps." Therefore, if you are talking in English to an American and you mean to say "Perhaps," you might accidentally say "No." This is confusing to the American.

Reserve "No" for situations where you absolutely must respond in the negative; use "Perhaps" for all other situations where you mean to give a gentle deferment.

— from the chapter "Turning American,"
How to Be an American Housewife

FOUR

I returned to the bedroom to kneel before my shrine, which I kept in a glass-shelved curio cabinet. When I left Japan, Father gave it to me, knowing there would be no Japanese churches where I was going. It was about the right size for a Barbie doll, maybe a little smaller. It looked exactly like a little wooden temple, with a glass door, writing, a tiny altar, everything. There were three small bowls for freshwater, uncooked rice, and salt.

The shrine had an envelope with special blessed tissue paper in it. I used the paper on anything that hurt. I wet it and put it on any sore spot, like a cut, and by morning, the sore spot had disappeared. The kids even used it on their zits.

Charlie dismissed it as toilet paper. Charlie was a Mormon. I did not believe in his God, he did not believe in mine.

Here I also kept my other small treasures:

a few Japanese dolls with real hair and silk kimonos; clay pots the children made; photos.

I clapped my hands twice for the *kamisama*'s attention, praying for my heart. I prayed for Mike and Sue to be happy. I asked that my granddaughter, Helena, do well in school. I wanted Charlie's knee to be healed. Most of all, for a good ten minutes, I prayed for my brother.

Charlie came in with more laundry. "Why do you already have your good clothes on? Your appointment's not until after lunch."

"I like get ready early." I sat on my dressing stool. *I want to go to Japan,* I wanted to say. *I want you to come.*

But Charlie was looking grumpy. He rooted around in his sock drawer. "Where are my thick white socks?"

"How I know? You do laundry," I reminded him. "Why you no go walk?" It would improve his mood. Besides, the doctor had told him to lose weight or get diabetes. His potbelly was so big it pitched him forward and rounded his posture. Nothing like the skinny corpsman I had met.

He put on some other socks and cheap tennis shoes from the drugstore. "My knee hurts." Charlie hated sweating. In Vietnam, his skin got tan — really his freckles growing together. He said that was enough outdoor time for him forever.

I wished that my knee was the only thing hurting me. "That 'cause you got two hundred extra pounds on it," I said. Charlie huffed and puffed and left the room. His idea of a walk was down four houses, up three houses.

I went into the living room. Charlie turned up Rush Limbaugh so loud you could hear it from outside. Sometimes I listened, too. Charlie nodded along, and I asked questions. "Why these feminazis love hate everybody so much? Why Rush got yell all time?"

Today, wanting quiet, I went in the backyard with my Sanka. Charlie had built a patio of old bricks; it was the best thing he had ever made, because he had done it properly, on a sand bed with a wooden border holding it in place. Overhead, I grew Chinese wisteria on the porch roof, the wild vines shooting up onto the house's roof, too. Purple flowers would be hanging down soon.

I fretted again about my trip to Japan. About my *hesokuri,* my hidden stash of money, and how I would have to ask Sue to buy the airline tickets on the computer. I sat down and formulated a plan for finding my brother at his last known place of employment, the high school where he had been principal. I had so much to tell him.

Taro was the only person left in my family, the only one who knew me, the real Shoko. We had our differences. What brother and sister didn't? But sometimes I swore he could read my mind.

That was all gone now. Taro had not spoken to me since I married Charlie, even though my father had endorsed the marriage. My brother hated Americans, and me as well, both for marrying an American and for other reasons I had long preferred not to think about. But fifty years was a long time to hold a grudge, even for someone who thought forgiveness was a weakness.

Japanese culture is different from American. We do not forgive readily. Sometimes we accept, which is different from forgiveness. In cases like this, where I'd done something Taro thought was evil, the taint would cling to me forever.

After the war, my father and I accepted the reality of the new Japan. Even after the way it ended.

I remembered the afternoon in 1945, jumping rope outside my house with Taro and Suki nearby. A cloudy, muggy summer day. Suddenly a bright light, then a shaking rumbling unlike any earthquake.

I dropped the jump rope and instinctively reached for my brother and sister, holding them tight. We didn't know what it was, but the sinking dread and nausea in my stomach told me everything I needed to know. I rocked my younger siblings until my mother came and brought us inside.

Nagasaki, fifty miles away.

We were spared for the most part. Except that many got sick, or died too young, like my parents. Mysterious blood ailments, hair falling out. Suki's heart and mine were likely sickened by this poison. And for all I knew, Taro's was, too. Perhaps that was why he could not accept the way things had changed.

It seemed to me that the Japanese should have surrendered sooner. We were out of food, our people were dying, and thousands more died in Hiroshima. It seemed that the Emperor would have every last man, woman, and child die in Japan before he would give up his holy throne. The price was too high, too high either way.

I drank the last of my bitter Sanka and went back inside the house. The floors were torn up, the carpeting halfway pulled back. Charlie had gotten a discount on hardwood flooring and had been trying to install it. Only half the room was floored, with jagged edges too far from the wall.

My husband fancied himself a great handyman. He would watch a home-improvement show on television and say, "That looks easy. I'll try it." But he always managed to leave out a step. As when he put in our sod — he put it over dead grass, then forgot to water it.

So this was why our house was crumbling. If we had money for supplies, we never had it for professionals to do the work.

I knew not to say anything about his flooring. It would only make him angry — angry that I had noticed — and frustrated with himself. "Charlie," I said instead, over the radio, "how 'bout you and me go on trip?"

He groaned, massaging his knee. I sat beside him and motioned for him to put his foot on my lap so I could massage it. "We've already been everywhere. Where do you want to go?"

"Different now. Back then, work all time. When we live Hawaii, we never leave Honolulu even."

"There was no reason to." Charlie didn't want to see the other islands, not even the volcanoes or rain forests, no matter how much Mike and I begged. "Oahu had everything we needed. It was too expensive to go all over the place."

I took my hand off of him. "I want go Japan."

He was quiet, like he didn't hear. Then he said, "Why do you want to go there?" like I had said I wanted to go to Iraq in the middle of the war.

"You promise me we go back. I no go back. Now we almost too old to move. My sister dead. I see Taro, before too late."

Still he said nothing. Maybe he was hoping I'd shut up if he ignored me. "How 'bout it?" I asked.

"Maybe next year," he said. "We don't have the money now."

"I do." I plumped the brown floral couch cushion. We didn't have money for furniture for fifteen years after we moved in here. Charlie had put a redwood patio chair set in this room. It had two seats, vinyl cushions, and a table in the middle with a hole for an umbrella. Mike was too embarrassed to have his friends over. He moved out as soon as he could. Sue was little and didn't know any better. "I save little bit here and there."

"Your brother won't even see you," he said. "All these years, you hardly talked about him. You said you're dead to him."

"He see me if I'm there. We both old now." I wanted to believe this. Taro may have softened with age.

Charlie shook his head. "I'm not coming."

"Because your knee?" He still said nothing. "You too proud. Not use cane. Not tell doctor you need new knee. Always wearing slippery shoes, falling all over place." Charlie liked to wear Italian dress shoes, too narrow for his feet. *"Baka-tare!"* Stubborn fool.

"Your doctor won't let you go," Charlie said. "You're too sick, Shoko."

"Maybe I no live through surgery," I said, saying what everyone was afraid to say. "I want go." I thought of something. "If Dr. Cunningham say okay, you say okay, too? You go with me?"

Charlie nodded, looking relieved. "But he's not going to say okay, Shoko."

"Deal," I said, sticking my hand out and shaking my husband's.

When you marry and integrate with Americans, it is only natural not to have friends. Most American women will dislike you. Perhaps looking for other Japanese women will be possible, but probably not. Expect to be alone much of the time. Children help relieve this melancholy.

— from the chapter "Culture for Women," *How to Be an American Housewife*

FIVE

In the afternoon, Charlie drove us home from Dr. Cunningham. He had said no to Japan, just as Charlie said he would.

"You'll need oxygen by the time you get off the plane." Dr. Cunningham crossed his arms and spoke as to a child. He was even more handsome when he looked stern.

"I do fine," I said.

He and Charlie exchanged looks. "If you put this off, you will die," Dr. Cunningham said quietly. "I'm afraid there's no other way to say it."

"I know that. But I always this way. No different." I spoke softly, but I wanted to yell. "I need go."

"He said no," Charlie said.

"Next year, when you recover," Dr. Cunningham said, touching my arm.

I grabbed my purse and stood up. Didn't they know I didn't care if there was a next year anymore? I felt dizzy and had to sit down again. "Take me home."

We always took surface streets, all the way from Balboa Park to San Carlos, through the terrible neighborhoods and potholes bigger than the Grand Canyon. "Take too long," I said every time. Charlie hated driving on the freeway.

"Less traffic this way," he said. Or he said nothing. Often I thought he didn't hear me. I knew he never listened to me.

Despite this, Charlie was a better husband than some other American men. He had a steady Navy job that was enough money, especially when we lived in Japan. He bought books for me and tried to learn Japanese. Another Japanese Navy wife I met in Guam had a husband who made her sit behind him in the car, like they did in Japan. But if Charlie had asked me to, I would have.

I would have done almost anything for Charlie to keep him happy. My friend Toyoko had shown me that. Back when Mike was a baby in Norfolk, I knew no Japanese Navy wives. There weren't many around in the early days. But one evening shortly after Mike turned two, Charlie arrived home with a broad smile and two extra people for dinner. "Shoko-chan, I have a surprise."

I got up from where Mike and I were playing blocks, already thinking about how I could stretch two chops into more and planning to tell him off later for bringing guests without telling me.

Then I saw who was following him inside. A Japanese woman about my age, maybe younger, and a black sailor. Her hair was cut short and permed into soft curls all over her head.

She bowed, taking off her shoes. In her hands was a casserole dish tied up in a purple scarf. "Forgive intrusion," she said, her voice high and polite and in English far better than my own. "I brought macaroni and cheese."

Toyoko and her husband, Jim, had just moved on base. They'd met as Charlie and I had, on the Iwakuni Air Base. Toyoko's eyes met mine and we smiled big as children.

"Welcome!" I said, wondering if we should switch to Japanese. No. It would be impolite not to include the men.

Charlie read my mind. "Go ahead and speak Japanese. We want to learn, right, Jim? Besides, the language sounds like music."

Toyoko and I did everything together for the next year. We tried to learn English better. There were no classes offered, at least none that we could easily get to, so Charlie got us a couple of textbooks, and we tried to study those. Most of the time, it was gibberish.

Our plan was to become citizens in five years. "That way, they can't get rid of us," Toyoko said with a sly grin, revealing a big gap between her front teeth. Most people thought that was unattractive, but on her it was good. Like a beauty mark.

The citizenship test promised to be difficult. You had to learn the Constitution and know all kinds of history, more than the average schoolkid. If I could pass that, I would be a true American.

But the next year, Charlie got transferred to Hawaii. I embraced Toyoko and promised to write. "We can do a citizenship correspondence course," I said.

In Hawaii, it was much easier to blend in. There were so many darker-skinned people that no one gave me a second glance. I made many friends there. More Navy men had Japanese wives in Hawaii. Pidgin English was quicker to learn than standard, especially because Charlie was gone too much to teach me proper English.

Toyoko and I wrote regularly for years. Jim got transferred to Yokosuka, Japan, and

I thought she must be thrilled. She was not. *The other Japanese wives won't talk to me because Jim is black,* she wrote. *I miss you, Shoko.*

Don't let them get the better of you! You're too good for them anyway, I responded. It had not occurred to me that these wives would treat each other like this, but I saw it more often in Hawaii, where there were more Japanese wives. Cliques formed based on what your husband's race was. Neither group would accept the other.

Then I didn't hear from Toyoko for a year. She sent me a postcard from Japan. *It was too hard,* she wrote. *Jim left me.* She was one of the lucky ones, able to return home, still childless. I wondered what had happened to those who weren't so lucky. They probably had to find another serviceman. That's what I would do if Charlie left me. It always nagged at the back of my mind. I tried to be the best wife I knew how.

We drove down the steep hill on Florida Street, to the dip that flooded with every light rain. We went over a pothole and I clutched the door. "Careful, Charlie!"

Charlie spoke. "Operation sounds good, doesn't it? Wonder if it'll help all the other things going wrong with your body."

66

"Maybe I run all over town again, huh? Then what you gonna do?" I poked at his belly. "Get you going again."

Charlie shifted away from me and turned up the radio. KPOP, hits from the 1940s and '50s. One thing we had in common, we hated newer music. "I'm too old to get going again."

"You not too old until dead." I chewed my lower lip in frustration. Ever since Charlie had retired from the Navy, he had acted as though he had retired an old person instead of just age forty-one.

We ended up in San Diego, Charlie's last station. Hawaii had been our favorite, but Hawaii, he said, was too expensive. And we didn't want to move all the way back across the Pacific, though I wouldn't have minded being closer to Japan.

The first thing we did was buy a house with a no-down-payment VA loan. It was the 1970s, when Sue was a baby and Mike was already twenty-two. Charlie wanted the house on the mountain side of the street, because there would never be people behind us. Jacaranda Street was lined with the flowering trees along the parking strips, purple clouds every spring. "Look like cherry tree in Japan," I had said when we were looking for a house. But still, there

67

were problems. With every big rain, the water poured down the mountain into our yard, and Charlie had to dig a ditch out to the street to let it out. Sometimes brush fires broke out behind us, too.

There was nothing built in the community. "Closest park five mile," I said to Charlie. "No good for kids." Developers were just beginning to push into eastern San Diego. I had no car; we could only afford one.

Charlie had looked exasperated. "This is what we can afford."

"They got older houses by park," I pointed out. "Can get loan on those, too."

"I want a new house." That was Charlie. He had caviar wishes and champagne dreams, like Mr. Robin Leach would say.

With us settled, Charlie went to college on the GI Bill. Originally, because he'd been a medic, he wanted to be a doctor. "But I'm too old," he said. He was. No new doctor was in his fifties, the way he'd be by the time he finished.

He settled on nursing. But when he graduated, no one was hiring. Not even a former corpsman he knew at a hospital who had been to Korea and Vietnam with Charlie.

Our times got tough for a while, and Charlie withdrew more and more. I tried to get him moving. One afternoon months after he finished school, Charlie sat eating a family-size bag of Lay's in his TV chair. A pile of old junk mail lay on the floor next to him.

I stared at the heap. All this work I had to do, trying to save us money. I washed Sue's diapers by hand. We never ate out. I dyed, permed, and cut my own hair. I dug up the hard clay earth and made a vegetable garden in the back, planting a fig tree and a tangerine tree to bear fruit. I saved rainwater in buckets — not that we got much rain — and used it to water the garden. Never did I think I would have to remember what my mother had taught me back in Japan.

Charlie was sitting there, getting chip crumbs all over the place.

I turned the TV off. "Why no apply job? What doing sit around all day?"

"Turn that back on." It was the days before remotes, but Charlie was too lazy to get up. "What're you doing?"

"All do is sit. Eat. TV. I throw TV away if you no get job soon. You no can sit 'round. You no old." I pointed to Sue, who lay in her playpen looking at us. "You got baby girl." I wished more than anything that I could go out into the world and conquer it for my family.

He blinked at Sue, as though seeing her for the first time.

I put my hands on my hips. "You apply every hospital in county? North, south, middle?"

He shifted in his chair, not answering.

"You apply Orange County if have to. We move. Who care?" I picked up his junk mail and tossed it high in the air. It scattered all over the floor. "Look at trash you make me."

Charlie pursed his lips, then closed his eyes. He inhaled. "It's hard, Shoko. How they look at me when I go apply. I'm so much older than everyone."

"Shut up. You got combat experience. What more they want?" I shook my head. Sue whimpered. I walked over and picked her up, putting my nose into her soft baby neck. She cooed. I smoothed back her hair, red at the time.

Charlie got up and picked the trash off the floor. He threw it away. Then he got changed into a shirt and tie and went out with his black vinyl briefcase full of résumés, all without saying a word.

Finally, Conroy Jewelers hired Charlie to work at the Mission Valley Mall one Christmas. Charlie had always liked jewelry. He learned how to do simple welding, and stayed there until his arthritis made it too hard for him to size rings for newlyweds and women whose fingers got bigger after childbirth, or to set tiny pearls some girl found in a Sea World oyster into a pendant. He made barely enough for us; with his Navy retirement, we got by.

Over the next twenty years, off and on, I tried to prod him into nursing. The job market didn't stay down forever. "Hospital got good benefit," I reminded him.

"I have Navy benefits. Besides, I can't move patients around anymore. That's the only reason they hire men." But still he sang all day and night, and if he wasn't singing, he had the radio or TV on, as though he could not bear to be with his thoughts.

Charlie sang now as he drove us home in the old Ford Taurus, the windows rolled down and the air-conditioning off. I tilted my seat back slightly, knowing he was in no mood to talk.

I wished we could get a new car with freezing air-conditioning. When we got this one brand-new, years ago, I had thought it was the nicest car I'd ever seen. It had gray cloth seats and maroon paint. It even had a real stereo with a tape deck, and air-conditioning, the kind of car I always dreamed about. I thought it was as nice as our next-door neighbor Lorraine's Buick Regal. When we bought it, I showed it to her. She told me how great it was. The next week, her husband bought her a brand-new Mercedes with license plates that said "ILUVLOR."

Lorraine wasn't really a friend, but she was the only person I knew who would talk to me. Everyone in our part of town was white, Christian, working-class, people like Charlie who watched *Hee Haw* or *Lawrence Welk*. The other housewives were a good fifteen years younger than I was. No time for someone like me, someone whose accent made her difficult to understand, and who never had anything worthwhile to say.

With no car, it was hard to do anything. Sue and I were on our own. Mike was going to community college part-time, still living with us but hardly ever home.

It felt lonelier than when Charlie had been in the Navy. At least when he was deployed, I got to use the car. Now I had to depend on Charlie or the neighbors for everything, which I hated.

When I got too lonely, I'd send Sue out to play with the neighbor kids and I'd go talk to Lorraine, who would be sitting in her plaid armchair, her feet bare on dark blue shag carpeting. She welcomed me into her house with a hearty laugh, brushing back her dark curls, leaving her soaps on the television and her magazines all over the glass and brass coffee table. "What new with you, Lor?" I asked on one of these visits. She gave me a glass of Coke and ice. I sipped it with relish. Charlie, being Mormon, didn't allow Coke.

"Same old, same old." She didn't care that she had a hard time understanding me. She talked enough for five people, never mind two. "Ken's flying the boys up to visit their grandparents while I'm stuck here waiting on Sears to finish our cabinets. Lordy, you wouldn't believe the mess they make."

"You got maid, though, right?" I prompted.

"I feel bad if she has too much to do. I clean before she cleans!" Lorraine yodeled a laugh. Lorraine also had a gardener who mowed her lawn, a pool guy, and a husband who didn't mind her TV dinners. They had more money than the rest of the neighborhood put together. She sat and watched soaps all day and called her friends to gossip. And ate.

This was how I thought I would be as an American housewife, except for the too-much-eating part. When I first married Charlie, we were in Japan, where the dollar

73

was strong. I had thought he was rich. I thought we would always be rich. I was wrong.

I nodded at Lorraine, my eyes falling to the women's magazines spread over the glass coffee table, the snack trash near Lorraine's recliner. She was like Charlie, I saw.

The doorbell sounded. "Come on in," Lorraine said.

It was the woman who lived across the street, Charlene. We smiled politely at each other. "Sorry, Lorraine, didn't know you were busy." She fiddled with her red curls.

"You're not interrupting at all," Lorraine said.

I glanced at Lorraine, hurt, realizing that for all the times I popped in, she never did the same.

"I was going to run to the mall. You want to come with?" Charlene avoided my eyes.

"Sure. Let me get my purse." Lorraine launched up from the chair.

I waited for them to ask me to go. Of course, they did not. I could have invited myself, but why? So I could tag along? "Thank you for Coke." I put the glass down on the table, where someone who was not Lorraine would pick it up later.

"You want us to get you anything?" Charlene asked. "We could stop at the grocery, too."

"I get myself. You girls have fun." I left, remembering what it was like to have girlfriends to giggle with.

Charlie and I arrived home on Jacaranda Street. In the next driveway, Lorraine was getting out of her Mercedes. She was bigger than ever and moved slowly. Her hair was gray now. She waved. "How you doing, Miss Shoko?" she called. "Not working too hard, are you? Your roses look beautiful!"

"Thank you." I simply shut the car door and turned away. In the old days, I would have stayed out and chatted with her. Finally I had realized it wasn't worth it. She was only a neighbor, not a friend. I no longer had the energy.

"I was going to get you out." Charlie tried to run around the car.

"I fine." I smiled.

He paused and looked at me. "I'm sorry about Japan, Shoko."

I glanced at his eyes. He really was. "Maybe next life, huh, Charlie?"

"There is no next life." Charlie turned and went into the house.

I followed, formulating a plan. I would have to call on my daughter.

75

The only question was whether she would ignore the request.

You must pay particular attention to raising daughters in the Japanese tradition. With American daughters, there are more ways to get into trouble, as she will want to be American. Teach her to resist this urge if you want to avoid the shame of having a daughter who runs with the fast American crowd.

— from the chapter
"American Family Habits,"
How to Be an American Housewife

Six

When the Americans first took over Japan, my father said to me, "Shoko. You must learn English. Now we all have to be like Americans."

"No," I said. "I will never be an American."

But he was right. He always was. Japan was going nowhere.

Our village was tiny, with only fishermen and farmers. There was nothing for young people to do but get married and work in low-paying jobs. Most girls sat around at home, waiting to get married. I dreamed about going to college, though there was no money for it.

I wanted to be a diplomat. I loved reading about different cultures, especially the European ones. I went to the library and found every book I could about France, England, Germany. I wanted to learn their languages, but my all-girls high school didn't have such courses. They had grammar and math, of course, but they also had flower arranging and dance as requirements.

Somehow, I thought I was smart enough to go to college and learn about the world there. My brother, Taro, told me that was nonsense.

"I make all A's. Do you think you're smarter than me?" I asked him.

"That's not the point. You could be the smartest woman in the world, but you're still a woman. A poor Japanese woman from a country that has lost a war. There is no way you could ever be a diplomat." He was right, and I knew it but didn't want to believe it. Taro, like me, spoke the truth, no matter how distasteful it sounded. "The best you could hope for is to go to college, pretend you're high-class, and marry a diplomat."

This was not how things worked out. I told my mother I wanted to go to college, and she said no, that there was no point in it for girls. My mother wanted me to marry one of the boys from our *shuku* — our community. People of a *shuku* worked together, and usually married each other.

Father disagreed with Mother. "She's too good for those *bakamono-shuku,*" he said, lifting his proud nose. "Too clever. She can do better."

Japan wasn't democratic like America. Who you were descended from counted for more than what you made of yourself. Our father was descended from the bearers of the imperial seal. We might live among the commoners, we might have no more money or property than they did, but father always reminded us we were better than them. Father, while he thought the people of the *shuku* were honest and nice enough, didn't want us to marry into them.

I was secretly very happy when I heard Father's decree. I had no desire to marry one of the village boys. A few of them were nice, but they had no prospects, nor did any of them seem concerned about this. They thought that they would keep on farming their little patches of land and that the government, like a samurai landlord, would take care of them. That was how the *shuku* system originated, in fact — from samurai. "If any of them were smart," Father said, "they'd take advantage of the Americans being here and make money off them."

For months, my parents debated about what I should do. Then finally it was my mother who sat me down one day when I was eighteen, a few months after I finished high school. With honors. "Shoko. You're a very smart girl. Too smart for your own good, I've thought."

I bowed my head.

Mother ran her hand over the lacquered black table. "We have decided it's time for you to work."

My mind raced. "Where am I going to work? With the fishermen?"

Mother's voice was flat. "We've heard there are plenty of jobs with the Americans. Good jobs."

"But what if I don't want to work for Americans?" My brother hated Americans. He wasn't a realist, like my parents were. But I was conflicted. I resented the Americans, but I thought about what it would mean to get away from my little village. To meet people who had seen more of the world than this little corner, to see what other places were like, through their eyes. I got excited, despite myself.

"It's best for the family. For you. We cannot keep you anymore." Mother folded her hands in front of her and looked at them. Mother looked at least two decades older than her forty-one years. Though she wore a hat every day, her face was still deeply tanned and lined, with darker freckles marring her hands. Her eyelids were beginning to wrinkle and droop. I wondered if she ever regretted that my father had given up his law job for the priesthood. I would never ask her; she would only tell me no. Besides, he could have lost his law practice during the war anyway, as so many had.

Mother continued. "You work and send money home. That way, we can pay for Taro to finish school. He is the son."

I understood. With a college degree, a boy like Taro could do so much more than I could ever hope. He would raise us all up. "I'll go right away."

It didn't occur to me to be frightened. Other girls were in my situation, too. Girls who saw opportunity where there had been nothing before. There was no reason to be afraid, only reason to hope. America was here, and like my father said, we had to get used to it.

I rented a room in a Kumamoto City house with my childhood friend, Shigemi. The owners were Japanese and made a living renting rooms to girls like us. I thought I'd be a secretary at the naval base, or get a job at a nightclub, something where I could meet powerful people. But I had to take the first job I could get.

Shigemi got me a job as a maid at an American officer's house in Kumamoto City, where she worked as his cook. It didn't pay much, but it was enough. More than I was used to. Enough to get my hair done at a beauty parlor and buy a few nice things for the first time in my life. I would rather have had a pretty new dress than a fancy meal any day.

The officer's home was the first American-style house I'd ever been in. It had wooden plank floors, big windows, no *shoji* screens, lots of heavy upholstered Western furniture. The officer, Captain Leonard, was married. His wife visited every six months or so, and her next visit was coming up soon. He wanted it to look very neat.

Luckily, Captain Leonard wasn't a messy man. He did keep his shoes on, though, which tracked in extra dirt. The first day I was there, I put on my starched white maid's uniform and tied a scarf in my hair. It would be another week before I went to the beauty parlor to have it set, so I wanted to keep it pristine. Then I put on the sensible black nurse's shoes. I went into the den with a dust cloth, singing in English, *"Let me go, let me go, let me go, lover."* I stopped short. I'd never seen so many books! Thick, leather-bound, gold-printed books lining dusty mahogany shelves. I picked one out, flipping through its pages, but I couldn't read English. A cloud of dust wafted up and I sneezed.

"Bless you," said a voice from behind me. I turned to look. A man in a casual brown naval dress uniform stood there. It was the first time I'd seen an American close-up. He looked a bit younger than forty, his hair just graying at the temples. He had soft brown eyes and a dimple in his chin, and was much taller than Japanese men. "How do you do?" he said, extending his hand to me and shaking it firmly. I smiled at him. He switched into Japanese. "I'm Captain Leonard. But you can call me Kyle."

The boss! I bowed my head, saying in Japanese, "My apologies, I'm sorry to disturb you."

He wouldn't let go of my hand. With his free one, he lifted my face. "You're very beautiful, with a wonderful voice," he said, and touched my cheek with the side of his hand. My heart beat fast. I blushed. "You know, you look like Machiko Kyo, the actress from *Rashomon*. You shouldn't be a maid." He gestured to a chair. "Sit down, won't you?"

People had told me I looked like her. I took it as a compliment, though my father said I was far more beautiful than she. I sat. The chair was wood and soft leather tacked on with brass studs. I crossed my ankles and folded my hands around the dust cloth. My hands were cracked and work-worn; I supposed Machiko Kyo didn't have hands like mine. But maybe Captain Leonard hadn't seen them.

He sat on the edge of his desk, directly in front of me. "What's your name?"

"Shoko."

"Well, Shoko," he said, "I think I might have other plans for you."

I perked up. Maybe he needed a translator. Or a secretary. My brain flew. "Like what?" Then I caught myself. "Forgive me."

He laughed in his smooth baritone. "Maybe you can be my personal maid. *Wakarimasu ka?*" Understand?

I was confused for a second. I thought men had butlers, not ladies' maids. Then I saw how he was looking at me, his pupils so big they obscured the color of his eyes, and comprehended. I stood. "I should get back to work."

He grabbed my arm and pressed me against him. "You really are lovely," he said.

I nudged him away. My father was always warning me against wearing clingy sweaters with those bullet bras. But I was wearing a maid's uniform, the most unflattering thing anyone could wear. This attention wasn't my fault.

"Shoko-san," he said, bowing his head. "Forgive me. I only want to be your friend. Surely you don't want to ruin your hands with this work. You're not meant for it." He put his arm around my waist, running his other hand over my back up to my dress's zipper.

"Stop," I said in English, shoving him against his bookcase, leather books clattering down. I bent my knees and got ready to punch him in the throat, like Taro had taught me.

He made a step toward me again, arms out to grab, but there was a sound of branches scraping the window. We both looked.

Outside was the dirt-streaked face of the gardener, my countryman come to save me, face shaded by a big straw hat. He raised one hand in greeting. "Sir!" he called out in perfect, unaccented English. "Where do you want these roses you ordered for your wife?"

"In the flower garden, of course." The captain went to the window and closed the curtains over the gardener's face. I ran to the kitchen.

"Shigemi! You'll never guess what happened!"

Shigemi turned from the sink, where she was peeling potatoes. "Ah, I know." She wiped her nose with the back of her hand. "You're the fourth maid this year."

"Why didn't you warn me?" I could have kicked her. "I'm calling the police."

"They won't do a thing." She shrugged, tucking back a stray tendril of black hair. Her plump cheeks were flushed. "It's not so bad. I'd do it if he wanted me. He buys nice clothes, gives you a bigger allowance than the whole maid staff put together." She grinned, showing her missing front molar. "You wanted out of Ueki."

I shook my head. "He's married, Shigemi. I want to get out of Japan, not only Ueki."

"An officer will never marry you," Shigemi scoffed. "Take what you can get, when you can get it."

She was probably right. I should be using my looks to get me somewhere, not working as a housecleaner. I leaned against the sink. "I would have been lost if that gardener hadn't interrupted."

Shigemi recoiled like I'd slapped her. "That gardener spoke to you? He's Eta!"

Eta, or *burakumin,* were the untouchable in Japan. As leatherworkers, who touched dead animal hides, Eta were the lowest of the low, set apart this way by the vegetarian Buddhists. A simple explanation for something very complicated.

Japan had had an official caste system for many years, but it was outlawed in 1871. However, like other caste systems, it persisted. After the system had been thrown out, people privately made lists of Eta families. When you got married, your parents checked to see that your fiancé wasn't an Eta.

Shigemi chuckled at me, potato peels flying. "These Americans don't know any better than to hire Eta. The Eta think they can work their way up, now that the Americans are here."

I took off my apron and tossed it at her face. "It's not worth me working here, Shigemi. I quit." I'd find a job somewhere else. There was plenty going on in Kumamoto City. I was no scarlet woman.

I left by the back door and started walking toward the road. The gardener came running up beside me, pushing a wheelbarrow full of roses. "Fine day for a walk, isn't it?" he said cheerfully. I ignored him. Then his foot hit a hole and he tumbled over, sideways, into a bush. The roses slid out after him.

Forgetting he was Eta, I held out a hand for him. He grasped it firmly in his own, which was lean, tan, and hard. Shocked, I pulled my hand away.

"You are marked now," he said gleefully. His hat had come off and left a ring around his forehead. His face was unlined and handsome, with sparkling black eyes, a strong chin, and a lean nose. He looked vaguely European, not like an untouchable. Besides, I corrected myself, untouchables looked like everyone else. "Ronin, at your service."

A *ronin* was a samurai without a master. Fitting. I smiled and discreetly wiped my hand on my dress. "Shoko."

"Nice to meet you," he said with a bow. "And where are you headed in such a hurry? Quit your job already, eh?"

I blanched. "I have another," I lied.

"Of course, it's not hard for a girl like yourself to get a new job just like that." He snapped his fingers. He righted his wheelbarrow and threw the roses back into it. "But if you are so inclined, I happen to know that the Kumamoto Hotel is hiring."

The Kumamoto Hotel had a lot of foreign business in those days. *That wouldn't be a bad place to work at all,* I mused. "Thank you, Ronin-san."

He looked at me as if I'd kissed him. "You're welcome." He watched me walk to the gate. I felt his eyes on my hips burn like a touch. My face reddened under my makeup. I turned around and gave him a little wave. It didn't matter, I wouldn't see him again. He raised his hand in return.

When I was a child we would sometimes see Eta living in the little encampments they had lived in for generations. "Who are they?" I asked when we passed by.

"Don't look at them," Mother told me. I stopped asking.

When I was three, while I waited for my mother at the fish market, an old man approached me with a toothless grin and petted my shiny black hair with a leathery hand. Mother had screamed so loud that I wet my pants. "Dirty Eta," she hissed. "Get away." She scolded me for letting him get so close. "You don't want to be tainted, do you? You can't get rid of an Eta touch."

It wasn't until during the war that mother changed her mind a bit. Food supplies were low. It was especially hard on the children. I knew one girl whose menses never came due to malnutrition; she remained forever stuck in childhood, flat-chested and barren.

At first, we complained of sore stomachs. Or Taro did. He was the only one allowed to. I, being eleven and female, was far too mature to make my parents feel worse about something they couldn't control.

"Quiet," Father told him in a voice much sterner than I had ever heard before.

A few months earlier, Mother had had a miscarriage. She had called me into the house while Father was away. I stopped at the door, alarmed. Mother lay on her bedroll, all the windows shut to make it night-black, blood seeping out of her onto old newspapers. Her face was marble white. "Get the midwife," she had whispered.

I ran into town and returned with the midwife. Mother held my hand as she pushed out the tiny baby boy, only five months along. He was perfectly formed, with long see-through nails and wispy eyelashes and the beginnings of dark hair.

The midwife, a woman who looked ancient with a humpback though she was probably only fifty, said a prayer. "Not enough food for her and the baby," she had said, wrapping him in a blanket as we waited for Father to return from church.

I held him, wiping the blood from his face with the blanket's edge. He was already cold.

Mother held out her arms to take him. "Go out and take care of your brother and sister," she said. "And take them to get Father."

Tokidoki," the midwife said sadly: Sometimes. Sometimes your fortune can turn on the drop of a pin. Good or bad.

I went outdoors, blinking in the brightness. Outside, a jay sang. I had forgotten it was spring.

Taro and Suki played in a muddy puddle, making small turtles out of the clay soil. "We've got to get Father," I said importantly, taking off at a run. The baby seemed like a dream to me. My legs were lead in the balmy air.

Father was meditating at the altar when we arrived. "Father," I whispered urgently, "the midwife is at home."

He opened his eyes and looked into nothingness. "Not again."

"Again?"

He shushed me.

Later, much later, I found out that Mother had had three miscarriages. This one had been the furthest along.

She named the stillborn boy Kenji, meaning "intelligent second son." This birth had taken everything out of her. Mother recovered in bed, too ill to move much for weeks.

I did the housework and cooked whatever food we had. "We can't hold out much longer," Father said. "The Emperor is talking about surrender."

"Never." Taro looked fierce. He probably

would have run away to be a child soldier if Father hadn't told him we needed him here. Taro hunted rabbits, but in the winter they got scarce. Besides, everyone was hunting the same thing. Our chickens even stopped laying, and we ate them though they were tough as jerky.

Mother grew weaker and weaker until one day Father brought home a cupful of rice. And the next day another and then another, stretching it into a thin gruel soup for all of us, until Mother got strong enough to rouse herself.

"Where did that rice come from?" she asked him on the fourth night in a low voice. We slept on two mattresses: Father, Mother, and Taro on one; my sister and I on the other, all pushed together so Taro was next to me.

"Neighbor." Father was lying. Even I could tell. He was too holy to be a good liar.

"What neighbor do we have left?" I could almost hear her eyes narrow in the darkness.

"Someone who came to me for a blessing." Father rolled over with a soft thud.

Mother was silent for a minute. "It was Haruko, wasn't it?"

I inhaled sharply and nudged my brother

93

in the ribs. He snored in response. Boys slept through everything good.

Haruko lived in the Eta village. She had been trying to come to church for years, only to be dissuaded by my mother. Father had taken to letting the Eta people gather in the garden for a service early in the morning. It was a compromise he had reached with Mother. Father saw the good in everyone.

Mother gasped. "I am ill. Why do you try to kill me?"

"I am not. You will be well." Father's voice was firm, a hand holding hers in the darkness. "I blessed the rice myself. You must find it in yourself to be strong."

"I cannot." Mother choked. "It's been too hard for too long. I cannot."

Father exhaled. "We will do what is necessary to live."

"Even if it kills me?" Mother muttered, but this time I could hear the humor in her tone.

"If it's not one thing, it's another." I heard him kiss her. "Good night."

The Eta woman kept sharing her rice — I think she got extra because she didn't report that her two young children had died from scarlet fever — and we kept eating it until Mother was up and about again. She still would not greet the woman if we saw her in the street, but she no longer crossed to the other side.

I went straight to the Kumamoto Hotel, not even bothering to change out of my maid's uniform. I had to get another job fast. I couldn't survive long without money. That Shigemi. I would have to find a new roommate, too. How could I live with someone who would throw me to the lions in a snap?

I walked through the big double glass doors and went up to the front desk. My heels caught in the thick, plush carpeting. Enormous landscape paintings of lands I'd never seen decorated the walls. The man at the desk told me the manager would be right out. I went and sat on the red velvet couch, staring at a painting of the Eiffel Tower. How nice it would be to visit France, drink coffee at an outdoor café.

I heard a low whistle behind me, and turned. I was startled to see my brother's childhood friend, Tetsuo, dressed in a bellhop's uniform, leaned over the back of the sofa. I hadn't seen him in over a year, and he'd grown into a handsome young man, with quick eyes and a strong, dimpled jaw.

"Tetsuo! I didn't know you worked here."

His eyes widened when he recognized me. "Shoko-chan! I can't believe it."

"Why are you whistling at strange girls, then?" I smiled. Tetsuo was my favorite of my brother's friends. He and I were like brother and sister. Until now, the way he was looking at me.

He hopped over the back and landed, cross-legged, beside me. His face broke into a grin. "You still playing baseball?"

"When I can." I smoothed out my skirt.

The manager appeared, a short, balding American with a potbelly. Tetsuo stood up. "Hello," the manager said in English. "I'm Mr. Lonstein."

"I can vouch for her, sir," Tetsuo said. I was surprised that he knew English so well. I only knew a few words. Stop. No. Please.

Mr. Lonstein gave me an appraising look. "You can start right away."

He put me in the gift shop, where I had to ring up purchases for the American sailors and others coming through. Mostly, the gift shop had glass cases full of figurines and cheap Japanese souvenirs marked "Made in Occupied Japan." Many servicemen stayed at this hotel. They also liked coming to the restaurant and dance club.

"Thank you very much," I said after each

96

purchase. I got to wear a beautiful cream silk kimono, decorated with pink camellias and climbing green vines. One lady even took a picture of me to show her friends back in the States, her arm around my waist, as though we were bosom friends. Americans were overly familiar. I got used to it.

Within a week of me starting the job, Tetsuo showed up at my counter. "How would you like to go out on Friday?" he asked.

"Let me think about it." Nice girls turned down the first request. "No, Friday I'm busy."

"Guess you'll miss out on the fun. Oh, well, I'll call another girl." Tetsuo pretended to leave.

I smiled. I needed fun. And no one was around to tell me how to behave. "I suppose I can go with you."

He leaned his elbows on the countertop. "Meet me at ten." He winked at me and snapped his fingers and pointed his fingers like guns at me. I winked back.

When you get your passport, you will notice that your race will be classified as "Mongoloid," although you are not from Mongolia. There is no point in debating this.

America consists primarily of Caucasians. It is understood without explanation or question that in the United States a Japanese person will not be considered an equal. If you married a non-Caucasian American, you will be considered in even a lesser light.

Therefore, you must work as hard as you can to prove yourself more than equal — the most polite, the best worker, an adept English learner, the most well-turned-out Housewife your husband could ever ask for. This is your duty, to both your home country and to your new one.

— from the chapter "Turning American,"
How to Be an American Housewife

SEVEN

I'd been dating Tetsuo for a couple of weeks when, one day, I went outside on my lunch break. The gardens at the hotel were nice, made to look English, with a maze about five feet tall made out of boxwood bushes.

I walked into this maze with my *bento* box, remembering Tetsuo saying there was a fountain somewhere inside. My brother and family were pleased that I was dating Tetsuo, my mother relieved. I was already nineteen, and many of the girls I went to high school with were married. However, I had many single friends, women like me who sought to improve their positions.

Every weekend night, sometimes even weeknights, Tetsuo picked me up from the one-room apartment I shared with another girl from the hotel, and we went dancing. Oh, Tetsuo could dance! He was the only man I ever knew who could. I lent him out to my friends, too. I wasn't even jealous when I looked up from my drink — Coca-Cola, of course, since I didn't like alcohol — to see Tetsuo slow dancing with my new roommate, Yuki, their eyes closed, cheek to cheek, dreamily moving under the orange and blue lights. Mitsui, another girlfriend of mine, nudged me. "You better watch her. She's a man-stealer."

"Yuki?" Why would I be jealous of Yuki? Her face was moon-round and her waist already looked matronly. "I guess some men might like that. Not Tetsuo."

And yet, when I danced with Yuki's boy-friend — not even a slow dance — Tetsuo cut in, enraged. He shoved the boy aside and drew me in to him. "I can't stand to have anyone else touch you," he said, putting his hand on the side of my face, gripping my jaw.

I drew my head back and forced a smile. "It's only a dance." I did not argue with him about Yuki. My mother said it was better that a man was jealous, to have him care about you more than you cared about him. It kept him close.

Tetsuo looped me next to his body. He slid his hand up and down my back. "Shoko," he sighed, and he pressed his pelvis close to mine. I tried not to jump. "Shoko, tonight?" He took my hand and brought it to his lips.

I thought quickly. Mother hadn't gone over this part of relationships. I'd been at a girls' high school, forbidden to date, and I was naïve in some ways. If I didn't give in, he might lose interest and move on. Tetsuo was too good of a catch. Handsome and smart and ambitious. But if I did give in, he might also lose interest. I decided to put him off a little longer.

I turned so my back was to him and swayed to the slowing drumbeat. "Soon," I purred over my shoulder. "Have patience."

He pulled me back to him again and put his lips on the soft skin of my neck. I shivered. "You drive me crazy, Shoko." He turned me around and bent down as though to kiss me.

I panicked. A kiss meant I was telling him he could have his way with me. This was how it was during my time. Everyone would see and know. He closed his eyes and his lips landed on the side of my hair. "I do care for you, Tetsuo. But you know I am a nice girl. The sister of your friend." I hoped that would inspire his sense of honor.

He held out his arm to spin me. As I whirled across the floor, my circle skirt flying out, I saw the eyes of everyone at our table.

■ ■ ■ ■

A few days later, I was walking through the hotel gardens, trying to figure out how to cha-cha. Back, forth, cha-cha-cha. My feet kicked up gravel. I went around the path again and again, my arm on the shoulder of an imaginary partner.

"Very good," a voice said from where the path forked to my right. I jumped, my hand at my throat. A man stepped into sight.

It was Ronin. Wearing his gardener's clothes, a hedge clipper in his gloved hands, he bowed. "So sorry to frighten you," he apologized.

I drew myself up, flushing. What was he doing here? I couldn't associate with him any longer. Holding my head high, I took the other fork of the path.

"That's not the way to the hotel," he said.

"No matter. I'll find my way."

He clipped at a bush. "You'll find yourself in Okinawa before too long."

I stopped. He was right. I would get lost. I spun around and headed back the way I thought I'd come.

"Still wrong," Ronin said in a low voice.

I looked away from him. "I'm not supposed to be talking to you."

He raised his eyebrows at me. "The Americans are here now. We're all equal."

I thought about what my mother would say, and my father, too, for that matter. He might have taken rice from *burakumin,* but it was another matter to have his daughter socializing with them. "My family is descended from the seal-bearer of the Emperor," I said.

Ronin leaned on his clippers. "It's a new era, is it not? Otherwise, you wouldn't be working as a maid for foreigners."

"I'm not a maid!" I said. "I'm a salesgirl."

He grinned. "You're too smart to work at that hotel. Why don't you go to college?"

This floored me. "I can't afford to."

He shrugged. "Me neither. At least, not right now. Tell you what. You show me how to cha-cha, and I'll show you how to get out of this maze."

I pursed my lips. "Fine. But you cannot touch me."

"Fine," he said, looking at me in a way that made my insides wiggle like tofu.

I knew I shouldn't, but I went walking in the gardens often after that. My job in the store wasn't taxing — in fact, it was so mindless that I wanted to sleep — and I needed the diversion of a friend. Ronin was merely an interesting man. Completely innocent.

I never tried to find Ronin, but he always found me, falling into step so quietly that I leaped up in fright every time, making him roar with laughter.

Then he started bringing food. "I bought it, so don't worry," he said, bowing his head.

Now that I knew him, I was ashamed that I'd treated him so disrespectfully before. "Of course I would eat your food. I'm eating with you, after all. It's no different."

He looked shamefaced. "It's just — I'm a rotten chef."

I laughed.

We sat in the sun, eating from our *bento* boxes. "When I was a child," he said, "this would have been unheard of."

"Eating lunch with a beautiful girl or working here?" I teased.

He looked about. "Where is this beautiful girl?" Ronin swallowed his fish hard, to disguise his laughter. "Both, Shoko. We lived in the Eta village and no one would have anything to do with us."

"Except other Eta."

"Yes. But no one like you or your family. It was like being a ghost." He put a cucumber into his mouth. "One day, my mother was at the market, selling the leather shoes that she had made. My mother was a beautiful woman. Almost as beautiful as you.

"She was doing her usual business when an English businessman happened by. He met her eyes and they fell in love.

"He was my father. He sent money, visited from time to time." Ronin smiled. "I suppose he did what he could. He left for England right before Japan attacked China. He asked my mother to come with him.

"She wanted to go and take me, but the country wouldn't let her out. They were gearing up to take over the world. No special considerations for her, especially as she was Eta." He looked into the shrubbery at something I couldn't see. "It wouldn't have worked out anyway. Englishman and Japanese."

"It's different now," I said.

"I hope so. I don't fit in here, I might as well try my luck elsewhere." He finished his lunch and replaced the red lid with a click. "I have a plan." He looked at me sideways. "America, here I come. The land of opportunity."

I was excited despite myself. "What will you do there? Cook in a Japanese restaurant?"

"Landscape. Like I do here, but bigger. I have big dreams, my Shoko."

How dare he? "I am not 'your Shoko.' "

He ignored that. "There is nothing for me here. I want to be my own boss."

"I wish you well." I finished eating my own lunch, demurely taking small bites and chewing slowly. I admired his dreams, but they were as crazy as my diplomat ones. I would not tell him this — what good would it serve? — so he continued to talk and to gaze starry-eyed at me, and I continued to feel guilty. "We are friends only, you know that," I said to him over and over.

"Friends." He grinned. "Whatever you say, Shoko." There was no disguising the hope in his eyes. I wondered if mine were the same.

My mother thought it was time for Tetsuo and me to get engaged. "You can't run around with only him unless you're engaged," she told me. "Everyone will think you're fast." Needless to say, she didn't know about Ronin.

Tetsuo made good money, and had been promoted to work at the front desk. Everyone thought he'd be a manager one day. My brain had to agree with my mother's logic. It only made sense, though my heart sank when I thought of spending the rest of my life on this island. She arranged it all with Tetsuo's parents, and we were officially engaged.

Then one day I arrived home from work a little early. I unlocked my door and saw Tetsuo's face, eyes closed, poised above my prostrate roommate. It took a minute for me to realize what they were doing, since I had never seen it done before. "Aaaah!" I screamed. Yuki screamed. I left the apartment and ran down the street.

"Shoko, wait!" Tetsuo called from the apartment window. "It's not what it looks like."

The engagement was off. Secretly, I thanked Tetsuo. I was free again. Then I began my American phase.

Though I flirted with the Americans (all the better for tips), I never had dated one. Plenty wanted to. Of course they did; they were a bunch of young servicemen in love with Japan.

It wasn't worthwhile for me. There was a ban on dating Japanese girls, effective for all ranks. Not that that stopped many. A girl, Mariko, who worked at the checkout desk did. She was two years older than me, with a long face and teeth a bit too big for her features. Still, she had a nice figure and a sweet laugh.

"She's seeing a staff sergeant and a lieutenant," Megumi, who worked with me in the gift shop, whispered. Megumi was a decade older, married to one of the lower-level managers, and the best gossip source in the region.

"Single guys?" I was doubtful.

"And they both want to marry her." Megumi's painted-on brows lifted in amazement.

"Pick the officer." I laughed and dusted another figurine.

Mariko disappeared one day. She didn't show up for work and no one was interested in finding her.

"What happened?" I asked Megumi.

Megumi shushed me. "She is not coming back."

"Did she get married?" I asked eagerly.

Megumi waved her hand in front of her face, indicating no.

I understood. Mariko had gotten pregnant and left. Would her family take her in? What would become of her? Poor Mariko. This was not going to happen to me.

Then something surprising occurred. Mariko had been far from the only one dating Americans. Finally the military decided they could no longer ignore the "problem." They decided to lift the ban on dating and marrying Japanese. Now, provided the

Americans got all the proper documentation, they could fraternize with and even marry Japanese. Of course, the military made sure it was nearly impossible to navigate the paperwork maze.

"A thousand signatures by a thousand different officials are required," Megumi remarked. "No one is getting married anytime soon."

Nonetheless, it was legal, and therefore possible. None of these Japanese men were going to do anything for me. *America is the way of the future,* I reminded myself of my father's words.

And Ronin? I couldn't deny how handsome he was, or how nice. Or how he made me feel, all fine and intelligent and vibrating with life.

But there was no future with an Eta gardener. It would mean everyone I had ever known shunning me. My father would likely get banned from his church. Our family would be ruined, even if I left the country.

My father heard about the ban being lifted. The next time I visited home, he sat me down. "Shoko, this is your opportunity," he told me.

"What do you think I should do?" I was afraid to hear his answer, but I was a practical girl and knew what was coming.

"You must casually see them, find out what you can about each. Then you can marry the best one. It's very simple."

"But what if I can't?" Speaking to men in a foreign language, saying not just the price of an item but having real conversations, seemed impossible. I was also thinking about Ronin, though I could not tell my father this.

"Many people have managed." My father's voice was warm. "Because I cannot meet them all, I have a suggestion. Take pictures of the ones you like the best and I'll help you choose."

I agreed.

At the gift shop, I began accepting the Americans' offers. I had a different date every night, and ended up seeing several casually. Dinner and a movie.

They were all very interesting men in their own ways. One was from Boston, one from Atlanta, one was a pig farmer from Iowa, one was a blond boy from Los Angeles. I dropped most of the ones who tried to get fresh.

I returned home again to see my parents. "The only problem is I'm not sure they all have marriage on their minds," I told my father as he had his tea. "They want fun."

"Not too much fun." He smiled and slurped at his cup, closing his eyes in thought. Perhaps he prayed. Then he opened them. "You will know, Shoko. You are a good judge of character."

I thought of Tetsuo. Not always, I thought. I went back to work.

Charlie became one of my Americans. He came into the gift shop one night with his friends, acting very nervous.

I had never seen anyone like him. He had red hair! No Japanese person had red hair. And he had freckles, and was skinny like a little boy. He was short for an American, but still tall for a Japanese. His blue-green eyes stared at me. He wore a blue dress shirt, blue tie, and black pants.

A Japanese girl clung to him, wearing too much lipstick and a low-cut blouse. Her eyebrows were shaved and then drawn in. She looked down her nose at me.

I smiled at Charlie, and he blushed beet red. He disengaged himself from the girl. I went over to him. "May I help you, sir?"

"Cigarettes?"

I got him a pack. He pointed to some chocolates and handed me some money. "The chocolates are for you."

"Thank you." I smiled nicely at him, trying to figure out his rank. Not confident enough for an officer, I decided. It didn't really matter. The American dollar was so strong that all the servicemen, even the enlisted ones, were rich here. The girl with him glowered. My heart beat faster.

"You speak English real well."

I bowed my head. "Thank you, sir."

His friends laughed. He blushed. "Call me Charlie."

"Okey-dokey, Charlie." I'd heard "okey-dokey" from another guy. I liked how it sounded. I started walking away, my wooden *geta* shoes clattering, but Charlie leaned toward me.

"Are you free later?" he asked.

I shook my head, an American custom I had observed. He probably thought I was another cheap girl.

Charlie smiled, and his face looked gentle and kind. "How about tomorrow? I'll take you to a movie."

"Yes, I can do that," I said, my eyes lowered.

Even though I was seeing Americans, I still saw Ronin during my lunch breaks. He was an interesting friend, that was all, I told myself. Not even a real Eta, since his father was European. I made all sorts of excuses to myself.

Of course, Ronin was still supposed to be off-limits, but he was right that in this day and age when Americans dated Japanese, it hardly seemed to matter too much. Old rules didn't apply. At least, not to this degree of casual friendship.

"Can you go anywhere and dance?" I asked him one day. We were sitting on the edge of the fountain in the middle of the maze. He had brought me a *bento* box packed by the hotel — a sticky rice ball rolled up with salt, covered in a seaweed wrap; steamed swordfish; and a spinach salad sprinkled with sesame seeds. The *hashi* — the chopsticks — were wrapped in a cloth napkin and secured with a tie.

"Of course." He lifted up half the salad with his *hashi* and popped it into his mouth. "People at nightclubs don't know who I am. No one would unless they checked my background. Like if I wanted to marry." He looked at me meaningfully.

"I could never marry an Eta." I took a bite of the cool rice ball. "My parents would throw me out."

"But you'd marry one of these Americans you run around with," he said, leaning close to me. "Someone you don't love, just to leave."

Before I could respond, he drew me in

close and kissed me. I knew I shouldn't let it happen, but I did. The kiss went on for what felt like minutes before I pushed him away.

"How dare you!" I said, getting up. I started running back toward the hotel.

"Shoko, wait!" Ronin said, coming after me, but I didn't stop. He caught my arm and whirled me toward him. "Shoko, we can go to America together. It will be a new beginning. I've already applied for my passport. I will take you there."

"No," I said, surprised at the shame I felt. There was a certain cachet in marrying an American, but not in marrying an Eta. Americans were up, Eta were below down. Even if it was unfair, I couldn't change it. "They'll never grant you a passport, Ronin."

He kissed me again, as if to try to convince me. His arms felt strong and safe, his body hard against mine. I inhaled the smell of him, cut grass, earth, and salt. "Meet me here tonight," he said. "Midnight."

"All right," I said. My knees actually felt weak.

I'd never felt anything like what I felt with Ronin. That night, and every Friday night for weeks after, I met Ronin in the garden. They were the happiest hours of my life, but I was also plagued with guilt, both for leading Ronin on and for what my family would think if they saw me. I would have to choose between my family and my love. Deep down, I knew I could not do this to my family. It was my job to marry well, not bring generations of shame to them.

Slowly I started dropping some of the American men I was seeing informally. Their laughter and easy ways no longer seemed as appealing. The time for superficial fun was over. I was not enjoying being single, with all these freedoms, as much as I thought I would. At the end of the day, my feet hurt and dancing became tiresome. My job at the hotel was so easy I could do it half asleep, yet there was no opportunity for promotion. I was twenty now, and because my situation would not improve on my own, I wanted to marry someone who could help it improve.

I took photographs of the men I thought were the best prospects, the ones who treated me respectfully, who held the door open for me and made efforts to communicate. I kept these in a special black lacquered box, inlaid with white mother-of-pearl cranes, to show my father later. I would marry the American of his choice, I decided. If I could not marry Ronin, I might as well marry any of these men. They were interchangeable to me. My father would at least have the guidance of prayer to help him, while my instincts seemed poor at best, leading me down difficult paths.

Charlie took me out several times. We went dancing, but Charlie was a horrible dancer, so we stopped that, to the relief of my feet in their high heels. We saw American movies, subtitled in Japanese. Mostly we sat and talked, or attempted to talk, over food, always ending with an American-style ice cream cone. If I didn't watch out, I'd gain too much weight for him to be interested.

One day, my brother came to see me and Tetsuo during his spring break, and stayed in a room at the hotel. They were still friends, even though Tetsuo was a cad. "Who can blame him," Taro said callously, "after he was stuck with an elephant like you."

I hit him in the shoulder, hard enough that he rubbed it. "I hope you're doing well in school, little brother," I said. He was in his final year. "Or else I won't pay for the rest."

"Don't worry," Taro said. "This hotel is nice. Maybe I'll have a party tonight."

"Be good," I warned. His room was nice, much better than his cramped apartment at his college. This was American-style, with a bed off the floor, carpeting, curtains to keep out the light, and a radio.

"Testuo will be here," Taro said, grinning. "Don't you want to get back together?"

"Mother already said I should not," I said, sniffing. "I had to get a new roommate because of him."

That night, I met Ronin in the garden again. It was to be our last time. I was sick of working in the gift shop, and the aircraft carrier, which had all my Americans on it, was due to leave in six months. That was just enough time to get married and settled before they left. I had to think of my family and of myself. I had to stop leading Ronin on.

Ronin sat stock-still in the moonlight after I told him. "Let's leave tonight," he said, grabbing my hands. I felt sick and hopeful at once. "We'll marry and leave."

"I have no passport," I said.

"We'll go to the north, where we're unknown. I'll change my name to yours." Ronin stroked my arm, sending shivers up and down it. "I have no reason when it comes to you, Shoko." He kissed me, tasting of rice and miso soup, his lips soft as pillows.

With the last of my resolve, I stood up

from the blanket strewn on the ground. "I have to go." From somewhere I heard laughter and music. "I won't see you again."

"Wait." Ronin hugged me, then touched my face with tenderness. I closed my eyes.

Then I gave way to weakness. I should have known I was asking for it, meeting him alone in the garden that way, but I couldn't say no again.

When you marry an American, it is not to be expected that every person in your family will be happy for you. Some still cling to old-fashioned precepts of Japanese-ness. They may shun you. It does not matter. You have embraced the modern reality of what it means to be Japanese. They are the ones who will be left behind. Remember this, and do not be ashamed.

— from the chapter "Turning American,"
How to Be an American Housewife

EIGHT

The morning after I said good-bye to Ronin, I went to work in the gift shop as usual. I put him in another part of my mind, behind a locked door. That didn't stop me from gazing into space a few times that morning, causing my boss to speak sharply to me.

At midday, my brother came into the gift shop. His face was a stern mask, heading into battle. I believed my brother's greatest regret was that he was too young to have been a *kamikaze.*

"Shoko." He already had a headmaster's voice.

"You look just like Father when you're mad," I teased him. "What's wrong?"

"I must speak to you in private." His voice was ice.

I got a bad feeling in the pit of my stomach. I'd never seen my brother's eyes so cold, not even during the war. And pained.

120

"Is it Mother?"

He shook his head and pointed silently to the door. I was so relieved that I followed without my usual smart remarks.

We went up to his hotel room, walking up the three flights of stairs, the sound of our shoes the only noise in the empty concrete stairwell.

Taro shut his door. "Did you think no one would find out? All the staff is talking. Tetsuo told me everything."

"I don't know what you mean." My response was automatic. I did know — Ronin. I sank into a chair.

Damn Tetsuo. Why couldn't he leave me alone? He owed me more, after what he had done to me. I had thought I was being so secretive. Now I realized it had never been a secret at all. Probably someone saw me with Ronin and had gossiped about it to Tetsuo. Of course he had to stick his big nose back into my business.

"It's bad enough, running around with Americans. But an Eta! An Eta!" Taro stood over me, his voice angry but not too loud. He didn't want the whole hotel to hear. "You have shamed your family, Shoko."

"Taro, I'm sorry. It's not what you think." I took a deep breath. "Ronin is a kind, hard-working man. In another life, I would marry him. But I broke it off."

I told myself this was true. Last night — I had slipped. I had woken, Ronin's arms around me, in a daze. We were still on the blanket in the garden; I had no idea what time it was. The moon had disappeared, but I could see every star from here to Mars.

"Ronin." I had pushed at him. He was deeply in slumber, a soft flutter around his lips. "I have to go."

His eyes were white in the darkness. "Where?" He grabbed my arm. "Let's make a run. Tonight. Right now."

"I don't have my clothes." What was I saying? I wasn't going anywhere with him.

"You don't need them. I'll buy you new ones."

I laughed bitterly. "Ronin. This is madness."

"It's not madness. It's love." He pulled me down for a kiss. "There. Do you feel that with any of your Americans?"

"Stop it." I pulled away. I needed to leave fast, before I destroyed my life. I thought about my parents. My brother, asleep in the hotel right next to us. I couldn't devastate them. I stood.

"If you go, I'll follow you," Ronin said. "Everyone will know anyway."

I didn't turn. "I know you. You wouldn't

do that."

He exhaled. "No. I wouldn't."

My head drooped so low it touched my chest. "Fool," I whispered to myself. Ronin deserved better than me. I was a coward. "Good luck in America."

I looked up at my brother in shock. Taro's shoulders were shaking, his eyes wet. I had never seen my brother cry before.

"I'm so angry I could kill you," he muttered, sitting on the bed. The covers were all messed up and I smoothed them automatically. "Once a maid, always a maid."

I knelt beside him. "You won't tell Father, will you?"

"Of course not. It would kill our parents to know." He grabbed my shoulder. "Have you really broken it off with him?"

"Last night. Father wants me to marry an American, and I agree." My voice sounded stilted. Taro heard it.

"Why couldn't you be a normal Japanese girl and marry a respectable Japanese man? What you've done is unforgivable." Taro shook his head. "This independence has not been good for you, Shoko."

I bit my lip, tasting the thick wax of my lipstick. If I were truly independent, I would have been on a train with Ronin right then.

"I didn't hear you complaining when I paid your tuition."

"I won't have that anymore. I'll pay my own way through." Taro lit a cigarette. "Tetsuo is still in love with you, you know."

I shut my eyes. "He should have thought of that before he bedded my roommate." If Tetsuo hadn't done that, I would still be with him, getting ready for marriage. Everything would be far simpler.

He blew smoke rings at me. "He means to have some words with your boyfriend."

I grew fearful. What did this mean? Words or fists? Tetsuo was notoriously hotheaded. I remembered how angry he had been when I danced with another boy. "Tell him not to! There's no need."

Taro shrugged. "I told him I would take care of it, that this was between you and me, but he ran off anyway. You know Tetsuo."

I hurried to the little house on the edge of town where I knew Ronin lived. On our walks, I had asked him to show me where he lived. Always he refused. "Even I know better than to bring you to such a place," he had said, merely pointing to the house with a small British flag being flown at his doorway. It was no more than a shack in

124

the middle of others like it, a poor enclave in the middle of this suddenly prosperous city.

Taro followed a few hundred feet behind me, worried, no doubt, about the reputation of our family being ruined by me venturing here. *He still can't run as fast as I can,* I thought to myself. *It's the alcohol and cigarettes.* I tried to lose him by wending through side streets and alleys, but he stayed within sight.

The Eta who lived near Ronin stared at me. I paid them no mind and rushed to Ronin's house. The door was open. A rat-nosed policeman in an olive-green wool suit was standing to the side, writing on a pad of paper. I snuck in behind him.

"Ronin!" I screamed. "Are you there? It's Shoko."

In my heart, I hoped he had left for America already. He had to have.

It was dark inside. It smelled earthy, tangy. Blood. Somehow I didn't retch. I saw a mostly packed suitcase leaning against the wall. "Ronin!" I called again. My mind wouldn't let me believe what was happening. I felt like I was in a movie, watching myself move through the tiny space.

"Get out!" The policeman hauled me backward.

"Let go!" At the other side of the room, I caught sight of a crumpled heap of gardener's clothes and two feet twisted in ways that feet shouldn't be.

Taro, arriving at last, skidded to a halt. "No, oh no," he breathed. "What did he do?"

"Ronin!" I shouted again, before I fainted. My brother caught me.

I awoke in Taro's room. Late-afternoon sun, the color of tangerines, bathed the Western furnishings with an eerie glow. I wondered if it had been a dream. It had to have been. Indigestion, no doubt.

Then I saw my brother, in a chair near the window. I sat up abruptly. "You killed him!" I shrieked, launching myself toward him. My fist caught him on the jaw; off guard, he lost his balance. I hit him again, not caring about the popping noise from my hand, punching his chest as hard as I could.

"I didn't know! I didn't know. Tetsuo is insane!" Taro said. I hit him again and again and he did nothing to restrain me, he stood like a scarecrow. I cracked him in the nose and he began bleeding.

My brother would only look at me. "You can hit me if it will make you feel better. I thought he would rough him up at worst, tell him to stay away from you."

I gulped and sat on the bed. The sight of the blood was making me feel faint again. "Did you tell the policeman who did it? Or did you cover that up for your friend?" Tetsuo — who would have thought he was capable? For a second, I had to count myself lucky that I hadn't married him.

"Yes. They're looking for him." He brought me to him in a hug. "I didn't know — I was trying to protect you."

"Then you should have been born first." I fell onto the bed, crying and beating my fists on the scratchy coverlet. What had Ronin done besides show me some kindness? This was all my fault. My vanity. I should have told him to go away and never return, or I should have gone with him. I was too weak to do either. Fickle. I berated myself and wept until I was empty. I stared up at the ceiling, eyes burning dry.

I stayed for two days. Taro came in and out, bringing soup, patting my back, pleading with me to get up. I ignored him.

When Taro couldn't rouse me, he told the hotel I'd taken ill and took me to my parents' home, me leaning on his shoulder as though I were deathly ill as we walked through the hotel.

The workers came out to say good-bye. "Come back soon." Mr. Lonstein touched my shoulder softly. I wondered if he knew what had happened, if he even noticed that his best gardener and desk man were gone for good. His eyes pitied me. I leaned against Taro even harder.

An important criterion in choosing your American mate is his blood type. Military men often wear identifying necklaces, "dog tags," which bear the blood type. Learn the English letters and recognize them.

AB — The worst kind. They do whatever they want whenever they want. They make horrible husbands.

A — They are reliable and calm.

O — They are social but sometimes need more pushing to finish what they start.

B — Very practical, but dull.

O goes best with other O's and AB's.

A can marry A or AB.

B can marry B or AB.

AB can marry anyone who will let them.

— from the chapter "A Map to Husbands,"
How to Be an American Housewife

NINE

A week after Ronin died, I awoke to see Father sitting beside me, a lacquered box of photographs in his hand. I had done as he had asked, dutifully sent him pictures of my Americans, every one I thought I could possibly live with, or who at least would want to marry me. "Shoko-chan, feeling better?"

I nodded slowly.

"It's time to look at your photos." He sounded cheerful, as though we were going to engage in a delightful task.

I sat up. As my father looked through the black-and-white pictures, he asked, "Is there one in particular you like?"

I could not have cared less. I told myself I had to get over Ronin. In relative terms, my troubles were tiny.

"Anyone?" Father prompted.

"No," I whispered. I closed my eyes. Father would pick this time, not me. I couldn't be trusted.

"I will look at their eyes." Father flipped through. "This one looks shifty." He tossed out the Iowa pig farmer. "Undependable." He threw out the man from Boston. "This one, this one has honest eyes." He stopped at Charlie. "Light in color. Are they blue?"

"Yes." My heart fluttered a tiny bit, thinking of Charlie's blue eyes and his easy laugh.

"Perhaps the eyes of your children will be blue. With a Japanese slant. How beautiful." Father slapped the photo down beside me. "He's the one. Has he asked you?"

"No." I lay back down. Did Charlie even notice I was gone? Had he gone to the hotel asking for me?

"Then it's time for you to go back to work. You ask him." Father pushed a bowl of rice toward me. "You like him, don't you?"

I felt like I could sleep for another century or so, but I roused myself. For the first time in a week, my stomach growled. "Yes, Father."

Charlie was a good choice. At least Father hadn't picked the pig farmer; I don't know what I would have done if I had had to breathe in pig shit for the rest of my life.

Charlie was a corpsman, or medic; he worked hard and made great money, or so I

131

thought at the time, compared to anyone else I knew. He was even a good blood type — O. I looked at his dog tags and reported what I saw to my father. "The best!" Father exclaimed with a chuckle. Charlie was also more ambitious than usual for his blood type, which was good. When he got out of the Navy, he said, he was going to go back to school and become a doctor. He was as bright as the doctors he worked for, so why shouldn't he? He never complained about anything. He was honest. He bought me things like small jewelry boxes and handkerchiefs. Pretty things. But he had never tried to kiss me, like the others had. I worried that he didn't like me that much. "He is simply old-fashioned, a gentleman," Father assured me, though he had never met Charlie.

I missed Ronin more than I could bear, but I put him aside. They never caught Tetsuo, and if they had, they wouldn't have done anything to him. We lived in a warrior culture. People would say that Ronin got what was coming to him. I'm sure that's what Taro told himself, if he thought about it at all.

I had to do what I needed to do now. Charlie's time here was halfway over. My options were running out.

If I stayed in Japan, what would I have? I couldn't go to college. I couldn't work at the hotel forever. Young women got replaced constantly with the newer, better models. Nor was finding a Japanese man that easy. My mother had exhausted her matchmaking abilities with Tetsuo; all the young men who had any ambition at all had left to seek their fortunes elsewhere. My hometown was a ghost town. I needed to get out or become one of those wrinkled spinsters, waiting at home for suitors who would never come.

Charlie took me on a date. We had ice cream cones and went for a walk along the harbor. Like two Americans in a movie. We stopped on a metal bridge over the water and looked at the Navy boats while leaning against the railing and eating our cones. I felt a little out of breath and sick to my stomach, as I often did since Ronin was killed. This time, I figured it was due to the ice cream — vanilla — because I was unused to cow's milk.

We looked down at the grayish-green water at the same time. Charlie and I tried to talk sometimes, but often we were comfortable in quiet. I wiped the sweat discreetly from my brow and hoped I didn't smell too bad. Charlie glanced at me with a shy smile. I smiled back expectantly.

133

"Humid today," he said, in his slow English.

I didn't understand. He made a fanning motion with his hand and pulled his shirt away from his skin.

"Oh, yes." I laughed. Charlie was really good at pantomime.

I waited again. He popped the rest of the cone back in his mouth. "Time for me to report back to the ship."

He was never going to ask me. "You leave soon?"

"Pretty soon."

I took his hand. It was cold despite the heat. Cold hands, warm heart, they say. I squeezed it. "You like date me?"

"Of course." He squeezed back, then put his arm around me. "I'm going to miss you," he added, his voice husky.

I rested my head on his shoulder. "You want to marry?"

He put his chin on my head. "Someday. Why?"

I stepped back, put one hand on a hip, and cocked my head to the side, pretending to be indignant. "Why you think I date you long time?"

He laughed. "Okay, then."

It took some people years to get the proper marriage paperwork. The Navy always changed the rules, saying if you filled out the blue form but not the green, then fill out the yellow with three copies. It was worse than taxes, they said. But Charlie filled out everything the next day. And then, with no problem, like magic, the Navy approved it.

About two weeks later, he took me to the courthouse. We signed our names on some papers in front of an official wearing horn-rimmed glasses, who shook our hands without smiling.

Charlie turned to me. "That's it."

I frowned. "What it?" No ceremony, no kiss, nothing? Was this American?

Charlie grinned. "We're married."

We rented a nice big house in town, where the richer people lived, using up all our money. "Two bedrooms!" Charlie said. "We had two bedrooms in my family for six kids and two parents!"

"Very nice." I smiled at him. I was learning English little by little. Charlie said when we went to America, he'd buy me a TV set and I'd pick it up in no time. We had no money left for furniture, so we had to wait for his next paycheck to buy that. Every payday after that, Charlie bought me lots of beautiful clothes. I went to a tailor and had

135

several fashionable American-style dresses made, a yellow silk suit, handmade shoes. My new husband loved pretty things as much as I did. I went to the beauty parlor every week to get my hair done. For the first time in my life, I didn't have to work. I felt rich. "I love to show off my beautiful wife," he said, giving me hugs. Charlie would always take care of me.

Around the time we married, I figured out I was pregnant. I was afraid to tell Charlie, afraid he'd figure out on his own that a baby born eight months after was not his. I decided to wait until after the danger of miscarriage had passed. I could tell him the baby was premature. I tried not to gain too much weight. A big baby would give it away.

I took Charlie home for a traditional Japanese wedding. To pay for it, I gave my mother a hundred dollars. One hundred guests, dinner, rental for the ballroom — one hundred dollars paid for it all.

As Charlie and I walked up our street, I pointed out my home. The kimonos on my mother's clothesline flapped in the wind. Not fancy silk ones that foreigners thought we wore every day. Plain cotton *yukata*. I wondered if Charlie would laugh, but he didn't. He came from poor, too.

"Welcome, Charlie," Mother said, managing to get the *l* sound out better than I could. She fixed my favorite, a rice curry, with extra-hot spice. Her hair had gone all white now, her skin devoid of any elasticity. In ten years, she would be dead.

I knelt on the floor. Charlie had told me this hurt his knees, and taking off his shoes all the time had made his arches fall, but he was getting used to it. He was a good sport about doing Japanese things. Like a lot of the Navy people coming into Japan, he had fallen in love with the culture as well as with a woman. "My husband even likes sushi," I said to Mother proudly.

She was impressed. "Most foreigners can't eat it at all."

Charlie took a bit of curry and his eyes welled. I gave him some tea to cool his mouth.

My younger sister, Suki, crept up to him. She was fifteen and still our baby, even though anyone could see she was a lovely young woman with long black hair, wearing her school uniform of a white blouse and long plaid skirt. I was happy to see she was a bit plump; this meant she was eating well for once.

Suki touched Charlie's hair. "His hair is fire!"

He pulled his head away. Charlie had his

curls combed into a jelly roll, one on each side of his head, put into place with a lot of hair ointment. "Yes, fire," he agreed in Japanese. He patted it back where she had mussed it.

He had gotten used to the attention. It was probably a lot more than he'd ever gotten in the United States.

My father knelt by him and watched him eat gravely, so intent that Charlie got nervous. His gaze meant approval. "It was a good choice, Shoko?" His hair was gray, too, and his skin already wizened. He ate slowly, as though he had all the time in the world to savor his food.

"Yes." I put my hand over Charlie's, the hand that had my sparkling new rings from the Navy Exchange department store. A diamond engagement ring, surrounded by a swirl of diamonds on the wedding band.

"Beautiful!" Mother picked up my hand to admire it. "Better than the richest ladies in Tokyo, I expect."

Father spoke to Charlie in the limited English he had been able to pick up. "Like Japan?"

"Hai." Charlie knew more Japanese than my father knew English. Charlie had gotten books on Japanese and studied them in an effort to communicate with me. He had a

kimono made for himself. He waited at the shrine while I prayed and wrote a prayer for himself in awful Japanese letters. He tried hard.

"Taro will be coming," Mother said, happy to have her children all together again.

I felt the sickness in my gut again. I hadn't seen Taro since he had left me here after Ronin. Taro had gone back to school, finishing out the semester with my money, and then gotten a job, refusing to take any more of it. My parents thought that was natural, because now I was married and out of the family, but I knew the real reason why.

"Does he know?" I asked my father. "Does he know we got married?"

"Yes." Father took a sip of tea. "He was hurt that he wasn't there."

"No one was there. That's why I'm here now." I guessed that Taro was only hurt because he had no chance of stopping me.

As though reading my mind, Father said, "Taro still wanted you to marry a Japanese boy." He waved his hand at my shocked face. "He'll accept it."

"Japanese boy?" Charlie said, that being the only expression he caught correctly.

I shook my head at him in a gesture he had taught me, and smiled. "Eat." Poor

Charlie, left out by my family chattering away.

My father felt bad also, because he leaned to Charlie and said, "You like Navy?"

"Yes, sir."

The door opened, shining bright light into the room. Taro stood silhouetted by sun. My little brother all over again. My heart ached.

He shut the door.

I stood. Charlie did, too. I bowed formally. "Please meet my husband, Charlie."

Taro stared at Charlie. Charlie held out his hand. "Nice to meet you," Charlie said in slow Japanese.

"Did you start eating without me?" Taro said to my mother.

"Taro, say hello to Charlie." Mother switched to Japanese.

"Hey, cowboy," Taro said in English, shaking Charlie's hand. "Japan is treating you real well, huh? Got a wife and everything."

Charlie blushed. Mother was shocked. "Taro! Be polite."

Taro pursed his lips, speaking to me in Japanese. "What makes you think he won't dump you when you get to the States? That's what happens. American servicemen can't get used to being married to a Japanese woman."

"I'm getting out of here." I leaned over to him. "Remember who got you out of this place. Me. Now it's my turn."

He made a rude noise with his lips. "You are disgusting. You'll do anything to get out of here, no matter how low."

"Taro!" my mother cried helplessly.

"If you could understand my position for one moment, you would know how hard this is," I said, squeezing my hand into a fist. I was glad that Charlie couldn't understand my brother. I hoped Taro wouldn't punch him. I would hit Taro first.

Charlie was nervous. "Have I done something to offend?" he said in Japanese.

I looked at Charlie helplessly, not knowing how to say, "It's not your fault." It wasn't Charlie's fault that while he was being trained to call us yellow-skinned monsters, we had been trained to call them fiends. I didn't have the English words for the bombing raids or the lack of food or the atomic bombs. To explain that some Japanese would submit in practice to being conquered, but not in spirit, no matter how much it only hurt themselves.

Taro clapped his hands slowly. "Very good, cowboy," he said in English.

My father had quietly watched this exchange. "We lost the war, Taro. It is time for peace, to accept the hand of fate. *Tokidoki.*"

Taro did not waver. He pointed at me. "You go to America and you are no longer my sister." He muttered under his breath, *"Pan pan."*

I bowed my head down, my heart breaking. *Pan pan* was a horrible insult, worse than whore, what they called prostitutes who sold themselves to the enemy to make money. "If that is what you want."

He bent down by my head. "All I wanted was a simple sister, a sister to be proud of."

Taro straightened and turned to my husband, his expression implacable. Charlie's forehead crinkled. "Good luck, Chuck." He bowed to Charlie, then turned and left my parent's house.

At our wedding in my father's church, Charlie and I wore traditional kimonos. As we were purified, as Charlie carefully read the Japanese words of commitment, as we drank our sake, I kept expecting Taro to walk in and take his place next to my mother. He had to. I was his sister.

I never saw him again.

It is important to support your husband's work endeavors. In America, the Wife tends to complain if the husband spends many hours at work. The Japanese Wife should know this is only good and natural. The American Wife is too demanding. Be sure to guard against this tendency once you are assimilated.

— from the chapter "A Map to Husbands,"
How to Be an American Housewife

TEN

The day after my visit to Dr. Cunningham, I awoke with my heart pounding and the taste of tin in my mouth, the image of Taro still swirling in my head. I would not be able to go to Japan. No. It couldn't be. I could not wait for another year, until after a surgery that might go bad. Until after I was dead. I got up and counted my secret money again, just to make sure it was all still there.

I looked at myself in the mirror, at my wild hair sticking up, at the new wrinkles on my forehead that had formed overnight. No longer was this the face of my mother — she hadn't lived this long. I thought about what I should do and who should do it. Someone to go in my stead. My stand-in.

Sue. My daughter. She was my only choice. Mike could not do it. He gave up too easily; if Taro turned him away, Mike would shrug his shoulders and disappear into the backcountry of southern Japan. Sue would be the one who would not give up. I hoped all these years of toil and disappointment had not worn her down too much, yanked her spirit out as it had Charlie's. No. She still had time. She would do this for me. I would pay. She couldn't say no.

My granddaughter Helena could do it alone, if only she weren't so young. She was a bright girl, smart, outgoing. The kind of girl who wouldn't be happy in the life that I had had. Or her mother's.

I took care of Helena often when she was young. Day care was tough on her; anyone could see that. She was left from six in the morning until almost six at night. Every time I saw her, even when she was two years old, she had bags under her eyes. I wished I could do more to help out.

"You can't take care of her. You don't have the stamina to run after a toddler," Sue told me over and over. I thought if I willed it, I could do it. "All she would do at your house is watch TV. At day care she plays with the other kids."

Sue would leave her here for short periods, though, and I would take her in the backyard, or on a little walk up the street. Her toddler pace, stopping at every crack and ladybug, suited me.

Last week, Helena had come over while Sue went to the gym. She was looking more grown-up these days, beginning to get hips and breasts, and her skin was still unmarked by the acne that had plagued Sue.

Helena surveyed my curio cabinet in the bedroom, which held my shrine and some Japanese dolls. "Aren't there more dolls?" she asked, twirling a lock of hair around her finger. "I remember Doll Day."

"Yes. Girls' Day." I smiled, pleased that she remembered. On March 3, I would have Helena come over and we would get out all my Japanese dolls. You were supposed to have the Emperor, the Empress, and all their retinue, but we made do with what I had: some wooden *kokeshi* dolls, simple wooden figures made on a lathe, with spherical heads on sticks poking into their bodies; and several porcelain dolls with delicate features and silk kimonos. I had them stored in the garage.

"Can I see them?" Helena was always curious about Japan, always asking me for stories. For show-and-tell in third grade, she had brought me in to talk about kimonos.

I got out the *kokeshi* dolls and set them up on the dining table. "These I got for your mommy and daddy," I said, pulling out the matching couple. They had cartoonish big eyes, painted black hair, and red lips. Their bobble heads drifted away from each other. "See, they look away from each other."

"That means they don't love each other, right?" She wasn't upset. She blinked her eyes innocently.

"Yeah, that right. But this only legend." Some people said that the *kokeshi* held the spirits of the dead; maybe some long-ago religion had used them. I had bought mine from a tourist spot near a hot spring.

I got out two more. These had kimonos made of a soft flocked material; Helena felt them with her index finger, as she always did. "These me and Ojisan." I put them on the table next to the others. Their heads bobbled, wavered, then looked at each other.

"You love each other!" Helena grinned. She twirled the head around on Craig's doll. "Can I take these home?"

I shrugged. "Your mommy no like them."

"They remind her of a bad time, I guess." Helena spun the doll head faster. "But I want them."

"You try cause trouble, Helena-chan?" I smoothed her hair out of her face. "Why no wear hair back, see pretty face?"

"I like it like this." She shook her mane. "I am not causing trouble. I just want the

147

dolls. Will you get me dolls when I get married?"

"If get marry." I smiled. "No get married until thirty year old, got it?"

"I know, I know." She rolled her eyes.

I peered at her. "You wear eyeliner? Your mommy know?" Good girls didn't wear eyeliner at twelve. What path was she headed down?

She leaned to me. "Don't tell her, okay?"

My heart melted. "Okay. Our secret." I smiled. "You want make cookie with me?"

"Sure." Helena put the *kokeshi* dolls by the front door to take home. I hoped Sue wouldn't be angry.

Helena was my do-over daughter. With her, I had the patience to do everything I should have done with Sue. Cook. Teach about Japan. Hugging. I would have even taught her the language, if I hadn't been certain I would mess it up. She needed to learn proper dialect, not what we used out in the country.

Maybe Helena could go with Sue, if Sue would agree to go.

I pulled on my clothes. I needed to go see Sue, tell her. My hands shook as I put on my makeup. Charlie could not know.

Charlie pushed the door open. I jumped. "Hey, I thought I heard you up." He sat down to put on his shoes. "I'm going to help Mike move the rest of his stuff."

"Good." I smoothed the guilty look over on my face.

"Where are you going?"

"Store." I brushed down my hair quickly. I knew he thought I meant the store that was a mile away.

"Get some Maalox while you're out, okay?" Charlie left.

"Okey-dokey." I put on blue eye shadow and my coral Revlon Moondrops lipstick that I'd had for the last ten years. I made makeup stretch. Then I added foundation — it was lighter than the skin on my neck, Sue said, but that's how I liked it — and was ready to go on my secret mission.

Sue's office building was a long way away. Though I had my driver's license, I didn't do much driving on my own. Usually I avoided freeways, but I had to take three to get there. I kept to the slow lane the whole way.

Her building was tall glass that reflected the clouds and sun. The company was so big, it took up all the office space. At the receptionist's desk, I asked where Sue worked.

"Second floor, New Accounts. You want

me to call her?" the girl asked. She snapped her gum. Rude.

Another young woman was already heading through the double doors. "I go with her, okay?" I walked in behind the woman before she could let the doors close.

"It's upstairs to the right," the woman told me. Her clothes were so chic; her perfume smelled expensive. It made me wish that we could switch positions.

I thanked her. My mind whirred with the stories I needed to tell my daughter, to get her to understand why I needed her. I should have called. Maybe she had a meeting; maybe this wasn't a good time. How could I work Japan into a two-minute conversation? This needed hours, days maybe.

I found my way to my daughter.

Sue hunched over her small desk, typing. I looked around. Fabric walls not as tall as I was stretched from here to the smoked-glass window. The only light came from dim green fluorescents. I shook my head. This had to be the wrong place. My daughter was a manager. Managers had offices overlooking the ocean, didn't they? And secretaries doing all their work for them.

"Suiko-chan?"

"Mom? What on earth are you doing here?" Her tone was incredulous and, I thought, annoyed.

As usual, my daughter had blue-black circles under her eyes, as though life had socked her in the face. Hereditary, she said. Not from my side, I said.

Her hair was pulled back into a messy ponytail; too-long bangs hung over her face. I bit back my urge to tell her to straighten up. How could she get promoted looking like she'd rather be anywhere but here?

"Come say hi to you." I sat down. My feet dangled in the chair. Sue studied my brown wool dress slacks and the cream cashmere sweater I always wore to the Commissary, along with my heavy gold rope chain. If I didn't dress up for the store, I would never get to dress up.

Her coworker popped up from the next cubicle, wearing more makeup than a prostitute would have back in my day. "Hey, is this your mom?"

Sue nodded. "This is Shoko. Mom, this is Marcy." Sue seemed relieved to be interrupted. I shifted.

"How you do?" I held out my hand, my pronunciation careful.

"I didn't know Sue was half Asian," Marcy marveled. "I thought she was Hispanic."

"Filipina, maybe look like." People thought all Asians looked alike. Even Sue had a hard time telling the difference. I had tried to describe what the subtleties were; she still could not pick up on it. If she ever lived in Asia, she would know.

"I don't know these things." Marcy disappeared back into her den.

I wondered if Sue was ashamed to tell them about me. About herself. I played with my diamond engagement ring. It was too loose, spinning around my knuckle so much I was afraid it would fall off. Sue stared at that, too, then at my face, at the sunken hollows under my cheekbones. My face burned.

"No office yet? I thought you manager." She had pictures of Helena all over her walls. Helena in a school play, Helena at the beach. None of me or Charlie. No men. I touched the plastic laminate of the desk and blanched. "So *kitanai*." Dirty. "They too cheap for cleaning woman?"

Sue's brow furrowed. I spoke again, quickly. "Not your fault, Sue." No matter how much I tried to help her, or how hard Sue worked, she could not get ahead.

Sue had always been bright, always in the gifted classes, but other parents were able to boost their children in ways I couldn't. One February afternoon when Sue was in eighth grade, she arrived home from school and threw her backpack to the side.

"Pick that up, Sue." Then I saw the worried look on her face, still flushed from the walk and still round with baby fat. That year she had grown tall, bigger than most of the boys at her school. "What happen? Boy bother you?"

"I have to do a project for the science fair, and I don't know what to do." She sat in our old armchair and pulled off the lace doily from the arm, twirling it on her finger.

"Teacher no tell how?"

She shook her head. Every night, Sue struggled with her science and math homework as I watched helplessly. English and art were her subjects. Her father was no aid, either. These matters were beyond us, especially the way they were taught in the indecipherable "new style." I thought quickly. "I help," I said to her.

On the base of the mountain behind the house, I knew of a hollow that filled with rainwater if we had a good wet season. It was an easy, short ascent that Charlie had taken us to before, but still I held on to Sue's shoulder as we walked the orange-brown dirt trail. I carried an old pickle jar. "We see if pollywog come yet."

"Where do they live?"

"Hide underground. Egg dry up." We crested the small hill. Yes, there it was, the small pond, bordered by boulders and wild shrubs and an old mattress someone had dumped. I sent her down with the jar. "Go find egg."

Sue grew the tadpole eggs in two jars. One she kept in a dark closet, the other in the light. Naturally, the one in the light grew better. It was as good of a project as I could come up with. Sue was happy with it, reporting on their progress every day. "When they turn into frogs I'll put them back in the pond," she said.

We made the science fair display board out of an old cardboard box. I cut it as square as I could with a pair of scissors, but it turned out crooked. Sue used her father's old typewriter to type out her findings. We carefully lettered the headings by hand and glued it all onto the board with rubber cement.

"It looks pretty good," Sue said.

"Course. 'Cause Mommy help you," I said. She smiled.

The morning of the school science fair, I drove her to school. We walked into the auditorium with the sign and the jars.

Instantly I saw that her project wasn't right. The other students had bought their display boards, so they were bright white and perfectly straight. The headings were made out of stickers. But that wasn't all that caught my attention. It was the quality. One had a big machine heart that pumped fluid from one plastic compartment to the next. One had chemistry-lab results posted, with charts and results from experiments that could never be done at home. Another had a huge working model of an engine.

"How do this?" I asked Sue, pointing to the heart.

"His dad's a cardiologist," she said. "That one's dad is a mechanical engineer. That one's mother is a chemist." She drew her arms into her body and slouched. I did not tell her to stand up straight.

In front of the stage, I spotted Sue's science teacher in a cluster of parents. "I be right back," I said to her, walking over to the teacher.

I had only seen him once before, at the Open House in the fall. He was a short man, even shorter than I was. He looked like a skinny garden gnome. " 'Scuse me, Mr. Moynahan," I said in my sweetest voice, tapping him on the shoulder.

He turned away from the other parents, who smiled smoothly and blankly. This neighborhood school had both wealthy and not-so-wealthy families, but these parents all looked like professionals to me. Well groomed, the women in short heels and slacks, the men in polo shirts and khakis. I looked no different, I thought, in my own slacks and sweater set with my string of pearls. I looked like I belonged.

Mr. Moynahan held out his hand. "Mrs. Morgan! Isn't the fair wonderful?"

I nodded. "Oh, yes. But why you no tell Sue 'bout what buy? How we know how do all this?" I gestured to the machines and charts. "How I know all this?"

He frowned, then shrugged his plaid-shirt-covered shoulders. "This is how science fairs are always done."

"But you no tell kid how do. I no doctor. I no scientist. How expect me know?" I tried to keep my voice polite, but I could not remember when I was last so angry. "No fair, parent do all work." I took his arm and walked him back to where Sue's project leaned crookedly on a table. She was nowhere to be found. "See? I don't know 'bout these boards you can buy at store."

"Haven't you ever been to a craft store, Mrs. Morgan?" He examined Sue's project.

"I don't got money for craft store." I tried to think of how I could express myself better and wished Sue would come help. I spot-

156

ted her in the corner with her friends, turned deliberately away from me. I leaned toward Mr. Moynahan. "You gonna give my daughter bad grade 'cause you no tell her how to do this? Huh?"

He took a red Sharpie out of his pocket and wrote a B on her board. "That's for the project, Mrs. Morgan. Not for the display. The display only matters if you go to the county."

"And you going tell people 'bout board and how make look pretty?" I wanted him to tell me that next year he would do a better job. Next year, maybe someone like Sue would be saved this trouble.

His face rumpled as he tried to decipher what I had said. "But it's already done. Don't worry about it." He patted my hand. "You know, science isn't for everyone. Sue's a nice girl. Too quiet. I barely notice her." He gave me a little salute and turned and walked away.

I stood and waved to Sue. She walked over, her short heels making a dull clicking noise on the tile. "What?"

"These people know nothing." I shook my head. "No help kid out."

"Mom. Lower your voice." Sue shrank herself down again.

"I tell you what, science fair not fair." I

watched the parents, undoubtedly congratulating their Ph.D. minds on completing an eighth-grader's work. The cardiologist dad slung an arm casually around his son. I thought about putting my arm around Sue to comfort her, in the American way, but while I was thinking about it the moment passed and Sue moved out of reach. "No good school," I said instead.

"Just forget about it, Mom."

I looked up at her. She was so beautiful, so tall. Only a few friends ever came around. Her teachers hardly noticed her. How could she be so invisible to everyone? "You got speak up, Suiko, get what you want."

She sighed heavily, opened and closed her mouth. I wondered what she had been about to say.

I watched the parents for a minute, trying to figure out who had money and who didn't, who was nice and who wasn't, and was unable to. I looked at my own clothes and felt like a pretender.

The bell rang. Sue moved around her tadpole jars. The parents began filing out. I stayed put, watching my daughter move aimlessly, her head down.

"Sue, I tell you. Not right, how they do this. I talk principal." I put my hand on her shoulder.

She shrugged away. "Forget it, okay?" She turned and strode off. "I'll see you after school." I waited until she left, then went home myself.

"Mom, what are you doing here?" Sue's voice startled me over the clicking keyboards and phone beeps in her office. Maybe I had been daydreaming too long.

I breathed in and out. What would Sue believe? The Marine base with the Commissary was a few miles away from her work. As retirees, we got to use it as much as we liked. I had never been there without Charlie. I looked Sue in the eyes, a lighter, more golden brown than mine. "Oh, you know, I go Commissary. Thought I say hi." I waved. "Hi."

"Where's Dad?"

I made a show of rolling my eyes. "Daddy never let me get good food. Always penny-pinching. I go alone, get what I want. Dad help Mike move."

Sue twirled her pen in her fingers. I could read her. *My mother has lost her mind.* "I'm surprised to see you, that's all."

"You no want me here, I go." I knew she would not tell me to leave. "Want to see where daughter work."

She glanced at her clock, calculating how

159

many more minutes she had to spend with me before she could politely say good-bye. It was something she had started doing early on, around age nine. I couldn't say I blamed her. I had done the same with her sometimes when she was younger, wanting only to rest when she was ready to play.

"Mom. I can take lunch now. You want me to come with you?"

"If you like." I took care to make it sound like her suggestion. "Maybe get food for you, too. I take home and put fridge."

"Mom, I'm fine. I don't need you to buy groceries." She was offended.

She was a single parent. Of course we would help her whenever we could. We didn't have much, but we had more than enough for food. "I like to. My treat." I inhaled again. *I must talk to her about Japan.* "Maybe good mommy-daughter time, huh?"

She gave me a strange look. True, I had never used such a term. And, true, I had never tried to do things with her, the way some other modern American mothers did. I never took her out to lunch. We never chatted on the phone. I felt my heart do a fast thump-thump, unexpected.

I needed to tell Sue the other bit of news before I told her about Japan. Aunt Suki,

160

my sister. I studied the desk. "Aunt Suki die."

"Today?"

"Couple month ago. Her husband just now write." I shrugged, not wanting Sue to see how hurt I was. "Always forget 'bout little Shoko in America, yeah?"

"Was it her heart?"

I nodded. "Poor little Suki. Always she was happy one."

"That's terrible." Sue put her hand on mine.

She did not know how terrible. Sue did not know the bond of a sibling. Not with Mike. For this I would always be sorry. Nonetheless, I did not want to upset her with my sadness. "*Tokidoki,* huh? We know coming for long, long time." I smiled at my daughter. "Now you take me Commissary or what?"

Miramar was right down the road from where Sue worked, past car dealerships and furniture wholesalers. I looked at the disabled jets on show from the street. "I live here so long and never go single air show or museum."

"I didn't know you were interested in jets." Sue drove my car carefully, unused to the controls.

"Nobody ask me, do they?" The gate guard saw my decal and waved us through. Exhaustion tried to take over, but I resisted.

All the way there, past Marines playing softball and washing their cars on lunch breaks, I tried to find the right words to tell her about my worsening illness and Japan and found words for everything else instead. My heart beat unsteadily. Deep breaths. Sue chattered about this and that, sneaking glances at me.

Perhaps I should simply say it. *I am probably going to die in the next few weeks. Will you go to Japan for me?* She would crash the car.

We parked in a handicapped space, me hanging up my blue placard. "People give me dirty look all time," I said as we got out. "Think I not in wheelchair, nothing wrong me. Look nothing wrong with you, either." I looked at Sue's arms, her biceps so well toned. Like that Madonna singer. Elegant women never used to have muscles like that. "Your arm big like man." I squeezed.

"That's what happens when you don't have a man around the house." She laughed shortly. "Maybe that's why I'm single."

I had not meant to insult her. My head spun a little and I took hold of a cart, leaning hard on it.

It seemed I could barely open my mouth without Sue taking it the wrong way. For Sue's senior prom, her father had bought her a treat: a big makeover. Hair, manicure, makeup. The works. I was a little jealous. It had been at least thirty years since I'd had anything like that done. Me, who used to visit the hairdresser weekly, had been fending with home perm and color kits since Charlie left the Navy, saving money for the family.

"I do your hair. Save hundred dollars."

"No way, Mom. The last time you permed it, it looked like I stuck my finger in a light socket."

Her expensive hairdresser did her hair in a style unsuited to her round face, which was shaped just like mine. I took one look at it and blurted out, "Make your face fat." Maybe I should have told her before she put on her ice-green Cinderella dress and was all ready to go, but I thought she still had time to fix it. I wanted her to look nice. Of course, I didn't think she was ugly — that would be like calling myself ugly. Mothers were the only ones you could depend on to tell the whole, unvarnished truth.

Sue's eyes had filled with tears. I hoped her mascara wouldn't run. For a second I thought she would curse at me. Instead she sniffled, her tears drying up even as her face reddened under the makeup. "Thank you for your kind advice." She left the house without another word as her date, Craig, came up the front walk.

"You're too harsh, Shoko," Charlie had said. It was as close to criticism of me as he would get.

"What matter? Nobody listen." If my own mother had told me this, I would have taken her advice in the spirit in which it was meant.

I thought once Sue was grown, I'd stop being scared for her. But I couldn't stop. She still wasn't happy, fretting over unseen worries. I wondered what secrets she carried that she kept from her mother. I doubted she thought about what secrets I had.

The Commissary cart had a squeaky wheel. I had to push down harder on one side to make it stop. "You come dinner tomorrow?"

"Sure. Why don't we get a frozen lasagna so you don't have to cook?" Sue walked beside me, slowly.

"No good, frozen food."

"Mom, it's really great these days. That chicken we had last time at my place was precooked."

I wrinkled my nose. "Little bit dry. Didn't want say."

At the Commissary, I came up with a list out of nothing. We needed food; what did it matter if I bought it now with Sue instead of with Charlie? I again searched for the right moment. My heart thumped slowly.

I watched her pick out vegetables and fruits, looking each over for bruises, smelling them the way I'd taught her. A little girl and her mother passed, carbon copies of each other. Sue had never looked like she belonged to me or to Charlie. Her hair was brown; her skin was pale and would tan.

The little girl gave me a chubby-cheeked smile, and I smiled back. I could hardly believe my own baby was here before me, thirty-two and a mother of practically a teenager.

Sue had been too young to be a mother. I knew because I had been, too. At twenty, you're still a child. She had told me of her pregnancy one October day. Over the phone, though she lived only a few miles away.

It had been better for her not to see my face. Even my voice, I couldn't control. I shut and opened my eyes for several moments. All of the hopes and dreams she had

had since she was a little girl flashed before my eyes. At five, an artist. At seven, the president. At ten, a chef. Twelve, an archaeologist. But, really, I wanted her to graduate from college, marry well, have a job she loved. Children would come later. Now she would have to make do with survival.

"Are you there, Mom?" Sue had asked anxiously. "I'm still going to finish school."

"Maybe." My voice had an edge. I tried to soften it. "Hard work, Sue. You think 'bout this?"

"It's too late to think about it now, even if I hadn't." Sue sounded disappointed.

Charlie had been thrilled. "People have been having kids young forever," he said. "All they need is one room and a crib."

I had looked at him — this man who had not been the one to wash poopy diapers and hang them to dry, who did not get up with sick children while his spouse was at sea — and said nothing.

At the meat section, I still could not think of the right way to talk to Sue. My whole life, my right moments had been few. Charlie had not asked me to marry him; I had asked him. That was one right moment. And when Sue had called me to say she and Craig were getting divorced, I had a right

166

moment.

She had been crying so hard I could barely understand her. "It's over! It's over. You were right."

I wanted to cry with her. *Sometimes these things happen for the best,* I wanted to say. I could not say I was sorry she had gotten married, for they had had my granddaughter. I could not say I was glad he was gone, for Sue was weeping. I wanted to say that she was still very young and that she would find someone else, but this might not come true. *"Tokidoki,"* I said instead. Fate steps in sometimes.

But most of the time, I talked first, thought later.

We stared at soy sauce bottles in the Japanese aisle. "I wonder real Japan food look like nowaday." I leaned against the cart. *Wouldn't you like to see for yourself, Sue?*

It was so hard to talk to her. She moved fast, in a hurry, a hummingbird pausing at flowers.

"They don't carry this stuff anywhere." She threw in packets of Japanese candies, chocolate pretzels, dried fish. Sue had always loved Japanese food.

"Hey, Sue," I said casually, though my mouth was dry. "You like go Japan one day?"

"Sure, Mom. Someday."

"Soon."

My eyesight became black at the edges. My breath quickened, quickened too much, into hyperventilation, then fear. I was going to pass out. I noticed I was sitting on the floor. I forced myself to take deep breaths in and out.

"Mom? Oh my God. I'll call you an ambulance."

Sue had called one for me before, once. When she was ten and home alone. She was so brave then. She told the paramedics all my medications and history.

My breathing slowed, my heart steadied. "No. I okay. Ambulance too *takai.*"

"It's not too expensive, Mom."

My eyesight sharpened. A small crowd had gathered around. Sue leaned over me, her forehead creased in worry. I touched it lightly. "No do that. Get wrinkles."

"Mom." Sue grinned, relieved. "Let me at least drive you home."

"Then how get back work?" I shook my head, embarrassed now, embarrassed at all the people waiting for a big show. "Get me wheelchair cart. I finish shop."

Spaghetti sauce is the easiest American recipe to make, as long as you remember all the steps and do it far in advance. Letting it sit overnight in the refrigerator is best for developing its flavors. Add sugar if the sauce is too acidic.

Your husband will be amazed when he comes home to a big pot of spaghetti sauce. It is also a crowd-pleaser. Even little babies and Japanese people like spaghetti sauce.

— from the chapter
"Cooking Western-Style,"
How to Be an American Housewife

ELEVEN

Back at home, I rested on the couch while Charlie brought the groceries in. He and Mike had come to get me after Sue called. "No way you're driving home," she had said.

Charlie had been mad. "You're impossible, Shoko-chan, you know that?" he had shouted. "You're going to get yourself killed!"

I had to agree. How could I go to Japan if I couldn't even make a trip to the Commissary?

But Charlie's anger passed, a brief rainstorm. The nice thing about Charlie was he never held a grudge in his life, even when he should have. Once a drunk driver hit our car and cried so hard that Charlie took pity and didn't report him. "Everyone needs a second chance," he said.

I wasn't like that. I believed that if someone wronged you once, they would do it again. They shouldn't be given the chance

170

to try. Taro was just like me.

When it came time for Sue to arrive for dinner, I waited for her in the yard, watering the brown-tinged ice plant. I feared I had neglected it too long this time.

I hoped Sue would like the spaghetti. It was once her favorite. But perhaps her favorite had changed and I had not asked what her new favorite was.

For Sue's birthday, every year, I would cook whatever her favorite food was.

No matter what it was, she would get it. Most children wanted pizza every year. Not Sue. Once she asked for a ham with pineapple slices stuck on it with cloves. Once for sushi rolls. And often for spaghetti and meatballs.

I always made her the kind of cake she wanted, too, devil's food with chocolate frosting, though privately I thought chocolate with chocolate was too much chocolate.

"Why is it devil's food? Is it evil?" she had asked when she was five. We were having a party for her kindergarten classmates. She had invited the entire class and it looked like they were all coming. I had Charlie borrow kid-sized chairs from his church, and we put a linen tablecloth over our coffee table for the kids to sit at. She wore a pink party dress and had her hair in a ponytail that was sliding out.

"Probably because make you want to be a big devil and eat whole thing, 'cause Mommy's cake *oishī*." Delicious. I laughed and so did she. I fixed her ponytail again. Back then, her hair was red and slightly curly. It had darkened and straightened over time. "Your hair too slick, Suiko-chan. Never gonna stay."

"I'll take it out." She pulled the elastic free. "It's pulling my hair, anyway."

All the little kindergartners sat around the table, just like a Norman Rockwell painting, wearing party hats and laughing. Even Sue, usually so shy and quiet, whooped and hollered. "It's just what I wanted!" she screamed after she opened each gift.

"Sit down, I'll serve the cake," Charlie whispered to me. I did, and watched later as he led them through Pin the Tail on the Donkey and then outside for leapfrog, Sue's face smiling in the sun.

Looking back, I wondered why we didn't do this every year. But later it seemed like her birthday came and went and the most I could do was make her a dinner, not a whole party. We were either too broke or I was too overwhelmed with my health, or both. Sue had other parties later, small ones when she could entertain her friends on her own. I forgot to miss that joyful little girl until she was already grown up and gone.

Sue and Helena pulled up, blocking the driveway. "Obāchan!" Helena called out, giving me a big hug. "Smells great."

"You taller than me, Helena-chan."

"I have been for three years." She smiled and went inside.

Sue stood around, looking at the dead plants, the old windows, the crack in the chimney. I turned off the hose. "Gonna stand around all night?" I made my lips smile, but she looked in my eyes and saw what I meant. *Quit looking around. Don't tell us about the house. We already know.* They say that Asians are stone-faced, but it's all in the eyes. "Gotta finish dinner."

We went inside. Sue opened the silverware drawer. "Wash hand first. Lotta good college did."

Sue merely smiled. In one ear and out the other.

I remembered when I taught her how to wash the dishes. She had been six or seven. When I had been her age, I had done the laundry alone. "Use hot water, so hot make hands red," I had said to her, pouring a good amount of Palmolive into the sink.

She had stood on a stool and dipped her

hands into it. She looked at me with her wide eyes. "It's too hot to touch."

"Not too hot for me." I put my hand in to show her. "Hot water get off gunk, see?" I dipped a plate that had dried beans on it into the water to show her. "Now take rag and scrub."

I watched her make mounds out of the soap. "Mom, this is boring," she said in a whiny voice after a second. "Besides, it's still too hot."

"You get used to." I showed her how to clean the plates in a circular motion. "Then feel plate, see if all food got off."

She tested it again. "It's cooler now." She washed a few, rinsing them in clean water and clattering them onto the drying rack.

I examined these. "No. Food on. Do again."

"Where?"

I pointed to a speck.

"Can't you just wipe it off with the dish-towel?"

"Learn do right." I put the dish back into the sink. I would not let her get away with doing things halfway as I had with her brother.

She huffed a sigh, running her hand over her sweaty forehead, and washed the plate over.

■ ■ ■ ■

I didn't wish to be short with Sue now. I stifled my impatience and made my voice pleasant. "You hungry, huh?" I put two pounds of pasta into the boiling water.

"Is Mike eating with us?" Sue asked.

"Think so." When Sue was little, she would ask about Mike, who would show up occasionally, eat, and leave, without a word to her. "Mike loves you," I would tell her. "He show in own way. Mike loner. Different."

"He should work for Animal Control," Sue said. "He likes animals more than people."

It was true. Once there had been a rattle-snake in the garage, come down off the mountain.

I screamed every time I saw a snake, even a garter snake. "Kill it!" I had shouted. But Mike had gone in there, no shoes, no shirt, only shorts, and gently pushed it out with a broom handle. "It's not the snake's fault we built here," he said. The snake hightailed it to Lorraine's house, where it got its head whacked off with a shovel.

Sue was watching me like she thought I would break into a billion pieces. To distract her, I said, "Suiko-chan, get my big green cookbook. Want make peach oatmeal crisp dessert."

I stirred the noodles and the sauce. Sue opened the deep drawer where I kept my books. "What's this? *How to Be an American Housewife*?" She showed the book to me. There was an illustration of a dark-haired woman holding a plattered turkey in one hand, a broom in the other, as her husband and clean kids applauded her from the dinner table.

My heart sped up. I fought the desire to snatch it from her. "Housekeeping book. You take. Maybe give good idea."

Sue flipped through the book. "It's written in Japanese and English?"

"Yeah, so can learn language. Got recipes, tell about housekeeping."

"Cleaning floors, laundry, getting along in America? Did people really follow this?"

"Mommy did." Oh no. The photo was still in there. "Maybe you try, too. Let me see." I held my hand out. I needed to get the photo.

But Sue had already found it. "Cleaning Floors" was bookmarked with a photo, an old black-and-white of a Japanese man, printed on card stock. "Who's this?"

Ronin. I had forgotten the picture. "Nobody. Some guy I work with have crush, give me picture." I kept my voice casual, even disdainful. "Too late make dessert." I went into the dining area and sat down. I would begin telling her now. Now or never. "Suiko-chan, how many times I go back Japan?"

"Never."

I used to talk about visiting all the time, when I still thought Charlie would get promoted and we would have the money for it. To show Sue where she came from, show Mike. I had stopped talking about it a long time ago.

The timer beeped. "Noodle done."

Sue went to get the pot, but Charlie practically pushed her aside. "I'll do it, sweetie."

Sue and I watched nervously as he limped to the sink. This man used to lift bleeding men from the ground to a stretcher. He would not admit to needing help with a pasta pot. He sloshed the water into the sink, the hot water splashing up at him.

Sue put her head by mine. "Mom, what were you saying?"

No. Not now. "Tell Helena and Mike time for dinner."

Charlie turned on the TV for the news. Mike came and sat with us, sticking his fork into his plate before his bottom touched the chair.

Sue smiled uncomfortably at her brother. "You liking work?"

"They could pay me more." Mike was already halfway through his plate. "I gotta go." He was out the door, a wind whipping through.

I poked at my plate. My hunger had been low lately. Sue and Helena ate steadily. I waited for them to be done. Waiting was my best skill now.

I should have removed that photo Sue found in the *Housewife* book. It belonged in a photo album, not stuck as a bookmark in a dusty, forgotten volume. Better that Sue had it and the book. I hoped she could use it.

For the first years of my marriage, it had been my handbook, my guide to doing everything. Rules for living, American style. Sometimes it was right, and sometimes it was not. Sometimes I liked it, and sometimes I didn't. But that was just like life. You don't always get to do what you want, do you?

In the Japanese household, it is assumed that the man will earn the money and the woman will manage it to accommodate the family's needs.

American husbands earn and manage money. Usually, an allowance will be given to his Wife to pay for household items. The Wife must stay within the household budget.

A Wife must not challenge his maleness by taking over budgetary matters. Do not fall into the trap of acting Japanese in this area.

— from the chapter "A Map to Husbands,"
How to Be an American Housewife

TWELVE

Sue stared at me from the couch in my living room. Her shirt had a bit of spaghetti sauce on it from the dinner we had just eaten. Like her father's always did after every meal. I decided not to point this out presently. "I got tell you something."

Charlie and Helena clattered in the kitchen, getting dessert ready. I had not discussed my plan with Charlie. With anyone. I did not need to. Nobody else had a say.

"Okay." She shifted her body warily.

I played with the crocheted doily on the arm of my chair. Probably she believed I was about to give her another lecture, another reason to tune me out. But her eyes were wide. Expectant. I realized that she was worried about me. I had seen her touch the dust on the table, eye the messes piling up everywhere. The same way I would have. Unlike me, however, she had said nothing.

Of course she was worried. Her weak mother driving miles to see her, almost passing out in the grocery store. How much I had kept from her. I shouldn't have. She was no child. Yet neither did I want to burden her.

I began my story, careful of my words. I measured how much I should tell her. So much history to be shared, all before Charlie could finish scooping out the bowls of ice cream. Not of Ronin. No, Ronin was my own. I did not want this shame to be hers, too. There were some things she was better off not knowing, just as there must be things I did not know about her.

I looked into my daughter's eyes and talked.

"Find my brother for me," I finished. There, I ended it.

Sue looked down and wiped at her eyes. Tears. Good. Maybe I had affected her enough to say yes to me. She cleared her throat and rubbed at the spaghetti stain on her shirt with her finger. "I can't go," Sue said finally, as I had feared she might. "Too much work. They won't let me take a vacation. And I don't know if Craig's parents can watch Helena."

I pleaded with her. "You must."

I felt weak, like crying. I hadn't cried in years.

"What about Mike?" Sue stared at the floor.

This truth spilled bitterly. "Mike no can clean bathroom, how he gonna find Taro?"

Sue twisted her lips. She knew I was right.

Charlie came in and added his disagreements. "You're not talking about Japan again, are you?"

"You know about this?" Sue looked from him to me.

"Shoko, you can't go," Charlie said to me.

"She wants *me* to go, Dad." Sue shook her head. "Mom, *you* were going to go and do this?"

"Why not? I from Japan. I know way around."

Sue considered me carefully, that same studying look she had used since she was a newborn and always had her eyes locked on me. Wondering if I would disappear, I thought.

Helena spooned ice cream into her mouth. "I want to go, too! Someone else can take my part in the play. They can assign me work. Let me go!"

This broke Sue down. She had a hard time saying no to her daughter.

"Good experience for Helena, yeah?" I

said hopefully.

Sue exhaled, blowing stray strands of her hair up. "I don't know, Mom. How do we know how to find Taro?"

"I have address of your cousin Yasuo. Suki son. He teach same school. He know where find Taro." I regarded my granddaughter. "She smart one, help you."

Charlie came over to me. "Sue can't go alone. It's too dangerous for women."

Charlie thought I couldn't tie my own shoe without his help. *More dangerous than leaving a Japanese woman alone in America in the 1950s?* I wanted to shout. Sue was not a little girl. I shot him an angry look. He took a step back. "Before I go, I make peace with Taro. You know this important. My family. I no can die without."

"No one's going to die, Shoko." Charlie moved toward me. "You're going to be fine and there's no reason for all this fuss. Besides, who's going to pay?"

"Me! Us. Who else?"

Charlie grumbled incoherently at this. I watched my daughter. The moment was slipping before I could grasp it. Please, Sue. Show me your spunk.

When she was in kindergarten, she got mad one day on the walk home and ran away from me, across a busy street alone.

She knew I could not follow. I watched, helpless. But she looked both ways. She was all right.

I would not beg. I had presented my case to her. Now if she didn't want to go, there was nothing I could do except mail my letter to my brother and hope it reached him, somehow.

"I'll go. We'll go." Sue's voice came out of a dream. Helena squealed. "I'll find Taro for you." She bowed her head at me, looking almost regal.

I clapped her hands, grinning. "No worry. We figure out." I held my arms out to her, hoping she would return the embrace. "I feel like I go, too. So happy."

If you married an American, it is likely you married a Christian. Most holidays in the United States are Christian: Christmas and Easter being the major ones. In general, these are times of good cheer and celebration. See the HOLIDAY section for recipes and details on decorating the house during these times.

For the sake of harmony, it is imperative that the good Housewife become a Christian as well. Japanese women should forget about their Buddhist or Shinto upbringing — these ways are not American ways. You will not be able to find people to worship with you. If you continue to insist on praying to Buddha statues, you will cause your husband to abandon you.

— from the chapter "Turning American,"
How to Be an American Housewife

THIRTEEN

During the next week and a half, I slept better than I had in months, though my heart was weaker. I watched Sue making travel arrangements as though I were the one doing it.

The day after the girls left, Charlie took me to the lab to get blood work done. At the Naval Hospital, you always expect to wait a long time. Even when there was no war, it was a long wait. Now, with so many injured personnel home from Iraq and Afghanistan, the wait stretched into hours and hours.

After the first hour watching scratchy TV in the blood lab, I wished I had a book with me. Charlie and I weren't big readers. Books were too expensive and library books were full of germs from all the people who had checked them out.

Charlie read an old *AARP* magazine and I looked at all the veterans, rows and rows of them in small vinyl-upholstered chairs, faces drawn, some coughing, some too weak to stand, too young to be here with us old people. I wondered what was wrong with them. Some kind of poison from the war? Cancer? Something else?

"Charlie," I said, "when you come back from Vietnam, were lot people sick?" Charlie hadn't talked about the war much to me, or about his job in the Navy.

"No," Charlie said. Always the short answer.

"Seem like lot of people sick here." I crossed my ankles, which swelled more each day. I hoped my surgery would be soon. I was getting uncomfortable. My doctor said I should use a wheelchair, but I hated doing that. Charlie could never push me up hills.

I smoothed out my outfit. Cashmere tan sweater, brown wool pants. Usually I wore my brown-and-white spectator pumps with this but I couldn't get my feet into them now. I had to wear black flats, old ugly ones. I might as well be wearing pajamas and slippers. I still put on the Mikimoto pearls Charlie had given me shortly after we married, and the dangling pearl earrings he gave me for my birthday. I'd only had my ears pierced because Charlie wanted to buy me earrings. In my time, only prostitutes pierced their ears. But now was different.

Charlie tossed the magazine onto the side table. "Mommy," he said, "I've been talking to Bishop Johanssen."

"Uh-oh." This was the guy in charge of his local church, or ward, as they called it.

"He said that maybe before this big surgery, when you could die" — Charlie looked uncomfortable — "I should ask you if you're ready to join us."

I laughed so loud several vets looked at me. "Be Mormon? You know answer."

"Well, maybe after you pass," Charlie said, "you'll change your mind in Purgatory. If you do, come tell me. It won't be too late to be baptized."

I gave him a hard look. It was true that both Charlie and I believed in ghosts — it was part of my culture, as natural as breathing to me — but this Purgatory business I did not believe. Besides, only the unhappy came back. "I haunt you night and day, Daddy," I said. "Boo!"

He shifted his body away from me, picking up the magazine again.

I could have become a Mormon a long time ago, but it was too secretive for me. When I went to my father's Konko church, I had to sit before my father, who at that moment ceased to be my father and was my

188

priest. We did something called *toritsugi,* a meditation. My father sat at the altar, with one ear toward that and the other toward you. You sat in front of the priest and simply said whatever you wanted to — a hope, a wish, whatever — for help with your problems, and the priest relayed it to our Tenchi Kane no Kami. Then you sat and thought about your problem and the priest gave you a message back.

The funny part of that was, of course, telling my troubles to my own father. When I was old enough to realize this, I was afraid. "Do not be, Shoko," Father said, "because I am also your priest. Whatever you say is between you and Tenchi Kane no Kami."

And indeed, Father acted like he never remembered what I said, whether I said I wanted to run away or had boxed Taro on the ears.

Once, as an adult, right after I'd married Charlie, I'd gone to see my father as a priest. "I am scared," I said in a low voice. "I don't know if this will turn out well."

Then I closed my eyes, searching for the solution.

It was at least five minutes before Father spoke. "You are right to be afraid," he said, "but where does this fear lead you? Nowhere. You must let go of fear."

That was my last meditation with my father. He never mentioned that, either.

Charlie had wanted to make our children Mormon. "At least let me take Sue to the youth group," he had said. "They do activities. She doesn't get to do anything."

I refused. This was difficult for me to say no to. In Japan, community is everything. Here I had nothing, no one, only my immediate family. I spent my years growing up poor, but we still attended every picnic and festival with the whole community.

Sue had had nothing until high school, when she was old enough to have friends who drove her to events. I felt bad for her, but I felt more strongly that I couldn't let Charlie make her into something I didn't believe in. I didn't know how the Mormons felt about Charlie being married to me, but since he was already married, they couldn't very well tell him to get rid of me.

Mormons were an okay bunch, on the whole. They helped each other out. Old Man Tattinger, who lived across from us, was a Mormon, and when he became unable to landscape his front yard, a big group of them came to do it. Free. I told Charlie he should ask Mormons to help with the floor, but he refused. Maybe they wouldn't

190

come because of me. More likely it was because Charlie hated to get help from anyone, freely given or not. I didn't know. There were some things I would never know about Charlie, just as there were things Charlie would never know about me. This was how it should be.

An orderly in a lab coat appeared. "Mrs. Morgan?"

I got up slowly. A young veteran moved his cane out of the way for me. The orderly rushed forward to help me.

"You can stay here," I said to Charlie, who hadn't moved. "Be right back."

"Want to get an ice cream after?" Charlie asked.

I shook my head. "No good for you." I took the orderly's arm. "Diabetic, want sugar more and more." The orderly nodded sympathetically, moving slowly with me along the narrow hall to the tiny bright room where they would take my blood.

Marriages arranged by parents often work out best. Parents know that sentiment is rarely the best predictor of long-term compatibility. Financial matters, temperament, and status are the objective criteria used to create successful marriages.

However, your parents will most likely not have arranged a marriage to an American for you. Perhaps they gave you input into choosing the right suitor, perhaps not. You may be unsure of whether you have done the correct thing, especially when your American husband acts in ways un-Japanese (keep this book near!). Do not be faint-hearted and never give up.

— from the chapter "A Map to Husbands,"
How to Be an American Housewife

FOURTEEN

A few days after Sue and Helena left for Japan, I began having trouble sleeping again. At first I thought it was because I was worried about them. Neither had ever been out of the country before. Anything could happen, I fretted. Charlie had been right.

This morning, I sensed something was wrong. My body knew it. All night I sweated, pain deep in my joints, unable to turn over or call out to Charlie, who slept deeply beside me. Finally the sun broke through the horizontal blinds and Charlie got up to use the bathroom. When he returned, my eyes were open and staring at him. I floated outside of myself.

"You all right?" he said in alarm.

My lips and mouth were parched. "No," I whispered.

He put his hand on my forehead. "You're paler than a ghost." He felt for my pulse in my neck. "We better go to the hospital."

They put me in the ICU, oxygen tubes stuck up my nose, a machine helping my heart pump, an IV shooting fluids and medication through me.

Dr. Cunningham arrived and didn't say much. He wrote something down on my chart and put his hand on my leg. "Feeling better now?"

"When can I go home?" My voice sounded weaker than I expected. It felt like a weight was on my chest.

"You're going to stay for observation."

I kicked my feet under the thin blankets. I hated staying there. "When you going do big operation? Pretty soon, huh?"

"Let's get you stabilized. Then we'll worry about that." He gestured to Charlie to come outside with him, probably to tell him I was really about to die and to make me as comfortable as possible, let me think I was going to be okay.

I wanted to scream, *I can know, too! I am an adult!* Anger caused my blood pressure and pulse to shoot up, and the on-call nurse rushed in. I didn't need to be told what was wrong. It was my heart, same as always. They would give me some new drug mix; I'd stay a couple of days and then go home. It would get stronger again. It always had. I had to keep believing that. I pushed all my doubts away.

Charlie came back in and sat down next to me. He patted my hand. "What did the doctor say?" I asked anyway.

"Not much." Charlie looked at me sideways. He was honest — my father had been right about that. A terrible liar.

"What, he say I gonna die today?"

Charlie leaned back, his eyes on a far wall. A nurse walked by. There was no privacy here. "He said you had to stay so they can run some tests."

"Great." I stared at my husband, willing him to tell me the truth. We'd been through so much together. True, I didn't love him when we first got married. But love can grow.

During one period in the Navy, Charlie went to Alaska with a spy group every few months. He stayed on the ground while pilots spied on the Russians. Charlie had said there was nothing much to do but sit around and wait for the planes to come back. He was there in case someone got hurt. The worst thing he ever treated was a runny nose.

He went walking on the beaches there. One morning, he found some jade. Real, deep-green jade. He took it home and had it made into earrings and a necklace for me. I knew that was how he showed his love.

In Vietnam, he rode in helicopters with the Marines through enemy fire to retrieve wounded men out of the jungle. But he never told me about the details, never wrote, "You wouldn't believe how many times we got shot at today! I saw the intestines coming out of five Marines!" Instead, he wrote, "You wouldn't believe how cheap the silver is here!" He brought back tortoiseshell bracelets, ebony salad bowls, hammered silver cuff links. Only once did he talk about it. Sue's hair got singed while she was blowing out birthday candles and Charlie got a faraway look in his eyes. "Nothing's worse than the smell of human hair burning," he said. "Smelled that and human flesh all the time in Vietnam. Put me off steak for a long time." Then he shook it off and smiled. "Not forever, though."

Deathly ill people filled the ICU. The man in the next bed died that night — from what, I didn't know. I never saw his face, only heard his machines and his rasped breathing through the thin polka-dot curtain separating our beds.

Charlie went home only once in two days.

I told him I was fine, that all I needed to do was sleep. "But you can't stay alone," he said fretfully, reminding me of an old woman. In fact, he looked more like one every day, his angular features filling out and softening, breasts forming under his shirt. I could not remember the last time we had been intimate. Years. In his religion, intimacy was for the purpose of baby-making, not for fun. I didn't know if the church had told him this or if he had decided on his own. I used to miss it, taking care of myself with the Hitachi magic wand that Charlie thought was a shoulder massager.

"I stay alone, Charlie. There nurses here."

"They take a half-hour to answer your call button."

"Only since they know you stay." He was annoying me, always hanging around rattling his newspaper or dozing off. He had never spent so much time staying close to me at home. I had had enough. Charlie never listened to me unless I was brusque. "I better faster if you go away."

He scratched his chin. He hadn't shaved in days. It looked awful, all salt-and-pepper whiskers that scratched my face when he kissed my cheek.

"But they should know . . ."

"Go home and sleep!" I said, wanting to get up and push him out. "Call Mike. I go home tomorrow. Too much fuss, eh? What matter with you?"

He paused a moment, and I thought he would tell me what the doctor said in the hallway.

I made a shooing motion at my husband. "Go away," I said, as fiercely as I could. "You want make me better? Leave me alone!"

He still stood there. "I'll call Mike," he said slowly.

"Yes." I didn't know if he would come. You never knew with Mike.

Charlie kissed my forehead, then left. Right away I wanted him to come back, but I didn't call for him. Now there were just machines beeping at me and Navy nurses sweeping by, some nice, some acting like hell demons. I felt like crying.

Child-rearing in America is a good deal more callous and cold than in Japan. Americans do not believe in letting the baby sleep with them, or carrying them all the time, the way a Japanese mother does. They take a far more disciplinarian approach to child-raising than we do in Japan.

Every mother must do what is best for her children and her conscience, as well as adhere to the wishes of her husband. Ideally, the father leaves such details to the mother, but this is not always the case.
— from the chapter
"American Family Habits,"
How to Be an American Housewife

FIFTEEN

Late that night, I awoke to find Mike staring at me, his chair only inches away from the bed. "Last time you in hospital is when I had you," I said, remembering decades ago like it was yesterday. I even remembered my Naval Hospital room, the big blond woman sharing it who screamed, "Take it out already!"

"Really?" Mike said, as though he had not heard this story a million times before. I knew I retold stories. I wasn't senile.

"I was in labor forty hours," I said. Charlie had wondered if this was why Mike seemed to be on his own planet, since his head had been squeezed over and over and his heart rate had dropped with each contraction, but I was sure the doctors would not have let me labor so long unless there was no danger.

He took my hand, which he hadn't done since he was four years old. "Are you going to be all right, Mom?"

Part of me wanted to tell him, of course, and the other part of me wanted to scream that I wasn't God. "I don't know," I said, for the first time since I'd been admitted. He looked down at the ground, his long dark lashes casting a shadow on his cheek. Such beautiful lashes wasted on a boy, I used to say. My poor daughter had skimpy ones, like mine. "Don't you cry like Daddy." I slapped him gently on the face.

He looked up and his eyes were clear. "Get some sleep," he said. He settled back into the chair with his book.

"It not too late for you, you know it?" I said. "Get out there, and get what you want, Mike. You waste your life sit around." In my hospital bed, I felt brave. I would never have said anything like that to my son before. He was stubborn and proud, and if anyone criticized him, he would turn away forever, like he had from Charlie when Charlie tried to make him stay in college.

Mike would have been happier as the son of a farmer. Just him and the land and some animals. No people to worry about.

In the past, I thought about what life would have been like with Mike and Ronin, if we had come here and started a company. No moving around for the Navy. Maybe it would have been better, maybe it would have been far worse.

But then — I wouldn't have Sue. Or Helena. I didn't look backward. The past was past.

When I thought of Ronin today, it wasn't with heartache. It was with fondness. Nothing could have been different in the circumstances I was in. The person I used to be could have made only one choice; the grown-up Shoko might have made a different one. That was how life was. You only figured out the right thing after you were old.

Mike shut his book and leaned into my face. Even though he thought I was dying, I was still surprised by his response. "I'll do better, Mom," he said simply.

"Good." I smoothed out the blanket with my hand. I'd done it so often I had a waffle-weave burn. My mouth felt parched, but the pitcher at my bedside was empty. I pressed the nurse buzzer.

"What do you need?"

"Water." No one was at the nurses' station. They were always so busy here.

Mike stood over me to reach the pitcher. His hair, already well streaked with white, fell into his eyes, and the stubble on his face was a week old. No wonder he couldn't get a job. "I'll get it, Mom." Close up, I could see holes in his jeans. They weren't the stylish kind. He smelled of cigarette smoke. I coughed. He left the room.

The nurse beeped the intercom. "What do you need?"

"Nothing," I said.

Mike came back and poured me a cup, handing it to me. Then he sat down and opened the fantasy novel he'd brought, like the ones I'd been shocked at when he was a teenager, with a huge-breasted lady on the cover, bursting out of her metal bustier and riding a dragon. Through the night he read, as I slept.

Forgiveness is a skill that, like cleanliness, should be learned early and practiced often. Whether it be forgiving the war, or forgiving your husband when he neglects to show up for dinner, you should bend like a willow tree in a fierce storm.

— from the chapter "Culture for Women,"
How to Be an American Housewife

SIXTEEN

Charlie came to see me in the morning, wiping tears out of his eyes.

"What happened to the big, tough Marine I marry?" I said. Charlie used to refer to himself that way, when he was in the war and attached to Marine units. It was a point of pride I wanted him to remember. Now if my husband cried, I had to be strong, and I wanted to be weak.

He didn't answer, just picked up my cup of ice chips and offered a spoon to me. I opened my mouth. My lips peeled dry and my mouth wrinkled like a prune. He applied Vaseline to them.

"I want Japanese food. Can go get some?"

"No sushi. The raw fish could make you sick," he said. "And nothing too salty. You're restricted."

"I know, I know," I said, picking at the white thermal blanket. "Get just noodles, then. Hate hospital food. Taste like paper."

All I ate were ice chips and Ensure. I did not even take soup. I lifted my hip up and grimaced.

He sort of laughed. "You need to *shi-shi?*"

"No." I said. I felt sorry to be so cranky to Charlie, especially when he was being helpful, but I couldn't help it. I wanted to be home, where I wouldn't get woken up by a blood pressure cuff at three a.m. I had to be nice to everyone in the hospital, polite and meek, when I really wanted to shoot them all between the eyes.

"Did they talk Taro?" I asked Charlie.

"I don't know. Mike talked to Sue, not me."

Of course Mike would never think to ask. Had Taro told them anything? Everything?

I didn't know if I wanted Taro to tell my story or not. In one way, it would be easier on me if he did. Then I wouldn't have to.

Telling Charlie about Mike had not been easy. Mike had been born a month and a half earlier than he should have been, by Charlie's calculations. This would have been all right had he not weighed nine pounds, four ounces, with the fully developed lungs of a baby born at term.

"I didn't know he would look so Japanese," Charlie marveled often the first month, sending me into guilty spasms. He wanted to believe Mike was his.

Finally, when Mike was six weeks, I couldn't stand it anymore. Charlie had a right to know. One evening, when Mike was asleep, I told Charlie everything in my poor English. I began crying as I did so, remembering it all, the stress of having this secret for months. I was the only one who knew. Not even Ronin knew.

Charlie simply sat and stared into the corner. I waited for him to storm out, shout at me. Then Mike woke and wailed.

"It's time for his feeding." Charlie prepared Mike's bottle.

I picked up Mike and changed him, still waiting for a reaction.

Instead, Charlie took Mike from me and sat down, holding the milk bottle to Mike's lips, cooing at him as Mike stared up, his black eyes watching Charlie's face intensely. The only sound was Mike's greedy eating, slurping in too much air.

Finally Charlie spoke without taking his eyes off the baby. "What's past is past, Shoko. All right?" He put Mike on his shoulder to burp him. "My name is on the birth certificate. He is my son." Charlie's eyes turned a brilliant sapphire and he glared at me with something like defiance.

I was shocked. I knew Charlie forgave and

forgot more easily than most, but this — I
had been expecting more. Instead he gently
rocked the gas out of Mike.

"No bother you?" I asked.

Charlie dabbed at the spit-up on Mike's
chin. "Of course it bothers me. But I knew
you had boyfriends before me. I knew about
your other Americans. But I can't do anything about it now. What is it you say, *tokidoki?*"

I nodded.

"So let's not talk about it anymore." Charlie stood.

"How can do this?" I still couldn't understand.

Charlie squished his eyes closed. He spoke
next in a low, authoritative voice, the sort I
had not heard him use. "I never want to
hear about it again, do you understand?"

I drew in my breath and nodded. "Yes.
Never."

Mike began crying. "Come on, big guy.
Time for bed." Charlie hummed a lullaby,
carrying him out of the room.

I exhaled. How lucky I was.

Dr. Cunningham kept saying, "We'll see,
we'll see," whenever I asked him about the
surgery. This morning when he came in, saying, "Knock, knock," before he entered, as

he always did, I asked him if I was too old to have the operation.

"It's not that," he said, hesitantly. "If we can get your blood pressure up, we'll be fine."

Always "we," as if we were a team that could control my body. "How about monkey heart?" I asked.

He grinned, but I wasn't kidding. "We'll do our best, Shoko, that much I can promise." Then he touched my foot. "I'll get you another blanket. You're freezing." He always said this. Although I always felt fine.

"I been here a week," I said, pouting. "When I get out?"

"We're moving you to Navajo Hospital," Dr. Cunningham said. "They have a special cardiology unit."

Charlie looked concerned. "Does the military insurance cover that?"

"You bet, if we order it." Dr. Cunningham frowned at Charlie, as though he thought Charlie would want to pay no matter what. But you never knew which benefits the government would cut, even though Charlie wouldn't have stayed in the damn military for over twenty years if he hadn't been promised so much when he retired.

I sighed. "You better tell everybody." I looked up at Dr. Cunningham's concerned, handsome face. At least Sue would get to meet him. I pulled the covers up to my chin and smiled despite myself.

At Navajo, my new cardiologist was Dr. Jenkins, a thin man in his sixties whose bald head shone.

"If I him," I said to Charlie, "I wear wig. Easter egg head."

Charlie laughed so hard he snorted. This made me laugh.

Dr. Jenkins came in, looking at his notes. "As soon as the blood pressure is stabilized," he said to the machine behind me, "we can get moving on the procedure."

"Who you talking to, the wall?" I said. Charlie had told me lots of good doctors had horrible manners, but I didn't care. "You going do it or what? No can wait forever."

"Dr. Su performs this particular procedure." Dr. Jenkins finally managed to lower his gaze to mine. His eyes were brown and tired.

I held out my hands. "Where Dr. Su?"

"When you're a suitable candidate, he will see you." Dr. Jenkins turned on his heel to go.

Charlie picked up my hand from where it lay limp on the scratchy white bedsheets. I turned it over and showed him my palm.

"Look here. Life line going away." To me it appeared to be fading, smoothing out.

He pursed his lips and said nothing.

"What, don't you think I be okay?"

"Yeah."

I took my hand back. "Help up. I wanna go bathroom."

"I'll get the bedpan."

I shook my head. I would have to prove to them I could handle the surgery or they'd give up on me, saying my blood pressure wasn't good enough or I was too weak. I could see it happening already. Transfer her there. Give her to this doctor. Wait and wait some more. They wanted to let me die.

"My feet not so swollen. Come on."

Charlie unhooked me from the monitors and put his arm around me. I swung my legs out of bed. His feet slipped a bit.

"Careful," I said.

"You're too weak," he said, out of breath, losing his grip. I started to fall and gripped the metal bed rail.

He caught me. "Sorry."

"Watch what doing." Slowly, carting the IV bag, we made it to the bathroom. He helped me raise my gown and sit on the toilet.

When I finished, Charlie turned on the

sink for me to wash my hands. I held on to the edge and looked in the mirror. My hair was half white, since I hadn't dyed it in so long. I needed lotion and there were big bags under my eyes. My face had lost its moon shape and my cheekbones stuck out. "I'm too skinny," I said wonderingly, touching my collarbone. "Heh, all my life I want be skinny, and now too much."

In the mirror, I could see Charlie's downcast eyes. Did he not want to look at me? "Help me back bed," I said.

A nurse appeared. "Where are you? You went off the monitors." She was African-American, older, short like me. She was a nice lady who brought me vanilla ice cream in a paper cup when it wasn't on the menu. She saw where we were and rushed to help me.

"We're fine," Charlie insisted.

The nurse came over to help anyway. "Good job, honey," she told me. "You keep it up."

I nodded, too winded to speak. I never thought I would have just as good a chance of going *shi-shi* by myself as I did of climbing Mount Everest with no oxygen. *Maybe the doctors are right,* I thought for the first time ever. Scared, I blocked it out of my head. I smiled at the nurse. "How 'bout some of that vanilla ice cream?"

The day after I went to the bathroom on my own, my blood pressure stabilized and Dr. Su finally came to see me. He was a friendly-looking guy about fifty years old, wearing wire-frame aviator-style bifocals. His hair was thin and bald in front, but he didn't comb it over. I liked that. Nice white smile, too. I decided that I would get my teeth bleached as soon as I got out of there. Have my own movie-star teeth.

Charlie and I held our breath as Dr. Su looked at my charts and at my blood pressure history. "Looks good, Shoko. We'll do it tomorrow."

"So soon?" I asked.

"Yes." Dr. Su said. "If your vitals hold." He made some notes on a piece of paper. "Sign this release, please."

I read it. It was the usual: you can die from this operation or from anesthesia, et cetera. I signed. "If my brain die," I said, "you let me go, right? No keep around."

Charlie nodded. "If you say so."

"I do." I handed the form back to Dr. Su. "Okay if I have Japanese food, Doctor?"

He shrugged. "Just lay off the *shōyu.*"

I saluted him. "Can do, chief."

I liked Dr. Su already.

Surgery didn't make me nervous. Being sick was what made me nervous. And being around Charlie while sick made me extra nervous, because he acted so different than normal. Why couldn't he be calm? Was this what he was like medevacing soldiers out of the jungle? I doubted it.

The procedure began at six. I closed my eyes as they wheeled me into the operating room and the anesthesiologist started talking to me about procedures. Over the years, Mother and Father visited me in my dreams. They held my daughter, born after they were dead. After Mike was born, I'd dreamed of Ronin talking to me and telling me how he was happy I had made a good life for myself.

Now I hoped I wouldn't see this trio as I slept. Today, it might mean that I had really died.

What would I tell Sue if I could see her again? Would I visit her in her dreams? And Helena?

The anesthesiologist patted my hand as he put the oxygen mask over my face.

"I don't want be ghost," I said.

He didn't hear. His face was shrouded by

the bright light behind him. "Now we're going to count backwards from ten. Ten, nine, eight . . ." and I was gone.

....

PART TWO:
BUTTER-*KUSAI*

....

As a young Japanese lady, you have been schooled in all the ways of housekeeping. Your high school taught you how to arrange flowers, the fine art of fan dancing, and how to launder and store kimonos.

Now that you have married an American, you might be at a loss as to certain American customs. How to iron a Western shirt. How to make a bed properly. If you were lucky enough to have worked as a maid in a Western-style establishment, you may already know these things. But for those of you who do not, or do not know the details of American culture, this book will provide all the higher education that you need.

— from the Introduction,
How to Be an American Housewife

ONE

I had always been an obedient girl.

When the doctors were sure my mother was gestating a boy, my parents declared they were wrong. I would be a girl. My mother could feel it in the way I made her crave enormous amounts of Hershey's Kisses, the manner in which I stretched and dropped down below her pelvis, pushing into her bladder like my brother never had. "A girl," my mother had said. I easily imagined her sounding resigned.

"Girls are precious," my father said. He bought a pink layette in preparation and chose a girl's name. Suiko, after a Japanese empress.

"Now it better be girl," my mother grumbled. "No can return all that stuff."

I, obeying, turned out female. It had not been a penis but the umbilical cord the doctors had spotted, the same one that tried to choke me to death during delivery.

Like any good little girl, I wore dresses when I wanted to wear jeans. I stopped climbing trees when my breasts started growing. When the boys in my classes yelled out answers, I stayed quiet. I tried as hard as I could not to be an inconvenience to anyone, at least not in a way that anyone would find out about.

In my memories of childhood, I remembered my mother always being present, whether she had really been there or not. It was her voice that was always there, whispering or shouting in my subconscious, tenacious as Jiminy Cricket. Even now, I always paused before I acted, to hear what she had to say, sometimes not hearing her until it was too late. "That no good. You *baka-tare* or what?" (*Baka-tare* means "stupid.") Or, more rarely, "Good girl, Suiko-chan."

When I was a child, I would do anything to hear the latter. I tiptoed around my mother and her constant exhaustion. I feared if she got angry enough, her heart would stop. Clean the bathroom while she was gone, diet down to a sylphlike size, play the perfect sonata on the piano. "I wish I play piano," Mom would sigh, and I felt victorious. I only wanted to see her approving nod and hear that statement. Finally I had done something right.

When I was fourteen, our relationship began its shift, a moving of tectonic plates that never fit together correctly again. It began with my subscription to *Young Miss* magazine. *Young Miss* sounded prim and proper, my parents thought. But eventually Dad began looking at the magazine covers and what was inside. He tore out the pages I wasn't allowed to read. "This is censorship!" I said to my mother on the afternoon that I discovered the deceit.

"Daddy know what bad," Mother said, indifferent to my red face and indignant tone. How could she calmly stand in the kitchen, drying dishes with a too-wet dish towel, when her own daughter was being discriminated against?

In the few stories Mom had told me about her time growing up, she cast herself as the renegade. The one smarter than the boys, more beautiful than the rest of the girls, destined for greatness, only thwarted by her circumstance. "Is that what you would have done when you were my age?"

She blanched, turning her back to me. Steam from the hot water rose to her face. "Thing different your time. Girl grow up too fast. Not same."

"It's not fair," I said, unable to articulate any better at that age. What else could I expect? My father wouldn't let me join Girl Scouts — he said they promoted feminist values. He probably wished women still wore girdles and gloves and left calling cards when they drove around in their horse-drawn carriages. But my mother — why wouldn't my mother take my side?

I thought of the mothers of my friends, the ones who sat down with them and talked about boys, about how the girls could break the glass ceiling when they grew up, while also frosting gingerbread houses at Christmastime. But my mother kept me both close and at arm's distance.

I turned away from her, leaving her at the sink, so she wouldn't see my tears. She did anyway. "What you cry 'bout? Nobody hit you." She clattered a metal pan. "Do what good for you, Suiko."

I focused and made my tears stop. It was a trick that I had learned early. "I'm not crying, Mom." I smiled at her. "See, I'm fine."

She shook her head as she bent over the dishes again. "You no like me," she muttered. "No can cry 'bout everything. People hurt you too much."

She was right. I did cry too much. I was weak.

This particular article was about birth

control. My parents wouldn't sign the consent form for sixth-grade sex ed class — nor did they give me an alternate education at home. They thought that if I knew about the mechanics of condoms, then I would run out and sleep with the entire middle school lacrosse team.

Or maybe my parents were all too aware of the hot intent lying beneath my demure surface. My friends' parents — even the one whose family never missed Sunday Mass — let them have posters of Patrick Swayze or half-naked military men on their walls. I hid my perversions, photos from *TeenBeat* of Michael J. Fox and Kirk Cameron, under the paper lining of my dresser drawers, the only place my nosy mother would never look.

What was it that my parents wanted for me? To go to college, pristine as the day I was born, and find Prince Charming hiding in a biology class. A future M.D. snagged while young and geeky.

But what I wanted was to live on an island in the South Pacific like Margaret Mead. Or to be Anaïs Nin living with Henry and June, or the notorious Bettie Page pinned up on soldiers' lockers. Mata Hari using her wiles to spy for the government, or a scientist like Rosalind Franklin, who helped discover DNA — only I'd make sure I got credit. I grew up counting the days until childhood ended, when I would no longer have to be good.

I needed to learn about condoms.

The birth control article was easy to find, tucked away among scraps of papers in the daily mail nest my father piled up by his easy chair. Its glossy page was a beacon. I slipped it under my shirt and went into the bathroom to read it. It's only information, I reminded myself. I futilely pushed down on the broken door lock.

I heard my mother in my head. "*Baka-tare!* Stupid girl. What you doing?"

"Shut up," I told that voice. "I'll do what I want."

I read the article, my heart beating so hard I could feel the pulse in my tongue.

A knock sounded on the bathroom door. "Just a minute!" I called out.

"What doing?" Mom's voice was suspicious, and I knew I'd been found out.

"Going to the bathroom, of course. Can't I have a little privacy?" I said anyway, sticking the magazine under the sink.

The door opened. Mom's eyes went to the sink cabinet, which she must have heard shut. She opened it up and took out the article. "I knew you go find this when I tell

224

you no." Mom gasped as her eyes fell on the photos of a condom being placed over a banana. "You no-good sneak. What's matter you?"

"They teach this stuff in science class!" I yelled. "It's no big deal."

She looked at me like I'd been caught robbing a bank. "You gonna be bad, huh?" She shook her head, then shut the door.

From then on, I was more careful. Dad, for all his blustering, was easy to fool. He forgot why he was mad in an hour. My mother did not. For a week, I didn't exist to her. She refused to talk to me.

When I was pregnant with my daughter, Helena, I made a list of Things I Would Not Do Like My Parents. Number One: I would not freeze her out to punish her. Number Two: I would teach her to do anything a boy could do. And more.

I finished high school without incident. I got good grades. I did my chores. If I ditched class, it was because I was an office monitor and doctored the records so no one found out.

I married the first boy I ever kissed. Exactly as my mother had told me I should. Because I, Suiko Morgan, also known as Sue, was a good girl. With morals that meant nothing to me.

And then everything really went to hell.

In the majority of instances, working outside the home is frowned upon. If your husband wanted to have an independent, working woman, he would have married an American. The Wife lives within the home, keeping it tidy and organized, preparing meals for the family, and keeping the children clean. In this way, you must live up to Japanese standards, not American. See it as a source of pride.

In some instances, it may unfortunately be necessary for a Wife to seek outside employment, such as when the husband is dismembered or is dead.

— from the chapter "A Map to Husbands,"
How to Be an American Housewife

TWO

Yesterday, I had been innocently wasting my life away at work, unaware that my mother was about to arrive, asking me to take her to the Commissary. I would have been less surprised to see a UFO land in the parking lot.

This morning I called my father as soon as I got to work. "Is Mom all right today?"

"She is. She goes through spells sometimes, just like she always has." Dad sounded reassuring, chewing food, the television in the background. Everything was normal, I wanted to believe.

"But why did she come up here alone?"

"I was busy." Dad crunched on something. "Sue, don't worry, everything's fine. We'll see you for dinner."

Now I tapped my pen on my desk, staring at the half-alive fern I kept near my monitor. Dad must be right. A seriously ill woman wouldn't be making spaghetti sauce from scratch, the kind you had to cook all day long. No, she would use a jarred sauce. *But your mother is stubborn,* I reminded myself, and pushed the voice away. Dad was there. My mother was, if not well, then the same as always.

The phone rang, then stopped before I could answer. I was a New Accounts manager, as soulless a paper-pushing processing job as you can get without actually turning into a zombie. People opened accounts, I input their information. I listened to employees ask for raises that I couldn't grant. The joke was that my company, PFD Financial, stood for Pays Fewer Dollars. I had worked there, I was ashamed to say, for nearly ten years. Ever since Craig and I got divorced. A steady paycheck and benefits were worth a little grind, though.

Every year I told myself this was the last. I'd start something new. Once upon a time, I'd wanted to teach. It was a modest goal, especially compared to my early daydreams. Yet it had proven unachievable so far. The night-class teacher education program cost too much; no use getting in debt for the sum of one's entire first-year salary. The cheaper state-school program scheduled classes during the day while I was working. I couldn't figure out how to manage. The only answer I came up with was to wait until my daughter had finished school. I'd still be young, relatively speaking, with twenty years left until retirement.

On this day, I looked at the coffee cup on my desk and realized that I'd taken fourteen breaks that day. Dreaming at the water cooler, looking into space. I heard the gasping cackle of the woman next to me, the low hum of the dim lights.

I thought again about my mother, arriving at my office the day before. A trip she had never made or asked to make, to see me. A trip to buy groceries that she would never dare make alone.

Ever since I could remember, Mom's heart had been no good. Always tired, always needing to lie down, barely enough energy to make dinner. Why had they had me, so late, at age forty-two? She had had a murmur before that; it had turned into something worse after she'd had me. "Your mother couldn't pick you up after you were a month old," Dad had said matter-of-factly. "You were too heavy." I had worn her down. How else would you explain it? Babies are hard on bodies. I knew this, and I had only had one.

And nobody could say what had happened to her with certainty. Genetics or environment, radiation sickness or scarlet fever, a simple virus — anything could tweak the heart, make it weak.

As though I needed to atone for my own strong heart, I began to run. I ran every morning, up at four, two and a half miles around the park next to my house, before Helena woke up. I ran even if I got painful shin splints, even if my knees got puffy. I ran fast, until I couldn't talk, until my heart thumped in my ears, hard rain on a tin roof. The doctor told me that when my heart couldn't speed up, that was the time to worry.

When I first began running, pushing Helena in her stroller, my brain wouldn't empty. Worries pushed up like weeds poking through good soil. I learned how to stomp them down. Now all I heard were my heart and my feet. No music.

Then I walked back down the short hill, slow, to my house. The air inside, so cold when I'd left, always felt hot and stale. Every day, I wanted to open the windows, but I worried that Helena would get a chill. I left them closed.

"I wish I run," Mom would say, every time she saw my running shoes by the door. "I use run faster than anybody. Beat even you."

■ ■ ■ ■

The phone on my desk rang again, and I did nothing. The endless years stretched out before me as though they had already been lived. I felt a lurching in my bones so violent, I thought we were surely experiencing an earthquake. I needed to get out of here.

Whenever I felt this way, I got another cup of water and distracted myself with chitchat. Today, I did what I felt like doing. What I thought my mother would do if she could, if she were me. I grabbed my jacket and ran.

The blue silk blouse stuck to my armpits. Late February and eighty degrees. A San Diego winter. I ran to the far end of the parking lot, that same glee I had felt when I ran as a child, my hair whipped back. I was sure that no one had seen me leave, and if they had, they did not care.

By the time I got to my car, my bad mood had disappeared completely. I would go pick up my daughter. We would have dinner with my parents — too much starch, which would make me sleepy. All would be well.

I cranked up a mix I made about ten years ago, probably for my ex-husband. It didn't matter. These songs were my favorites. I bobbed my head and sang along to the Smiths, waved at the cute guy wearing Ray-Ban Wayfarers in the convertible to my right. He rewarded me with a grin.

As usual, traffic was backed up in Mission Valley by the time I got to Finney Plimpton Middle School. No worse place existed for a school, sandwiched between shopping malls and business parks. Helena loved it, though, and with my husband's parents footing the bill for a private education, I couldn't turn down the opportunity.

I parked by a banana-yellow Escalade. The kids were in the auditorium, rehearsing their sixth-grade play, *South Pacific.* Helena was playing Nurse Nellie. Somehow I, Suiko Morgan Smith, had raised a kid who was everything I was not — ultrabright, ultra-talented, ultraconfident, ultranice. I held my breath for her thirteenth birthday and hoped she wouldn't morph.

When I went back to work, Mom had been scandalized at day care. "You gonna let *stranger* take care kid?" she had demanded. "What if shake death?"

"She's not going to get shaken to death," I had said, though of course the thought insinuated itself as a late-night worry, eyes wide open. *You never know,* my mother's voice whispered in my head.

"What am I supposed to do?" I had asked her. "*You* can't take care of her."

"Yes can." Mom had tried to convince me to leave my baby with her, but that was impossible. They were in their sixties by then, and their ailments made them seem older than their years. I would not leave her for more than short periods. Day care had treated her fine.

I watched my daughter, her long hair shampoo-commercial shiny, in the middle of a pack of girls. "Hey, you. Look who's here early."

Helena broke away. Her caramel-colored eyes, the same shade as mine, were bright with tears. I put my arm around her. "What happened?"

"Amelie's having a Disneyland weekend," she sniffed. "I can't pay for tickets."

We got in the car. "I bet Grandma and Grandpa will foot it. You could do some chores for them." I meant Craig's folks, or Grandma and Grandpa Trump, as I called them.

Helena clicked her seat belt shut. "They don't want chores, Mom. They want me to watch old British comedies and be the fourth for their old-fogey bridge parties."

"Consider it character building."

"Amelie thinks she's all that because she

got her period months ago and is already in a B cup," Helena blurted out. "Kiana just got hers, too. When am I going to get mine?"

"You'll get yours, honey. Don't be in a hurry. Believe me."

"Mom. You don't understand." Helena shut up and stuck iPod buds into her ears.

I do, I wanted to tell her. My own parents were like my grandparents in my childhood, older than everyone else's parents and tired out from living. But Helena and I were only twenty years apart in age, and I remembered what she was going through all too well.

My awkward phase had been something for the books, lasting approximately fifteen years. I was shy, afraid I would shatter at the sound of my voice in public, which might have had something to do with the fact that I couldn't see two feet in front of me and no one noticed until third grade. I hated my nose, which spread out over my face more than other peoples'. I didn't grow a bridge until I was thirteen.

The really bad part began in fourth grade. My Dorothy Hamill haircut, combined with huge, thick glasses, actually caused a girl to scream when I went into the girls' room. "I thought you were a boy," she said.

The misery continued into junior high. Dad's idea of what a young lady should wear to school was business attire, as though I were going to work on Wall Street. "No jeans," he said severely when he took me clothes shopping at Penney's. Apparently he believed that it was still the 1950s, when only disreputable greasers wore denim.

Mom hated shopping. "Spend too much, get tired," she grumbled. "Daddy take you."

I looked longingly at the triangle emblem of the Guess jeans a passing girl had on, rolled up with white Reeboks. "School is your job and you need to dress like it." So instead of jeans and sneakers, I was forced to wear middle-aged dresses with big shoulder pads and nylons. My *Dynasty* years, I joked now.

Helena would be saved from this same fate, if I had anything to do with it, but with her father's looks and her own sense, my daughter was not in need of saving.

We arrived in Allied Gardens, a couple miles north of San Diego State University, a Mayberry of small bungalows. The park had a year-round heated pool and a library, people handed out hot chocolate and apples during trick-or-treating, neighbors watched your house while you were gone. It was a good place to raise a child.

My phone beeped. Work had called. Perhaps someone had noticed my early departure after all. My stomach roiled.

Our house was about a thousand square feet, consisting of a living room adjoined by a kitchen and a hallway, with two closet-sized bedrooms and one bathroom. Our house was the only thing of value my ex and I had had at the age of twenty-two, mostly paid for by his parents; and I got to keep it in the divorce, as I had kept Helena.

It was decorated with a colorful mix of stuff my parents didn't want anymore, like the Japanese screen my parents brought over in the 1950s, hand-painted with bright peacocks. Their old shiny black Japanese dining table with the removable legs was our coffee table, where we often ate in front of the TV.

Housekeeping was low on my priority list. Lower than even my job. Dust bunnies, clean laundry waiting to be put away, dirty laundry waiting to go into the wash, everything out of place. I hated having people over. "I'm a single mother," I announced before people could say anything, think anything. "No time for housekeeping."

Mom would have none of that. Last Easter, she had showed up for dinner with a mop and a bucket, wearing old clothes, her nice clothes on hangers. "*Ai! Kitanai* your house. I no can eat 'less clean up."

Why couldn't she say, *I thought you might need some help, dear?*

"It's only a family dinner," I had said, following her into the bathroom.

"We no good company?" Mom filled up her bucket in the tub. "I bring you wood-floor soap. Good floor." She squirted a generous amount into the hot water. "You got time plenty thing: run, eat out all time. Why no clean?" She attacked a corner of the room behind a door. "No pride," she muttered. "No pride in house, have nothing!"

When I was growing up, despite her tiredness, Mom maintained a punishing cleaning routine that would make Martha Stewart cower in her well-turned heels. Every day, a different part of the house was tackled. Mom got down on her hands and knees and scrubbed floors, using a rag and plenty of Borax dissolved in hot water. In between chores, she lay on the couch and napped.

Laundry day was a whole other production. Mom had a washer and dryer but said the electric dryer cost too much to run. She carted the heavy, wet laundry in a two-wheeled shopping cart from the garage at the front of the house, around the side yard to the back, where she had erected two wooden crosses with hooks and eyes across the bars. My job was to thread a heavy white rope back and forth across to make a clothesline, then take it down when she was done. "Japanese like sun," she said. "Sun not use too much *denki* like dryer. *Denki takai.* You know how much *denki* bill was? I save big money."

She hand-washed dishes for the same reason, though I tried to tell her the dishwasher used less water. "Sue, why don't you help your mother?" Dad said every night after dinner as he watched TV from the couch.

"You could help her, too," I grumbled. He and Mike were served like kings. If I ever had a son, there would be none of that. My theoretical son would set the table before I asked, clear my plate and his. My theoretical husband would wash dishes alongside Helena.

Boys of my own had not been in the cards for me. Sometimes I thought I was giving up too soon on the whole finding-a-man-and-having-more-kids idea.

But what if I did get married again and the same thing happened, and I was a single mom to not one but two kids? Or more? How could you know that someone wouldn't leave?

Helena walked into our house and threw her books down on the coffee table. "What's for dinner?"

"We're going to Ojīchan and Obāchan's house, remember?"

"Oh, yeah." Helena grinned. "Spaghetti, I suppose. At four."

"But of course." My mother always made spaghetti when we visited. It was as dependable as her cleaning schedule.

I went into the bedroom to change my clothes. This room was no neater. No money to buy the nice little fabric organization boxes or closet systems that I longed for. Just a full-sized bed, big for this tiny room. Books were stacked in corners, dusty. *Math Achievement in the Classroom. Teaching Grammar and Punctuation to English Learners.* Fiction books I hadn't touched for years. Why did I even bother to keep them? Suddenly the clutter was overwhelmingly claustrophobic. Disgust seized my throat. I wanted to throw everything out the window. I walked around and began picking up what I could put away easily.

A box of old greeting cards stood on my dresser. Birthday cards from every year since I turned six, cards from Craig, hand-made cards from my daughter. Proof of love. I picked up the box and shoved it into my closet, then sat on my bed and unbuttoned my blouse.

My mother's visit to my office yesterday still nagged at me. No matter what Dad had told me, there was something wrong. I could feel it. I replayed the scene with her again, eyes closed, my mother telling me that she had simply driven twenty miles on her own to go to the Commissary.

My eyes opened. That was it. My mother had looked me in the eyes. My mother had been lying. She had something to tell me, something important.

Mom usually refused to meet my gaze. It was rude in Japan to make eye contact, and somehow I had learned this habit from her by osmosis. I grew up being told by my teachers, "Look adults in the eye when you talk to them." My mother would get angry with me if I did. "No respect," she would mutter.

She was maddening in that way, how she parceled out information as though she were a government spy declassifying documents. I was on a need-to-know basis, and it seemed I never needed to know anything until Mom was ready to tell me. Never mind whether or not I was ready. I was sure that if I asked her directly, she would claim no knowledge of what I was talking about. "Wild ideas, Suiko," Mom would say. "Better keep quiet."

Perhaps this time she would remember to look away while she was talking to me, so I wouldn't know she was lying.

I threw my blouse into the dry-cleaning hamper. I heard Helena flush the toilet, call out to me. I wanted to crawl into bed and hide. Not face my mother again, my mother with her precious spaghetti and her wounded heart. Not hear what I felt to be coming, news of her mortality that I was not ready to hear. I pulled on jeans.

"Are you ready?" Helena was at the bedroom door. "I'm starving."

I cast off my mood and smiled at my child. "Of course."

Some Wives who emigrate to America have the opportunity to visit Japan with their new families, causing the Wife to worry about the reaction to her half-Asian child. In America, the half-Asian child may be scorned. However, Japanese believe the half-Asian child to be pretty. Most love them, especially if they are lucky enough to inherit the round Western eyes while keeping some Japanese features.

— from the chapter "The American Family,"
How to Be an American Housewife

THREE

Two weeks later, I stood in Tokyo International Airport. The place contained more Mom look-alikes than I had ever seen in all of San Diego, in all of my life. Although none of these people were related to me, I felt safe here, like I could go up to anyone and they would help me with the same big smile Mom gave to strangers.

I had never expected to be able to go to Japan, certainly not to meet the family I only knew from the occasional New Year's portrait postcard or funeral or birth announcement. I had enough trouble putting a few dollars into my 401(k) without dipping into the grocery budget. Yet I had still hoped I could go one day, taking college Japanese classes, sponging up whatever Japanese culture my mother meted out. Being here now, so suddenly, was like awakening in an alternate universe.

Monitors played soundless music videos

and commercials with giant dancing bubble-gum balls; blue screens announced flights. This was what I wanted, if I could only translate the letters quickly enough. The screens scrolled through the English lettering too fast for my tired eyes.

"Are we there?" Helena shifted her red duffel. "You don't know where you're going." I sensed rather than saw the eye roll, which was so frequent that I didn't register it as disrespectful. My mother would never have allowed it. But I was not my mother.

The truth was, Helena was right. This was the first big trip I'd ever been on. I never even took the bus at home — how was I supposed to find a connecting flight? I had no idea if we were supposed to take a shuttle or the subway or whatever it was they had at this airport.

Helena pointed. "Terminal Fifteen. Flight 267 to Kyushu. That's us."

I smoothed her golden brown bangs. She dried her long hair stick-straight and would wear eyeliner if I gave in. "What would I do without you?"

"Probably die here in the terminal." Helena took my hand — she hadn't held my hand since she was little, and her hands were big and adult now — and walked confidently down past the terminal numbers. "Stick with me, Mamacita. I'm the brains of this operation."

It is not advisable to teach your American-born children Japanese. It will only confuse their language development. Children who learn Japanese and English will speak English like their mothers — with an accent. This is, of course, not desirable.

Teaching two languages may also confuse them as to their identity. They are Americans and should learn only English, as Americans do.

> — from the chapter
> "American Family Habits,"
> *How to Be an American Housewife*

FOUR

We finally found the connecting flight and boarded, clutching wrapped sandwiches from an airport shop. Everyone took off their shoes and put on paper slippers. The Japanese were very hygienic, like Mom, a fastidious hand-washer and non-cross-contaminator. Some would say Mom was too hygienic, but I didn't get a cold until I was in second grade. Her house was like living in a bubble.

As though awakening from a long half-dream, I noticed everything. At home I moved through my surroundings as quickly as possible, never seeing who was around me, always intent on doing what I needed to do. I listened closely to the chatter of Japanese, both familiar and foreign, picking up only a few words. I marveled at the well-mannered way everyone got onto this plane. No one yelled at any flight clerks, no one pushed or line-jumped.

Helena kicked off her sneakers. "I love Japan so far. And I did most of my homework on the plane, so I don't have a thing to worry about."

I frowned. "There must not have been much work."

"No joke. Can I be homeschooled? I mean, that was nearly two weeks' worth of work. What am I spending all that time at school for?" Helena took a piece of gum out of her Hello Kitty denim backpack, handing me a piece.

"Sure. If you can find someone to homeschool you." I yawned despite myself, flipping through the airline magazine.

"I can homeschool myself." She smiled. High cheekbones, like Mom's, irises outlined with darker brown so they glowed in the sun, a perfect slim nose like her father's. When she and Craig were together, you knew immediately they were related.

Craig and I had met in English class, his eyes catching mine as we filed in on the first day of junior year. His eyes were so blue, his irises ringed with black, that they seemed to glow.

Freshman and sophomore years, I was quiet. Unnoticed unless someone needed help with their English paper or calculus problem. The only bad marks I got were for not raising my hand. At last, in junior year, I'd gotten a salon perm and contacts. I began to smile at people. My skirts got short and my baby fat disappeared. Boys finally saw me.

Craig slid into the desk next to mine and gave me his trademark half-grin, the one that got him elected Cutest Sophomore in the yearbook. "Hey," he said.

I blushed. "Hey."

Craig leaned forward, sandy blond hair falling over his forehead. "I'm a real idiot in English. I hear you're smart. Think you can help me?"

I looked straight ahead, afraid I was going to be shy again, but somehow I wasn't. "Sure, but the class just started. Don't you want to see how hard it is first?"

He laughed. "Believe me, I know how hard it is." I blushed.

My previous experience with love had been with the New Kids on the Block posters in my locker. This guy, who played football and baseball and oozed testosterone, was all too real. I was floored.

Craig waited for me at the door, walked me to my locker, talked to me more in his bantering guyspeak. He followed me like a lovesick duckling, not caring about his popular status. People called to him, waved from every sideline. I felt like a star. Just like that, I was in his circle. Sneaking out at night to meet his friends at Sunset Cliffs beach to smoke pot and drink beer, Craig pushing his motorcycle for blocks so my parents wouldn't hear. He kissed me for the first time at that beach, wrapped me up in a blanket he had brought, in between sandstone cliffs where his friends couldn't see. I did worse in school and he did better. And then we started at State, still bound at the hip.

Marriage happened even though Craig's parents advised degrees first. "Living together first wouldn't be the worst idea ever," his mother told us. "Share expenses, see if you can get along."

I blanched. My parents weren't nearly so liberal.

"You live with him, no married, you kill Daddy!" Mom shouted at me when I brought it up. "We stop pay college if do that!"

I went back to Craig with the news. "If we're going to get married, we might as well get married now."

"Why not?" Craig agreed. Craig used to agree to everything I said.

My father looked sad when I told him.

"I'd hoped you wouldn't marry so young," he said. I waited for guidance, but that was all.

Mom was furious. "I send college find man, not marry boy drag through high school!"

"But you told me we had to get married!"

"No. Say you no can live with. Not same." She squinted at me. "Why, you *have* get married?"

"I am not pregnant. You told me that living with him was wrong, but I want to be with him. I give up. There's no pleasing you."

The disintegration of my marriage came about not with flying fists, alcoholism, felonies, or anything that my parents would consider a good reason for divorce. No. It was our two-sentence conversations, our staring blankly at each other when we were supposed to be out having fun, nothing left to say. When I finally began talking to other people in my classes, I found that I could have a better conversation with a random state college boy than I could with my own husband.

When Craig began staying out with his friends and sleeping in instead of getting up with our baby, I knew it was coming. When he told me, when Helena was two, that he was quitting college to be an actor, I didn't do much to stop him. When he said it would be easier to live in L.A. than commute from San Diego, I agreed. The relationship petered out as quietly as it should have when we began.

There was the sound of movement to my right and a male voice. "Excuse me?"

I looked up from the airline magazine. A young Japanese man inclined his head and smiled. Though historically I had been attracted only to all-white Wonderbreads, I couldn't help noticing that he had beautiful straight teeth and skin like Werther's cream toffees. I blushed.

"I believe I'm sitting next to you," he said in accented English, sliding his slim frame into the seat on the aisle.

He had to be twenty-five, tops. I hadn't been twenty-five for a hundred years. I smiled briefly at him and concentrated on the magazine.

Helena leaned over me. "I'm Helena and this is my mom. We're here to find our Japanese relatives."

"Really?" The man smiled. "Have they been lost long?"

"Since before I was born," I said quietly. My tongue felt thick from fatigue.

He extended his hand. "Toshiro."

"Suiko." I almost never identified myself by my Japanese name, not even in college, when doing so would have been chic.

We shook hands. His was very warm.

"Your English is great," Helena said. "Does everyone in Japan speak it?"

"We learn it in school. And I took classes from an American. Now I work for an English-teaching company." He buckled his seat belt. "I'm going home for a visit, like you."

Like me. "We're from the States."

He inclined his head. "Your ancestral home. I see you are mixed. You are part Japanese and part what?"

Somehow his question wasn't intrusive, the way it would if an American like Marcy asked it. *Japanese ask personal questions to get to know you,* I recalled from the little guidebook I'd brought along in my purse. It had also said that Japanese didn't talk to strangers unless they were introduced; yet this man was. Perhaps it was because he taught foreigners. I relaxed. "Irish."

"Ireland." He clapped his hands. "I've always wanted to go. Have you been?"

I shook my head. "My father's family came to the States generations ago. We don't have any family there."

Helena nudged me. "That's a good idea, Mom. Ireland next year. We can find our long-lost relatives on the Internet."

Toshiro and I laughed at this. "Your daughter is bright, yes?"

"That's what they tell me," Helena said. "Bright as a button."

Toshiro rested his hand on the armrest between us. His fingers were touching my arm. "Tell me how these relatives of yours got lost."

I inhaled. Talking to strangers made me uncomfortable. I could talk about the weather or the high price of fuel, but nothing of the real me. The real me was a horrifying swamp of insecurity. "It's complicated."

"You have a captive audience." He grinned. "Perhaps I can help."

I glanced at him. He waited. Whether he was genuinely interested or only mildly bored, I suddenly didn't mind telling him everything. Perhaps it was because I wouldn't see him again. I told him all about my mother, my uncle, and me. My job and my wishes to teach. I talked until I needed a glass of water and Helena was staring at me with complete surprise at all I was revealing.

"Taro sounds like a difficult case." He

kept asking questions whose answers I didn't know. Where my uncle lived, why he wouldn't talk to my mother after all these years had elapsed.

His eyes flicked from my gesticulating hands to my face. The flight and this conversation would end in one hundred minutes, but somehow this effort was all worthwhile. I smiled at Toshiro.

The last time I went on a date had been two years earlier, with a man who rented the house across the street from my parents. Thank God he moved soon afterward.

Mom had called me up, eager. "You never guess who in Larramie house. Good-looking guy. Single!"

"And?" I had closed my eyes in dread.

"And I go over there, tell all about you. You most beautiful girl ever. Could marry big-time businessman if live in Japan." *Instead of Craig,* I heard silently.

"Mom, of course you say that. You're my mother." I imagined her chasing the poor man around his cement front patio, moving boxes still in his hands. *Date my daughter.*

"I show him picture. He interested. Eyes get big."

I was afraid to ask which picture. Probably her favorite, from when I was nineteen. I had long hair down my back and a seductive smile. The best photo I'd ever taken, or ever would take. "Girls most beautiful at this age," Mom had said when she saw it. "Then go down the hill."

"He gonna give you call, okay?" Mom was excited. "He own Internet company."

I made a skeptical noise. "That could mean anything. Anyone can open an Internet company." I agreed to go out with him anyway.

Jake met me at the sushi restaurant he had suggested. He was unremarkable: dark brown hair, medium build, brown eyes. "You're even prettier than your picture."

I laughed. "I was afraid she showed you my junior high school portrait with the bad perm."

"She did." He pulled out my chair. "Just kidding. No, as soon as your mom came over and started talking about her daughter, I knew I had to give it a shot. I have a thing for Japanese women."

Oh. He was one of those. "You *otaku?*" It meant someone who was perhaps unhealthily obsessed with Japanese culture. The word had negative connotations, but I used it anyway. I had met men like him before, who thought my mom had raised me right, that I would trail behind them in public and be some sort of sex slave who also kept an immaculate home.

He blanched. "No. Well, maybe a little. Wasn't your dad?"

That gave me pause. Dad had pursued a woman who couldn't speak his language. I didn't want to date anyone like my father. "Maybe, but he knows better now. I'm American through and through. So's my mom."

"Didn't seem that way." He smirked. "I can tell."

I got up. "A real Japanese girl would have sat here, pretending to like you. I prefer the American method. Direct." Then I left.

My mother wouldn't speak to me for a week. "I no can go outside," she moaned. "No want see Jake."

"Mom, he's a renter. Don't you want me to date someone with his own house?" I knew that would get her to leave me alone.

"That true." Mom sniffed. "Maybe no good anyway."

The flight attendant brought coffee, tea, and hot chocolate packets. I chose a coffee and powdered hot chocolate to make myself a mocha. It tasted like thick, powdery chocolate sauce, and something else I couldn't place. "This is different than what we have at home."

Toshiro dipped his tea bag up and down in hot water. "No offense. You must be butter-*kusai*. Not used to things with no butter."

I smiled. "Helena, remember Obāchan saying, 'Butter-*kusai!* Get in shower'?" We smelled like butter because we ate so much of it.

"Obāchan is butter-*kusai* by now, too." Helena stuffed her sandwich into her mouth.

I still couldn't place what was in it. It must have been an ingredient I was unfamiliar with, or a slightly different way of making the hot chocolate mix.

"But do you like it?" Toshiro pressed.

I nodded.

"Then that is all that matters." He sipped his tea.

I realized Toshiro was correct.

Kumamoto City was in Kumamoto Prefecture on the island of Kyushu. We bade goodbye to Toshiro, who handed me his business card. "If I may be of assistance, do not hesitate." He bowed. I bowed back. Then he extended his hand and shook mine. "I mean this, Suiko-san."

"Thank you."

"Best of luck." He looked toward the

ground. I wished for a moment that the Japanese were cheek-kissers. Instead, with another bow, Toshiro disappeared into the crowd.

I watched him go for a second longer than necessary.

"Let's go, let's go." Helena moved off impatiently.

We had to find the bus into Ueki, a suburb. At first glance, Kumamoto City looked kind of like California: power lines, mountains in the background. Except there weren't any palm trees, and no big cars. And it smelled like powdered sugar and pine, mingled with the cigarettes everyone smoked. Helena coughed a little. The driver stowed our baggage underneath. "I hope they leave the windows open."

"Not every place is like California," I reminded her, "with smoking laws everywhere."

She looked around the bus. People chattered to each other behind their hands, glancing at us. "What are they saying?"

"I can only tell snips and bits. *Foreign women. Half and half.*" There probably weren't too many Westerners venturing into the outskirts. Still, I didn't expect us to be greeted with such curiosity.

Helena leaned into me. "I bet you in a

week I speak better Japanese than you."

"That's a sucker bet. No way I'm taking it." I glanced at my daughter. Her legs were crossed with one ankle over her knee. I remembered another cultural tidbit I had read. "Put your foot down," I whispered. "Japanese sit with their feet on the floor."

She looked at the other people on the bus to find them doing the same thing. She corrected herself.

"You really should believe your mother," I said. "I know some things."

I looked at the address of the inn I had booked the week before. "We need to get to San-bon Machi." In halting Japanese, I asked an elderly lady, her gray hair tied back in a navy blue scarf, what stop we needed.

"Stop Shodo, close by. Two block," the woman responded in English. "You speak Japanese very well."

"*Arigatō.*" I smirked at my daughter. She made a face.

The woman launched into rapid Japanese with her seatmate, a nearly identical woman. This didn't sound like the Japanese I had heard in class, and Mom had only spoken a few words here and there. I realized what I was hearing. "In school, they teach standard Japanese. This is a dialect, what Mom would speak," I told Helena.

"Like an accent?"

"More than an accent. Different words for things, too."

She shifted. "I wish I knew the language."

I smiled. "I wish I knew the language, too."

Mom hadn't believed in teaching me Japanese, fearing it would irrevocably contaminate my English. She and Dad did, however, use plenty of random Japanese words, usually baby words like *shi-shi* instead of "pee."

One of my favorite Japanese games was rock-paper-scissors, or, as Mom had taught me, Jan Ken Poi. "In Japan, use this for everything, even businessmen," Mom had told me.

Jan Ken Poi became a special game, done to break ties and decide between an eight o'clock and an eight-thirty bedtime.

"Shodo, Shodo," the woman next to us yelled, pointing at the stop cord. I jumped up and pulled. The bus shuddered to a halt.

"Arigatō." Helena waved.

"Gūddo rākku." The old woman returned it with a weathered hand. Good luck.

Our driver retrieved our travel backpacks from under the bus. He bowed.

We stood on the sidewalk for a moment, Helena looking expectantly up and down the road. These street signs were hieroglyphics to me. A 7-Eleven stood a block down. "Let's get directions."

Helena grinned. "Can I get a Slurpee?"

"Sure."

Inside, it was like any American 7-Eleven, except there weren't any Slurpees, and there were things like rice balls and fast food made of fish. I inhaled the familiar smell of coffee and wondered if all the 7-Elevens in the world got their beans from the same place.

The storekeeper, a short man in his mid-fifties, bowed. *"Irasshaimase!"* he exclaimed, waving his cigarette at us. Welcome.

Helena immediately headed for the junk food aisle. "Excuse me," I began in Japanese, "can you tell me how to get to Sanbon Machi?"

"Two blocks down" — he held up two fingers — "make right, three blocks, then left, one more block, right. Got it?"

"Can you repeat that?" I reached into my purse for paper. He took a map from the display at the front, whipped it open, and marked the route in red ink.

Helena dumped a Halloween booty's worth of candy on the counter.

"I don't think so. If you're hungry, get some *onigiri*." I pointed to the rice balls, cold sticky rice wrapped in black seaweed

263

paper, encased in a cellophane packet.

"Fine." She started putting the candy back.

"Ah." The storekeeper patted her on the head. He switched to English. "You like sweet?" He hand her a wrapped peppermint. "Your Japanese very good," he added to me.

"*Arigatō,*" Helena said with a big smile, unwrapping her candy. "People in this country are so nice."

We walked the half-mile or so to the Shodo Inn, near the Tsuetate hot springs. It was a traditional Japanese inn, in a fortlike compound of log buildings. It was set another half-acre off the main road, up a dirt path.

I chose this inn so Helena and I could get a true Japanese experience. Though we were here to see Taro, this trip was very possibly a once-in-a-lifetime event, at least for me, and I wanted us to get all we could out of it.

Instead of the Western bed and bad art that has been in every hotel or motel I've ever encountered, there were *shoji* screens, *tatami*-covered floors, and a futon with a hard head roll that looked like a cylindrical pillow.

"This is supposed to be a pillow?" Helena flopped onto the futon and tossed the head roll aside, wadding up her jacket under her head.

"Obāchan had one lying around — don't you remember? You used to play with it. It's traditional."

"I hope this isn't going to be one long history trip." She turned over. I stifled my annoyance and desire to lecture, which would only lead to an exhausted fight. Instead I joined her, tucking the head roll under my neck.

Helena moved her head roll under her neck, too. "This hurts."

"If your grandmother could sleep like this, so can we."

"We're soft, spoiled Americans, Mom." She giggled. "This is like a sleepover."

"Mm-hmm." My body ached.

She shifted toward me and whispered. "I want to have a sleepover party for my next birthday."

"Sure. But check with me again tomorrow. I might be talking in my sleep right now." I kept my eyes closed.

"And I want to have it be coed."

I laughed shortly, fully awakening in an instant. "Think again."

"Why not? It's totally platonic. Everyone does it." I could hear she was going to try to wear me down with research. "I don't see what the big deal is."

"You know very well what the big deal is, young lady, and if you ask me again, you won't have any party whatsoever. Is that clear?" I made my voice final. "Now, please, can we sleep?"

She was quiet for a second. "Can we get a pizza and have the closet makeovers like we did last time?"

"Don't get ahead of yourself. Your birthday's still a ways off."

I had always enjoyed Helena's slumber parties. At the last one, I'd bought a bunch of cheap cosmetics and had the girls pair up and go into a dark closet to give each other makeovers. Though Helena had gotten eye shadow in her eye, it was all great fun.

When I was a child, I wasn't allowed to go to slumber parties until I was ten. Once I turned twelve, I was forbidden again. Mom said, "You never know. You pretend spend night at someone's house and be somewhere else."

"But I would never do that!" I swore up and down, finally appealing to my father for assistance. He told me to respect my mother.

I shouldn't have been surprised. Mom wasn't like any of the other mothers. My friends came over with a mix of anxiety and anticipation. "Will we have to bow? Take our shoes off? Kneel on the floor?" my friend Shauna asked.

"Just the shoes," I said.

Mom was always pleased to see my friends show up. "You popular girl, huh? Only popular girl have so many friends."

"Please, Mom, I have like three," I'd say each time. This was true.

"Tell me what new at school while Sue get ready." Mom would try to waylay them as they came through, inviting them to sit on the couch beside her.

"I can't understand half of what she says," Shauna would tell me afterward, right in front of my mother, as though she were deaf instead of accented.

"Tell me about it," I would say, deliberately ignoring the hurt on my mother's face. I regretted my cruelty now.

It was a particularly sharp betrayal since so many of the English speakers she encountered daily treated her this way. In fourth grade, I made a new friend, Cindy, who invited me over to her house, which was about twice the size of ours. "Gotta meet mother first. Never know who people are," Mom said. She took me to their house, wearing her finest dress-up clothing.

Mom rang the doorbell as I nervously

waited. The mother answered. "Come on in." She wore shorts, a T-shirt, and white Keds and had wide blue eyes. In the background, Cindy jumped up and down. "You didn't have to get dressed up for me."

"I always dress up," Mom said, which was totally untrue. She stepped indoors and took her shoes off.

Cindy's mother grimaced but didn't say anything. "Well, come in and sit down. Have some tea."

Cindy and I began playing Barbie on the floor. Mom sat on the couch and reached for a piece of coffee cake. She put it on a napkin.

"Oh, don't you want a plate?" Cindy's mother picked up one of the tea plates from the table.

"Napkin fine. Less dish wash." Mom took a bite of cake with her fingers. Cindy's mother sat down and put a piece of cake onto her plate and ate it with a fork. I felt horribly embarrassed, but said nothing.

"It's great that you're trying to learn English," Cindy's mother commented. "You must not have been here very long."

Mom smiled coolly. "I here longer since before you born!"

Later, I would invite Cindy to my house, but her mother always had an excuse for declining.

Now that I was a mother, I understood how excluded my mother must have felt, at least in part. Last year, I was at a PTA meeting. We were eating store-bought cookies afterward and chatting.

"We're going to Cabo for Ski Week this year," one mother piped up. Ski Week was what they called the school's vacation week surrounding Presidents' Day. Public schools gave two days off, but Helena's school gave the entire week off. The mother's clothes were casual jeans and a T-shirt, but the sort of casual that sets you back several hundred dollars.

"Only you would go to a beach for Ski Week, Stacey!" another mother chimed in. She shifted on her too-high pumps. "We're going to Sun Valley. It's Jim's favorite place." She turned to me. "You going anywhere, Sue?"

I could never tell if they were being polite and trying to include me, or if they were baiting me. It had to be obvious to anyone with a pair of eyeballs that I wasn't the one paying Helena's tuition. "We're going to kick it here in S.D., old-school," I said. "Maybe we'll go to the Mission Beach roller coaster." I tugged up the waist of my own Target brand jeans, which always started out tight and got too loose by day's end.

"Is that even open in February?" the mother asked.

I shrugged. In reality, Helena would be spending the week with her grandparents while I worked. I didn't get a Ski Week.

The circle of conversation closed around me, and I backed away with my chocolate-chip cookie, unnoticed. I stopped attending PTA meetings. No one ever asked me why.

Helena and I, instead of taking a short nap, ended up sleeping through until the next morning. At eight, a quiet knock sounded. Slits of sun bordered the wooden blinds. A gray-haired woman bowed over a tray of food. Unfolding a low table from a corner, she set the food down. She smiled. As we stood, she rolled up our futon, opening the shutters to bright light. Then she bowed and left.

"Oh my gosh. What is this?" Helena poked at a square white bowl filled with brown beans on top of steamed white rice. As she lifted her chopsticks, trails of goo stretched like long ribbons of snot.

Nattō. I'd heard of this acquired taste — fermented soybeans. I'd also read that there were a lot of Japanese people who hated it, never mind *gaijin* like us.

Helena shuddered and put down her chopsticks. "No, thank you."

I gulped and decided I would try it. "*Nattō.* It's a traditional Japanese breakfast food." It tasted like very slimy edamame beans. "It's not so bad."

I wondered if my mother had ever eaten *nattō.* If she had, she had never mentioned it, nor bought it. She only made Japanese food at New Year's — sushi and all kinds of pickled foods she set out in lacquered boxes. But she wouldn't show me how to cook.

I had loved to be in the kitchen with her, on a stool by the island, watching her chop up onions or frying potatoes on the stovetop, her hair held back with a bandanna. "Always cover head. If you go restaurant," she pronounced, holding her small knife aloft, the same knife she used to cut everything from vegetables to large roasts, "and people no have hairnet, get out."

There was one cookie in particular Mom made that I loved, a tiny raisin-filled tart. When I was eleven, I asked her to teach me how to make it.

Mom had sighed. Dad, from his easy chair in the adjoining family room, tsked. "It'll be good for her. Go ahead."

"Read ingredients, get out everything first," Mom told me. She put her apron on, and I tied my little apron with Dutch flower girls embroidered on it around my waist. "First, wash hand."

I did as she said, then pulled out the flour, the sugar, the raisins, the baking soda.

Mom cleaned the countertops where we'd roll out the dough.

"I can do that," I said.

She handed the cloth to me and observed. "Don't forget corner. Spray there."

I scrubbed harder, knowing that if I missed any spot on the yellow Formica, she would see.

"Can I measure?" I noticed the look of displeasure, but she nodded. Nervously, I measured two cups of flour.

"Scrape! Scrape!" Mom cried, as though I were running into traffic. I scraped the top. "Must be even. Smooth."

My hands quaked. I spilled the flour on the floor.

"Now see what happen you not careful? Not old enough. Sit." Mom got out the broom. "Easier do myself."

"Honey," Dad said, not looking up, "she's just a kid."

"You teach, then. Your kid, too." She swept up the floor.

"I'm sorry," I said in a small voice.

She nodded. I felt her disappointment in

my pores. "You play. I make cookie. You eat, okay? That your job." She dismissed me from the kitchen.

That was the last time I asked her to teach me how to make anything. I wanted to know how she made her spaghetti, her fried chicken, her sushi, and especially her pizza. I waited for her to offer, but she never did.

When Craig and I got married, his mother asked what I wanted for a wedding gift. I asked for cookware: All-Clad pans, baking dishes, a bright green enameled Le Creuset Dutch oven. Then I got some cookbooks and taught myself how to cook.

Even this would not impress my mother. A few years ago, as part of dinner, I made my parents baked Brie in phyllo dough. "*Ai!* Sour," Mom said. Dad did not comment, but put his fork down. Now if they came to dinner, I made the simplest of meals or ordered takeout. It was too hard to please them. Helena was the only one who knew of my secret Julia Child experiments, the one who watched me cook now, and whom I taught how to cook.

My mother once had similar aspirations. Usually, she presented us with the meat and potatoes Dad liked. But sometimes I saw her leafing through her big green cookbook, looking at recipes, marking the ones she wanted to try, cutting out interesting ones from the newspaper's food section. Coq au vin.

"Where are we going to get an old rooster?" Dad couldn't believe she wanted to cook coq au vin. "And I can't have wine."

"Alcohol cook away!" Mom tossed the recipe down, dejected. "Use chicken. Same thing." She smiled. "Maybe raise chicken backyard, huh?"

"The coyotes will get them." Dad laughed. "How about chicken and grape juice?"

My mother made coq au vin with chicken and grape juice that she soured with vinegar as a wine substitute. It tasted, if not like the original, then passable as another dish entirely. My father was delighted. "Best chicken ever!"

I wondered why she had not continued to try new recipes. Perhaps it was her heart; perhaps she had simply lost interest. But I still wished she would teach me how to make her signature dishes, the way only she made them. Even the chicken and grape juice.

Mom had also taken care with her cooking for class potlucks. While everyone else slapped together a casserole or a green salad, to Mom the potluck was a point of family pride. She would either borrow the neighbor's giant pasta pot and make a boatload of spaghetti, or make pizzas from scratch. All day she'd bake or stir the sauce. "Enough for army," she would say happily. "Nobody else do it, huh? Mine is best." I was filled with pride for my mother as my classmates clamored for her food.

I did the same for Helena. Even if I had to stay up into the wee hours, I would make a homemade mac-and-cheese casserole that the other mothers raved over, or homemade cupcakes instead of store-bought for her class parties. And I took special pleasure in it, just as my mother had. *At least in this I am best,* my plate of cupcakes said.

I played with the remaining *nattō* on my plate, wishing it were a cupcake instead.

"Aren't you going to finish it?" Helena asked.

I wiped my mouth. "Another thing to know. In Japan, if you want to have more, you eat it all. If you are done, leave a little food on your plate."

"All these rules." Helena rubbed sleep from her eyes.

"Think of all the unspoken rules we have, Helena."

"Like finishing our food?" Helena picked up the rolled egg omelet with her chopsticks. "A doughnut wouldn't kill anybody."

"Maybe tomorrow." I smiled at her and finished my breakfast, still remembering my mother with every bite.

When assimilating into America and making new acquaintances, remember that Americans are a somewhat aloof group of people. They may avoid conversations of a personal nature, unlike Japanese.

This repression is difficult to become accustomed to, especially given the too-gregarious nature of other American habits, such as public hugging and back-slapping. It is puzzling to the Japanese person: why is it wrong to talk about personal subjects, but not wrong to hug someone you have just met?

It is best to smile and go along with what the American wants.

— from the chapter "Turning American,"
How to Be an American Housewife

FIVE

The small house was easy to find. Two lines, one above the other, stood for number two. It was close to its neighbors, built out of weathered wood with a simple tile roof. It looked very old, like modernization didn't quite make it this far. The door practically opened onto the street, and it was window- less at its front. Behind was a rectangle of fenceless land. White towels and boxer shorts fluttered in the wind.

"Mom." Helena waved her hand in front of my face. "Are we going to stand here forever?"

"Go ahead and knock." I nodded to the door.

"You do it." She shrank behind me.

I felt her anxiety. What if he shut the door in our faces? Or worse, was dead? It was strange not to know an entire side of the family. Dad's family were on the East Coast, but at least they were on the same continent, and had always been easily available by phone.

I knocked. No one answered.

"He couldn't even hear you." Suddenly brave, Helena pounded with two fists.

I grabbed her shoulder. "Stop."

Someone shuffled to the door and creaked it open, Haunted Mansion–style. A salt-and-pepper-haired Japanese man, probably in his early forties, blinked at the sudden light. He drew his kimono close around him. Was this our cousin Yasuo, Suki's son? I momentarily held out my arms to embrace him, then remembered. Japanese did not hug. As my mother did not. *"Sumimasen,"* I said, *"Watashi-wa Suiko."*

He interrupted in flawless English. "Aaah. Your pronunciation is terrible."

"Yasuo?" I bowed.

His smile cracked his face, a plate breaking. "Yasuo doesn't live here anymore. He moved to Kikuchi City." He started to shut the door.

"Wait." I stuck my foot into the door, certain the wood was old enough to break. "Surely you've got an address."

"If you have business with him, you should have his address, not me." He pushed my foot back with his bare one.

"We've come all the way from America."

Helena turned her big eyes up to him, tearing up. She was either exhausted or an excellent manipulator. I suspected the latter. "My mother is his cousin."

The man relented. "Ah, yes, his American cousins. He has spoken of you."

"You know him?" I said, hopeful.

"Yes." He contemplated us.

"We're on a mission." Helena drew herself up importantly. "We need to find Great-Uncle Taro."

"Taro?" The man's laugh turned into a shuddering cough. "Go to Ueki High School. Yasuo teaches art part-time. Good-bye, now." He quickly closed the door, hasping the lock.

"Where's Ueki High School?" I asked the closed door.

"Not even a cup of tea or anything." Helena's unlaced Converse kicked up dirt on the road. "I thought he'd invite us to a tea ceremony."

"The man obviously wasn't feeling well." I wondered how he knew Yasuo.

"Where to now?"

Good question. Helena watched me expectantly. "We'll go back to the hotel and ask for directions," I said. I had no idea if the high school was a quarter mile away or ten miles away. We would find it no matter

280

what, even if I had to carry Helena on my back.

I attempted to retrace our steps to the hotel, but all the buildings had changed. I was leading us down a trail of blown-away bread crumbs.

"We're lost," Helena said.

I opened the map. "If I look carefully at the symbols, we can find our way back." I tried to match up the map with the street signs. Slow work.

Helena trudged after me. The streets became narrower, until we arrived at what appeared to be a town square. On a platform in the middle, a large gong hung from a wooden altar. "That's what they ring at New Year's to chase away the evil spirits." I walked up the steps of the platform. "There's one in San Diego, too."

"Have you ever been?" Helena touched the gong.

"I don't go out on New Year's. You know that." I smiled at her. "Maybe we'll go next year." Funny how, now that I could go out on New Year's, I no longer wanted to. New Year's was the most important holiday to my mother, not an excuse to party. In high school, I'd get the occasional invitation to a bash and have to turn it down. "Stay home," Mom said. "Never know what gonna happen, crazies run around. Besides, New Year for family."

I would spend the evening watching my parents snooze in front of Dick Clark. Mike had long gone. When he was a teenager, my mother had said, he went out on New Year's. "Boys different," she said. "And maybe was mistake. Mike too wild. We do right thing for you." I had to pay for every time Mike watched too much television and failed a test, or smoked a reefer at the park and got picked up by the cops.

"I want to ring it." Helena looped around. "Where's the hammer?"

"It's not New Year's." I didn't want all the locals staring at us for breaking a taboo.

"It could be for any time. It's in the middle of the square."

I exhaled. "Please just listen to me for once."

"Oh, Mom. I always listen to you." Helena crossed her eyes and grinned. "I'm a good little girl."

"We'll find someone and ask where the high school is."

Around the perimeter of the square were dozens of cherry trees, topped with clouds of pink, continuing all the way down the next road as far as we could see. Underneath, people picnicked on blankets spread out over the green grass. It was an Impressionist painting. My eyes filled.

"It's so beautiful," I whispered.

Helena shrank back. "Mom, what are you crying about? I swear, if it's not a Hallmark commercial, it's something else." Nonetheless, she patted my hand.

I blew my nose into a tissue. "Get the camera, honey."

"Only if you stop embarrassing me." She reached into her knapsack. "Sheesh. They're only flowers."

"Stand by the trees." I held my hand out for the camera.

She shook her head. "Of you. You never let me take pictures of you."

I hated getting my picture taken. Invariably, I was squinting, I had a double chin, or my mouth was twisted into a gargoyle grimace.

Dad had dozens of photos of Mom posing, shoulders back, bust out, hands on hips, red-lipsticked lips smiling like Lana Turner. From her twenties until now, her pose hadn't changed. It said: Look at Me. Mine said: Don't. Please.

Nonetheless, I stood by the gong, arranging myself into a Shoko-like stance. Helena snapped the photo. "Perfect." She showed me the image. "You look happy for once."

"I'm always happy, Helena." And for once, I felt this was mostly true. I was happy here, even as we got lost and my feet blistered and I didn't know where we would be the next night. I felt as calm as if everything were already taken care of. I waved to a passerby. "Let's find this high school."

American males, like Japanese males, have lives outside of the home, at work, in hobbies, and in other arenas. They often wish to keep this part of their lives separate from their domestic lives. This is normal and natural and not to be taken as hurtful.

The good Wife will not question where her husband has been or what he has been doing, or with whom. Such pryings will drive your husband away. It is important to mind your own business and stay within the arena of domesticity.

— from the chapter "A Map to Husbands,"
How to Be an American Housewife

Six

Ueki High School was a few miles down the bus route, a gray rectangle three stories high, with pine trees shading the lawn into oblivion.

In the office, a woman about thirty with a flipped-up bob worked behind a computer. Her red lips smiled. *"Ohayō; gozaimasu."*

"Ohayō. Sumimasen," I began. *"Yasuo Tanaka . . ."*

"Tanaka-sensei?" She bowed and we bowed back and she bowed again. I held my breath, afraid that this would continue like a Marx Brothers gag until Christmas came. She continued in English. "How do you call yourself?"

Helena's white teeth flashed. "We're American cousins." The lady smiled again and motioned to the bright orange plastic chairs.

When I was in college, my work-study job one semester was being a teacher's aide to a high school English class. I had taught adverbs versus adjectives to a mostly uncaring classroom; yet at its end, the students made me thank-you cards, and most passed the final. "Did you make them do this?" I asked the regular teacher. He had not. I had gripped my sheaf of handmade cards and decided to become a teacher.

I thought about this as I sat down, feeling a pang as I watched a couple of students pass by. Around the office, photo portraits of serious men and a few women hung on the walls, obviously a gallery of the school's principals over the years. One of these must be Taro. I studied them, looking for resemblances to Mom, but found no one.

A few minutes later, the office door opened and a trim man in a pink-and-purple argyle sweater vest, purple button-down shirt, and dark slacks entered. His graying hair was cut close to his head and bald in front. He wore wire-rimmed glasses and carried an art portfolio. "Suiko?" He bowed. "This is most unexpected." An understatement.

"Yasuo?" He had Mom's same broad forehead and pointed chin. And he knew my name. I smiled at him. "This is my daughter, Helena."

He stared at my face, too. "Ah!" Suddenly

he leapt forward and hugged us both. I hugged him back, touched. "I thought I wouldn't see you until I died. My dear, dear cousins."

We followed him into the teachers' lounge, furnished with round tables. "Sit, sit." He hustled to the counter. "Coffee? Tea? Or me?" He laughed. "Are you on a tour?"

"Tea, please. I'm getting used to green tea, Mom. Even with no sugar." Helena swung her feet.

"Tea also, please." I cleared my throat. "We came here to find Taro."

Yasuo stopped pouring for a second, his eyes raised to the black cabinets. Perhaps I had been too abrupt. What a strange, sad look came across his face. "He used to be principal here. Now he is retired, a priest. Konko religion. Like our grandfather. He lives in Uwajima now." Yasuo brought over the tea. "You don't need to see him."

"I do need to see him." I told him about my mother's heart and what she had asked me to do.

"Same as happened to my mother. I am sorry to hear it." He nodded slowly. "Such is the cycle of life. One dies, one is born."

My mouth went dry. "She's having surgery. She'll be fine."

His eyes were doubtful. "The radiation

weakened the heart, I'm afraid."

"Radiation?" Helena took a teacup. "From what?"

"Nagasaki," Yasuo replied.

I leaned forward. "Her doctors always say the cause could have been any number of things."

"You never told me that." Helena's eyes became huge. "She never told me that. She told me about other stuff from Japan — happier stuff." She stared into her cup of tea. "Poor Obāchan."

"She doesn't think of herself that way, Helena. You know her." My mother, persisting with her garden and her backbreaking laundry chores. "She never gives up."

My mother and her iron will, forged during World War II. The most I had ever had to contend with was minuscule in comparison. "You have easy life," Mom would tell me often.

"So you think she won't survive." Helena looked at Yasuo. Her voice was flat.

Yasuo's chest moved up and down. He glanced at me instead and said nothing.

I reached out and gripped his hand. "I need to do this for her."

Yasuo smiled briefly. "I do not want to give you false hope." He gazed pensively over his teacup. What was he leaving out? "I have Taro's address at home. If you have time, I will take you."

Yasuo lived in downtown Kumamoto City. His apartment was two rooms, separated by a sliding rice-paper wall. We took off our shoes and padded across the light-colored hardwood to a low table. "I like traditional Japanese design," Yasuo said, inviting us to sit on cushions, then going into the kitchen. "Clean, simple, nothing to dust."

I agreed. I had always liked what I knew of Japanese design. Westerners put the colors all over the room; the Japanese were more monochromatic, with colors concentrated in one spot. The Japanese way seemed so much simpler: a framing of views, using what you had, not creating clutter to tire your eyes.

We heard water running. A door opened and a man appeared. He was Yasuo's age, his dark hair clipped in a buzz cut, wearing a white button-down, untucked over trousers. *"Ah, sumimasen."* He bowed, backing up. "Yasuo, you didn't tell me we had company," he said in Japanese, then switched to English. "I am Hiroshi."

"Sorry. I am Suiko and this is Helena, my daughter." I shook his hand. "We're Yasuo's cousins." He had to be Yasuo's roommate.

Yasuo returned with a tea tray and set it on the low table. "They want to know about Taro. They are on a mission from Shoko." Hiroshi looked doubtful. "Tomorrow, I can take you to the boat to Uwajima, on Shikoku, where Taro lives. It is only an hour from Kyushu. I do not believe the boats run late in the day." Yasuo poured tea and offered little cakes resembling green Twinkies.

"Are you Yasuo's boyfriend?" Helena asked.

"That's not any of our business," I whispered. Helena clamped her mouth shut and blushed.

Yasuo froze. Hiroshi inclined his head. "You are observant, little girl."

I gave Helena a cake. She put it in her mouth, still blushing.

Hiroshi changed the subject. "Have you kept in touch with Taro?"

"Not at all." I sipped some tea.

Tomorrow we would see Taro. My stomach fluttered. I was not used to meeting relatives. I had only met my Maryland relatives once in my whole life, during a trip to see my dying grandmother when I was four. It had been a long time since Dad went home, too.

All we had was our immediate family. No one visited at the holidays. No one even bothered to send Christmas cards anymore. Not even me.

Hiroshi leaned over. "Yasuo, you did warn them about the terrible ogre, no?"

Yasuo looked at us. "I did, but they still want to chance being eaten." He smiled. "Today, I thought you might like to see where our grandfather was priest, and where your mother grew up."

The Konko church was imposing. Stone steps, guarded by two creatures that looked like lions crossed with dogs, led up to a traditional Japanese building with a red tile roof curving toward the sky. I touched a statue that I remembered from a photo of my grandparents, taken on these steps. Had my grandparents touched it, too, or my mother, when she was a child?

I imagined what my mother looked like as a child. The only photos of my mother from grade school were of her entire school group, and even in a crowd of a hundred identically clad Japanese girls, I had easily picked out her face. It was oddly mature, a smaller version of her adult face, with the same solemn look and sculpted cheekbones.

We walked around the back to an open-air pavilion. Yasuo extended his arm toward it. "Many rites take place here. It is open to

nature, to *kami. Kami* is everything sacred."
He gestured to the landscaped grounds of
pine trees, grass, and flowers. "In the back
is the cemetery. I thought you would like to
see where our grandparents are." We followed him down a path that veered sharply
left.

Hundreds of headstones and short stone
lanterns were built into a hillside and on a
small, flat piece of land below it. Yasuo
tapped a lantern. "These are *torī.* They are
the gateway between sacred and profane.
Between our world and the next, I should
say."

He stopped at a headstone marked with a
plain gray *torī.* "Here are our grandparents."

"Are those their names?" I pointed to the
symbols.

"Yes."

I put my hand on the stone, feeling the
coarseness of the unpolished granite scratch
my palm. "Our grandmother died well
before I was born, but I knew Grandfather.
He was a fine man," Yasuo said. "He always
had time for me, to take me fishing, tell
stories, play ball. He taught me to observe,
and how to draw."

I had never known a grandfather. Yasuo's
gentle smile reminded me of what I would
never have. What would he have done with

me, his granddaughter? I thought of what Helena's grandfathers did with her. Bounced me on his knee, told me stories? "Did he give you candy?" I asked, my voice low.

Yasuo's grin broadened. "Always. Foil-wrapped chocolates. Why do you ask?"

My father liked to have butterscotch candies for Helena, producing them from his pocket to hear her delighted yelps. "I'm trying to get a picture of him, know what he was like." Know what he would have been like with me.

Helena smiled at me and put her hand on my arm. "You okay, Mom?"

I nodded. Swallowing hard, I asked, "Did he ever talk about our mother?"

Yasuo nodded, dusting off the top of the headstone with a handkerchief. "He was always sorry that Taro and Shoko didn't get along. Grandfather would have been glad to see her again. We all would have. But America was too far and expensive for us to visit."

Our mother had never seen her parents' graves. On the anniversaries of their deaths, Mom always said a prayer for them and put their favorite fruit — tangerines — in her shrine. She said they spoke to her in her dreams. No one spoke to me.

"You have a camera? I'll take your picture." Yasuo motioned for us to stand by the headstone. "In Japan, we take pictures at funerals. You know that?"

"Yes, sometimes relatives send them to my mother." Until recently, it had been Aunt Suki's duty. Now I supposed it belonged to no one, unless I asked Yasuo to do it.

He snapped the photo, then checked his watch. "Time to go. Hiroshi-san's famous sukiyaki will be ready soon."

Returning home for visits is not a business for the faint of heart. The culture shock you will feel upon returning to Japan is as bad as when you left it. We do not, therefore, recommend returning unless absolutely necessary. Visits may lead to symptoms such as melancholy and longing for things which can no longer be.

— from the chapter "Turning American,"
How to Be an American Housewife

SEVEN

Over Hiroshi's delicious sukiyaki — a pot
of thinly sliced beef, vegetables, and broth
simmering in the middle of the table over a
gas flame — I told Yasuo more about how
we got to Japan and how we went to his old
house.

Yasuo shook his head. "The man you saw
at my old house is named Kobe. He and I
broke up. He was very angry about it and
told Taro. Luckily, Taro was no longer the
principal, or he would have fired me." Yasuo
sighed. "I had kept this secret from the family until then. Now Taro has disowned me."

I had thought my mother would disown
me for getting a divorce. She had told me
from a young age that marriage was forever.
At the very least, I expected an "I told you
so." When she found out — in a crying
phone call late at night — she was calm.

"He gone?" she asked. "I come over."

Then Mom surprised me by listening to

297

all I had to say. "If he leave, not nothing for you do, huh?" she said philosophically. *"Toki-doki."* Then she sighed. Nonetheless, I couldn't shake the feeling that Mom viewed me with disappointment, as though she were measuring up her old hopes for me against the reality and finding it short. I would feel her eyes on me in quiet moments. "What, Mom?" I would say, and she always said, "Nothing," and went back to whatever she was doing.

We finished all the sukiyaki. "It's fine with me if we never see that old badger again," Hiroshi said while carrying in graham crackers, chocolate bars, and marshmallows. "You know what these are?"

"S'mores! What happened to traditional Japanese food?" Helena popped a marshmallow into her mouth. "Better than *nattō* any day."

"Good for you for trying *nattō*. I never have." Yasuo offered us bamboo skewers, then put his own marshmallow over the gas flame. "I fear Taro won't be any more forgiving of your mother than he has been of me. When he has hard feelings, they last forever."

This was not unlike my mother. She had a mental list of who had wronged her: the kid up the street who stole a rose from her garden; the neighbor who put his bags of grass clippings on our side of the property line; me for any number of things. I always chalked it up to her life spent trapped, peering out onto the street from behind the living room curtains. Perhaps it was cultural. Dad always said, "It's in the past. Move on!"

"Taro wrote a nationalist curriculum for the schools." Hiroshi retrieved a Japanese textbook from a shelf. "He is rewriting history. Saying the Rape of Nanking never happened."

The book was as big and heavy as a college textbook. "They actually use this in schools?"

"Not all. Some." Yasuo wiped chocolate off his fingers. "We have not used it since Taro retired."

I looked at my daughter to see how much of this she was taking in. All of it, of course. She said, "So Taro is like one of those Holocaust deniers? My teacher talked about that. Why can't he just admit that it happened and move on?"

Yasuo nodded. "It is not so easy. Japan suffered a lot during the war and after. Where once we were proud, we had to bow. Some, like Taro, had a very difficult time doing this. It was hard enough to admit defeat to Americans. To admit all these other atrocities as well — I'm afraid Taro may not be capable."

"But my grandmother forgave." Helena violently squished a marshmallow between two crackers. "She married an American. And if she hadn't, I wouldn't be here."

Hiroshi put his hand on Helena's arm. "There are some who cannot live in the present, Helena, and we should feel sorry for them rather than angry."

"Maybe he's softened since you've seen him." I thought of my mother's father, by Mom's account, a gentle man and a priest for the same church. Surely he raised his son to be the same. I reserved judgment. I had no other choice. Otherwise I would have to give up and go home.

Hiroshi bowed his head. "We hope so."

The next morning, a Sunday, fog made the mountains disappear. I checked us out of the inn, and Yasuo and Hiroshi picked us up to go to the dock. "We will make a stop. Where our mothers grew up," Yasuo said. He took us to a little plot of land that stood between two large, modern homes. "Their house was torn down long ago, and the land divided between these two owners. But our house stood here." He walked several hundred feet into the land and turned to look at us.

I stared at the terrain, picturing the house. This was where all of Mom's stories took place. I imagined my mother as a youngster, laughing, putting up laundry on a line. Maybe that field to the west was where she and Taro had to take cover from the B-24s. Here was where Dad returned with her as a bride, where her fate was decided on the basis of a blurry photograph. Melancholy, pure and liquid, flooded me. I wanted to sit, but instead crossed my arms.

Helena took a picture of the countryside. "I didn't know it would be so . . . different."

"Obāchan never told you stories?" I thought she had, during one of the many times Helena spent with her. Helena seemed to be much closer to my mother than I could ever be. But perhaps she was no closer than I was.

"Not many. She said they were too boring for me." Helena considered the land. She walked away from us, staring through her viewfinder at something I couldn't see.

"Is it hard, being a single parent?" Yasuo stared at the horizon.

"Only every day." I flashed a smile, picking up a round black stone from the tall grass. It was cold. I closed my fist around it.

"You were in love?" he prompted.

I glanced at him, startled by the question. No one had ever asked me this. I stuttered. "Too young, I suppose."

"I was married once, too." Yasuo gave me a kind look. "Right after college. It was a marriage of convenience. She knew what I was like." He shook his head. "In the end, she wanted more than I could give."

"Sometimes things don't work out."

"It hurts, even if it wasn't meant to be."

For a moment I stood and committed the scene to memory. Dark dirt and stones and knee-high grasses. The occasional glint of broken glass. Aunt Suki, Mom, and Taro running through the fields, before the war. My own heavy heart. I put the stone in my pocket and walked to the car. "Helena, time to go, love."

She followed.

We drove to the east side of Kyushu. "The jet foil takes one hour." Yasuo hugged each of us. "Catch the bus to Uwajima — it's four miles south. I do not know his exact address, but it is not hard to find. There's not much on Shikoku."

"Thank you." Helena hugged him again impulsively. "So far you're my favorite

302

person in the country! I wish you could come with us."

Yasuo laughed. "I wish I could. But I must work. I hope we will meet again." He gave me a piece of paper. "Here is my e-mail and home address. Please, if it doesn't go well, come back again. Stay with us. Good luck to you." We squeezed onto the water taxi with the other people heading to Shikoku, and waved as it roared away, the front of its hull lifting out of the water.

According to my guidebook, Shikoku was the least visited of all the Japanese islands. The main attraction was an eighty-eight-stop Buddhist temple tour, or pilgrimage, which the book said took between one and two months to complete.

As the sun broke through the marine layer, the sea revealed itself to be a gorgeous turquoise, dotted by small islands with mountains. The air was warm for March, humid with salt. I inhaled, feeling sunshine on my eyelids, a spray of seawater hitting my face. This I could get used to. Helena was absolutely green. "Please tell me we can drive back."

"Lean over the rail if you have to." I stroked her hair.

We docked in Masaki, north of Uwajima.

A white lighthouse perched atop a hill in the distance. We straggled off the boat and waited for Helena to get her land legs back. Up the shore stretched white sand beaches bordered by evergreen trees beyond. In America, there would be mansions replacing the trees.

Helena recovered, popping a piece of mint gum into her mouth. "Is this it?" The shrine had a wooden platform and *torī* gates, which were two poles with two beams across. Tourists milled about, cameras at the ready, spilling out from three tour buses parked nearby.

"No, Yasuo said it was down the road. Maybe this one is part of the temple tour." I looked at the bus schedule. Half an hour to kill. We climbed up the steps to investigate.

Helena got to the top first, and jumped back. "Holy cow!"

There was an enormous wooden penis, carved out of a giant tree, laid on its side, complete with monstrously sized veins. I flushed and grabbed Helena's shoulders, spinning her around. "Okay, Helena, it's just a tourist trap. Let's go see if we can find a snack stand. I'm starving."

Helena twisted out of my grip. "What *is* that thing? A tree?"

"Yes." I headed down the steps, hoping irrationally that she would follow. Instead she ran back to the top.

"That's a penis!" she shouted.

"Shh." Try to remain calm, I told myself. I returned to her and made my voice clinical. "It's a fertility shrine, obviously."

"So that's what one looks like," Helena murmured.

"Helena!" I was the panicking mother that I never wanted to become. "Calm down." I was really talking to myself.

"What?" She crossed her arms, blushing a deep red. She pulled her short-sleeve cardigan together over her tank top. "I didn't say I *wanted* to see one, you know. Sheesh, Mom."

I pulled myself together. She was almost thirteen. It was natural to have that curiosity. "It's a bit — exaggerated."

Helena rolled her eyes. *"Obviously,"* she repeated.

I took out my little guidebook and found the shrine entry. *"Those who want to be blessed with fertility, or who have been blessed as a result of a previous visit, write their notes or prayers on little white papers and fold them into the dry splits of the wood,"* I read aloud.

Helena backed away. "These people are so superstitious."

Her tone was contemptuous. "These people," I said tightly, "are your people."

"I didn't mean it like that, Mom. But you've got to admit, Obāchan's a big fan of old wives' tales."

I smiled. "I would admit that."

To my mother, the number four was bad. "Never take four," she admonished me when I took four dumplings once at dinner. "Mean death. Or two. Bad manner. One or three or five." Same with sticking your *hashi* straight up and down in the rice bowl. "Only at funeral!" Mom admonished.

Mom also advised me to clean the toilet bowl when I was pregnant, "so have pretty baby." Spiders shouldn't be killed in the morning; they were good luck. At night it was okay. Flowers had to be arranged in a trio. "It for balance. Sun, earth, sky."

People were putting coins into a wooden box and pulling out small sticks with writing on them. "*Sumimasen.* What is that for?" Helena asked an older man, pointing to the stick in his hand.

"*Dai-kichi.*" He bowed with his stick, his face crinkling into a smile. He gestured at the box.

I dug into my pocket. "It means good fortune." Five hundred yen. I dropped the coins in for both of us. We each took a stick.

"I can't read it." It was in *kanji,* the symbolic alphabet. I could barely read the phonetic alphabets. "We can ask Taro to translate."

"Are they like a fortune cookie?" Helena stuck hers into her little knapsack.

"I would assume so."

"I can't wait to see what mine says!" She whipped out her small digital camera and took a photo of the penis. I mentally groaned. "Imagine seeing this in America, right next to a cross. There'd be so many lawsuits your head would spin." She took a picture of me next to it. I set my mouth in a disapproving line.

"Let's walk," Helena said, shifting her traveling backpack. "It's only a couple of miles, right?"

"If you can make it, I can."

A sign pointed to the sex museum up the street. I steered Helena away. "Let's get going before this fertility magic rubs off on me."

"Don't you want to give me a sibling?" Helena asked as we walked back to the road. "I always wanted one."

"You did?" Helena had seemed content on her own, a mini-adult among us. "But you're too old to have a sibling now. Look at the age difference between me and Mike.

We're not close."

"That's not because of age difference, Mom. It's because he doesn't like kids. Or people." Helena stopped to tie her shoe. "I'm different. I'd babysit and everything."

"I decided to stop with perfection." I gave her a hug.

"Why didn't you ever marry somebody else?" Helena straightened. "Like a billionaire hedge-fund trader."

I laughed, a hollow sound. We began the walk down the road. "Guess not many men are in the market for a single mom."

She gave me a hurt look. I squeezed her shoulders. "It's not that, really, honey. It's me. I'm — me. Nothing special. I go to work and I'm your mom and that's enough."

"Mom." Helena shook her head. "Everybody's always told me what a beautiful mother I have. I always dreamed I could be like you."

I laughed again, genuinely. I could not believe this for a moment. After all I've taught her, she would still want to be like me? "You don't want to be like me, Helena. You're already different. That's a good thing."

She huffed a little as we got to the steep part of the hill. The sun had come out hot. On our left, a meadow led to a mountain;

on the right, a drop down to the ocean. "You're always telling me how extraordinary I am, but what about you?"

My shoulders slumped. Everyone had dreams when they were young. But they slumbered, were put off, and sometimes they died. I could not confess this to my daughter, with her face upturned to the sky. I could not tell her the truth. "Helena."

"What about you?" Her voice echoed forlornly across the meadow.

I spoke quietly. "I do the best I can, Helena."

Helena stopped moving. "That's just it. You do — just enough. Enough to get by. You're" — she jammed her finger into my chest — "lonely." She started moving. "I worry about you, you know."

"I don't want you to." I wished that she were a little girl again, unbothered by my worries and ambitions, unaware. I wished I could pick her up and distract her with a lollipop and a kiss.

She walked faster. I caught up. "Did you ever have any dreams?"

I paused. From up here, the waves churned tiny foam. "Of course I did. But they changed." My words sounded hollow even to me. Helena was right. This life was not enough. Soon enough, my child would be off. And I would have nothing.

Helena sat, too. "I ruined your life."

"Of course not." I reached for her and she pulled away.

"You should have just had an abortion."

"I wanted you." I remembered the day I found out I was pregnant. "You were a surprise, but I wanted you. We both did." I took the pregnancy test in the bathroom with its old pink bathtub and toilet, Craig and I waiting in anxiety. It wasn't the first pregnancy scare we'd had, but this was the first time we'd had real cause for alarm. A vacation when I'd accidentally left my birth controls pills in my dresser drawer at home.

"What is it?" Craig's boyish face leaned over the toilet.

"Two lines." I spoke too softly for him to hear.

"That's a positive." He put his arms around my waist and kissed my neck. I looked at us reflected in the mirror, our faces unlined, slender, in love.

I leaned into my knees and searched for the right words for my daughter. "Things don't always go the way you plan when you're young, Helena. But I want you to know." I cupped her face with my hands. Her eyes gleamed. "You have never been a sacrifice to me. Do you understand?"

"Yes."

I dropped my hands. "Don't you forget it."

"I won't if you won't." She glanced at me sideways. We continued our walk, quiet, each of us staring off into the expansive sea.

We came to Taro's church after a twenty-minute walk. It was similar to the one in Ueki — tiled roof, guardian statues on either side of wooden steps, a wooden pavilion-like structure. A garden, a weeping willow bending low over a koi pond, was visible to the right. I felt the urge to do some plein air painting, though I hadn't attempted such a thing since college art class.

A Japanese woman in a big straw hat, on her knees, weeding near a small pine, was the only other person around. She wore overalls and a long-sleeved white shirt with cotton gloves. She rose and saw us. She smiled. Her skin was very fair, her eyebrows and hair charcoal against it. "Hello," she said in English.

I waved. Maybe she knew where to find Taro. We approached. In the pond, koi in brilliant fall colors swam. The young woman took a plastic bag filled with pellets out of her tool basket. "Food." She pointed. "Like to feed?"

"Arigatō." I took the pellets, unsure how to proceed. Helena pinched some in her fingers.

"No, no." She forced Helena's hand open, the pellets in the middle of her palm. "Put hand by water."

Dubiously Helena knelt, dipping the back of her hand into the water. A gold-and-cream koi stuck its head out and plucked the food from her hand. I tried it. The fish sucked gently at my fingers.

"It's like feeding the bat rays at Sea World," Helena smiled. She turned to the woman. "How long do they take to get this big?"

"Many years," the woman answered.

"Ojīchan and Obāchan used to have a koi pond," I said. "When I was a kid." Dad dug and cemented it; a bonsai pine stood over it, cut into flat levels. Most of the time the water was so brackish, we couldn't see anything, unlike this crystal-clear pond.

"We had goldfish in there. Koi were too expensive." I sat back on the grass. "We had one for seven years; he was about eight inches long. Then something, probably a raccoon, got him. There was nothing left but a pile of scales." I fed the koi a few more pellets. "Mom said she'd never have fish again. We filled in the pond."

312

The woman listened with interest. "How very sad."

"Guess raccoons have to eat, too." Helena fed the fish more, too. "You should have put something around it to keep the critters out."

"That would ruin the nature of the pond." The woman gestured around her. "No fence here. Sometimes we lose a fish. You cannot control."

I smiled at the woman. She seemed in no hurry to return to work. She knelt near me and wiped at her brow with a handkerchief.

"Do you come for services?" Her accent was much thicker than Yasuo's. "There are none today."

I plucked a blade of soft grass. A clump of dirt clung to the end. "I am looking for the priest."

"Which one?"

"Taro."

"Yes, yes." She nodded. "Not here, down road. Not far."

"I'm his niece," I said in Japanese.

The woman's inky eyebrows shot up. *"Sō desu ka?"* she exclaimed. *"Watakushi wa ma-gomusume!"*

"What?" Helena asked.

I stared at the woman's face. She grinned at mine. "She's his granddaughter," I repeated in English, disbelieving. Another blood relative discovered.

"Hai." She bowed, then spoke in rapid Japanese. I had a hard time following her. She had heard a little of us. A very little — she knew that we existed. Through Aunt Suki, until Taro had his falling-out with Yasuo and, consequently, Aunt Suki.

"Come," the woman said in English. "I am Sumiko. Come meet him."

American households do not have the tatami mat as Japanese households do. Nor do Americans remove their shoes before entering a home, the result being that their floors become filthy as all manner of mud, grass, and unmentionables are tracked inside. It is a common problem for American Housewives to be ashamed at the state of their floors; do not let yourself become one of them! Floors absolutely must be dry swept on a daily basis, to prevent the overwhelming accumulation of despicable dirt. At least weekly, your floors should be thoroughly cleansed, not by mop, but by hand, the Japanese way, as proper husbands should expect.

— from the chapter
"American Housekeeping,"
How to Be an American Housewife

EIGHT

We followed our newly discovered cousin to a tiny maroon Honda. I wedged myself in the back, next to a car seat. Helena got in the front. "Do you have a child?" I asked.

"Three-year-old boy."

"How cute!" Helena clapped her hands. "Japanese children are adorable. They look like little squishy apples!"

"And you say I'm weird." I folded my knees up to my chest. I wondered why I didn't take the front seat. I was the parent. Maybe it was a holdover from my self-sacrificing mother's example, who would give herself the chipped plate at dinner and the piece of meat with the gristle. If my daughter could be comfortable, I would make it so.

Sumiko bumped the car down the country road. I gripped Helena's seat. Sumiko could have been a New York cabbie.

A mile or two later, she ground to a halt

316

in front of a wood-framed house. Behind it stretched a square acre of land planted with a large vegetable garden and fruit trees.

"Ojīchan!" Sumiko called as we entered the home. I took off my shoes. "Ojīchan! Visitors!" She spoke the word in English. "Welcome, welcome, have a seat." Sumiko pushed indoor slippers toward us to use on the hardwood floors.

The inside of the house consisted of one very large room, separated into smaller rooms by sliding *shoji*-screen panels — rice paper and wooden lattice in a honey color. The main room had a low dining table set on a mat, with red cushions set around it. Light came through a screen printed with the silhouette of a bonsai tree. Two round white paper lanterns hung down over the table. In the corner, there was a flat-screen TV. One wall had a large *tansu* unit of dark wood — cubes and drawers for storage and display that stair-stepped toward the ceiling.

Through an open screen, I saw a small room whose floor was covered in tatami mats, and a big window looking to the garden, providing most of the light in here, as well.

"Why the English, Sumiko-chan? *Gaijin imasu ka?*" a jovial voice said from another room that I couldn't see.

"Foreigners, he's asking," I whispered.

"I knew that from the first five minutes we were here, Mother." Helena smiled and sat on a red cushion.

"*Iie,*" Sumiko responded in the negative. She glanced to us, at a loss for what to call us, then flashed a quick, reassuring smile.

A chubby-cheeked boy wearing Spider-Man underwear whipped open the *shoji* screen and ran screaming into the room. "*Okāsan! Okāsan!*" he screeched, leaping into her arms.

"Taro-chan!" A man in his late sixties rushed after him, holding a pair of shorts and a T-shirt. He stopped at the sight of us.

We took each other in for a moment. His gray hair was thick on his head, and his eyes were deep brown and nearly disappeared under his bushy black eyebrows. His cotton kimono was dark navy, with a white *kanji* symbol repeated all over.

He bowed, covering up his surprise and turning to Sumiko, then back to us. "*Hajime-mashite. Amerika no kata deshō ka?*"

"He-llo," I stammered, forgetting my Japanese altogether. Helena clasped her hands together and, instead of bowing, dipped into a low, dramatic curtsy.

"Hello," Taro said in English. "*Nihongo ga*

318

dekinai," he said to his granddaughter scorn-fully. *They don't speak Japanese.*

"Sukoshi," I said. *A little.*

Never before had I seen one of my moth-er's immediate relatives in person. I couldn't stop staring at his face, which looked a bit like my mother, and a lot like the photos of my long-dead grandfather. He was more stoutly built than my grandfather had ap-peared, his chest a barrel and his legs thick, his feet flat and wide. Peasant stock from my grandmother, my mother would say. Hard to push over.

"I will speak English, then," Taro said. "Sumiko, these are your friends?"

"Yes. No." Sumiko pulled Taro-chan's shirt over his head. "It's a very strange oc-currence, Ojīchan. These are your nieces."

Taro's brow furrowed.

"Shoko's daughters."

"This is my daughter, Helena," I corrected Sumiko. "I am Shoko's daughter." I bowed now. It seemed the right thing to do.

He glowered. "Why do you come here? Money?"

I felt heat rising from my neck. Yasuo had warned us.

"Why would we come all the way to Japan for money?" Helena crossed her arms. "Do you know how expensive plane tickets are?"

Taro's eyes flickered with amusement. "Ah, true. You are here for another reason."

I collected myself. "May we sit down and talk?"

Taro did not hesitate. "Tell me so I can decide whether to have you here or not."

"Aren't you the least bit glad to see us, Uncle?" Helena spread her arms out dejectedly.

Sumiko put one arm around her. "Ojīchan, they came to reunite. It is wonderful."

Taro grunted. It reminded me of Mike.

Everyone was a stranger to me. The family I had grown up with. The family I had just found. I knew them, yet they were no closer to me than a casual acquaintance. Only Helena was mine, and even she became, by turns, a stranger as she neared her teens. My lip trembled and I made it stop. "Shoko's sick, Uncle."

Momentary concern passed over Taro's face before he controlled it. "Caught some American disease, eh? I am not surprised."

Sumiko covered her mouth with her tiny hand. "Ojīchan!" she said. "Sit down, Cousins, please. Let us have tea."

"No!" he said. "I will not have these traitors in my home." He ranted in Japanese until even little Taro was agog.

320

Helena was near tears. I drew myself up and looked him square in the face. What I saw there was not anger, but fear and exhaustion. He knew this was silly. He knew, but his pride wouldn't let him admit it.

I bowed. "Of course we will leave if you wish, Uncle. But my mother wanted us to give you a message. It's in my bag. Would you like it?"

He bowed back. "Do as you wish. I must be leaving." He glanced at Sumiko.

"This is my house, my husband's house," Sumiko said. "They stay."

"I will see you at a later time, it seems," Taro said stiffly. He put Taro-chan's clothes down on the mat, put on his shoes, and left.

"He's going to the church." Sumiko dressed her son. "I am sorry for his outburst. I knew he had difficulties with your mother, but I did not know he would act so." She bowed. "Forgive me."

Helena lay on her stomach and rolled a red race car toward Taro-chan. "It's not your fault."

"One can be sorry without it being one's fault." Sumiko gestured to me. "Please, sit. I will bring out food." She went into the other room.

"Mom, what is going on?" Helena asked.

"How can he just throw us away after we came all this way to see him?"

"He was surprised. Maybe he needs time to recover." I wanted to believe this.

Sumiko returned with a tray of sliced persimmons, coffee, and cakes. "This is all we have," she said, handing us hot, moist towels. "I apologize again for my grandfather. Even though he is priest and Konkokyo says that all mankind gets along, he is still like that." She picked up the persimmon. "It's from being principal. He had to be strict with the students." Taro would have been at home in South Central. "Where do you stay now?"

I brought up my shoulders. "Where's the nearest hotel?"

Sumiko clasped my hand. "I would like you to stay here. You are welcome. My husband is a fisherman, out to sea most times. Ojīchan lives with us. His wife died a couple years ago."

I bit into a persimmon. It tasted like a juicy date. "He won't like it, Sumiko."

"This is my house, not his." She stood. "You are my family, too."

I smiled at her. Only once had anyone from Dad's family come out to see us from the East Coast — my grandma Millie, when I was about ten years old. Mom had spent two weeks getting ready for her visit. She fixed up a mattress on the floor of the spare room for me, giving Grandma my bed. "More comfortable," she had said.

Then, after Grandma arrived, Mom wouldn't let her do anything. Mom made elaborate meals and catered to every small need Grandma might have. "Let me do the dishes, Shoko," Grandma would offer every night, looking concerned at the amount of energy my mother was displaying. Grandma Millie was in her sixties, gray-haired, and had commenced living a nomadic life in which she spent a couple of months with each of her children on the East Coast. Not us — we lived too far away, she said. She had Dad's same blue eyes. I thought she was fascinating because she removed her teeth every night.

"You guest. No help," Mom said, even as the strain made her lie down for longer periods.

"I'm family, Shoko. Family helps out." Millie would watch her anxiously, then whisper to me, "Help your mama out, Sue. I can't stand watching her do that."

I watched Sumiko start clearing away the remnants of our snack and stood to help. "Sit, sit, you guest." She brushed me aside.

"Tomorrow I'm family, and I help. Okay?"

She looked taken aback. "If you would like."

We spent the rest of the afternoon and early evening looking at the family we didn't know we had: pictures of Taro's two sons and daughter getting married; the birth of Sumiko; Taro celebrating anniversaries with his late wife, Keiko; photos of Taro as school principal; and all the other milestones families always have pictures of. Sumiko had her own photos in neat albums; Taro's were stuffed into three shoe boxes.

Taro looked entirely unlike the man we saw earlier: in these he was smiling, his arms always hugging those around him. There were a few of their grandparents and some of Suki and her husband and her children.

"Where are Taro's children?" I picked up a photo of Taro holding a baby, many years ago.

"My parents live in Kumamoto City. My aunt went to Tokyo to be a singer — a jazz singer."

"Really?" Helena was trying to put Taro's photos into chronological order. "Can we go see her?"

"You can hear her." Sumiko went to the *tansu* and put a CD into the player. "God Bless the Child" came on, sung by a sweet, high, thin voice, backed by a piano.

"Wow." Helena's eyes widened. "Mom, you never told me we're related to a professional singer."

"I didn't know myself." I smiled. "What I don't know about this family, Helena, could fill two books."

"And my brother is a judo champion," Sumiko added, returning to us and flipping an album to a photo of a diminutive, yet very solid, man on an Olympic podium, gold medal around his neck.

"We're related to a celebrity!" Helena shrieked. "That is so cool."

Taro-chan, lying on the floor and watching cartoons, stirred. Sumiko kissed Taro-chan on the cheek. "He is tired."

Would Sumiko and the rest of the family be as pleased to see pictures of us? Did they ever think about Mike and me, and my mother and Helena, out in America? Or were we gladly forgotten?

Mom had rarely spoken of Taro. From his actions, I guessed that Taro had spoken of her even more rarely. Maybe talking about it hurt too much. Maybe he simply didn't care any longer.

We had no singers or athletes in our little section of family in San Diego, or even on the East Coast, as far as I knew. Perhaps our Japanese relatives would be ashamed of our mediocrity, of my parents' falling-down house and my own ramshackle one. Or maybe they would want to visit, just because we were not too far from Disneyland.

Helena yawned, and I did, too. More had happened in the past day than it had for the last half-decade of my life.

"Mom?" Helena stretched out beside Taro-chan. "I'm having a great time. Thanks."

I smiled at her. "You're welcome."

It was seven now. Taro had not returned. Possibly he would not for as long as we stayed. The letter sat in my bag. I could leave it for him, but Mom wanted a reply. I did, too.

Sumiko smiled. "Bed?" She pointed toward the tatami room. "I will unroll your futons."

One thing Americans and Japanese have in common is their can-do spirit. In America, you will find your hard work rewarded as it is in Japan. How fitting that America should have been the only one who could defeat Japan.

— from the chapter "Turning American,"
How to Be an American Housewife

NINE

I awoke to a sharp pain in my back. Taro-chan's small foot was planted in my spine, his mouth open and drooling. Helena was on my other side. Sumiko slept on another futon across the room. Light filtered in brightly through the sheer blinds. The room was bare except for some shelves on the walls. Uncluttered. How different from my bedroom in San Diego, with old overflowing dressers and light-blocking dusty drapes.

From the other side of the *shoji,* I smelled breakfast. Eggs. I got up to use the bathroom, then went into the living area.

Taro sat at the table, reading a newspaper and drinking tea. He gave the barest nod, terrifying me. I couldn't help thinking he had a weapon stashed in his kimono, even if his only weapon was an insult.

"Sorry," I muttered, ready to return to the sleeping room.

"Sit. Have some tea. If you prefer coffee,"

he added, "I'm afraid you will have to wait for Sumiko. She is the coffee drinker."

"Your English is excellent." Of course his English was good. He went to college, unlike my mother. An education for which she had largely paid.

His eyebrows went up. "Yes. I have studied it."

"Why? Don't you hate Americans?"

"Keep your friends close and your enemies closer," he quoted, amused.

I sat down. The remains of a plate of scrambled eggs sat in front of him, along with an untouched platter of chocolate croissants. My stomach growled.

I wanted to act like my mother would, but I couldn't think of what she would have done. Yelled? Thrown something? Hugged him? I squared my jaw.

I had to give him the letter, stuck in the pocket of my bag, Mom's elegant chicken scratch so close together, it looked like a pattern.

I waited.

"I have been in meditation all night." Taro put down the paper and folded his hands.

He examined my face, probably seeing my mother in me somewhere, in the longish shape, the jaw, the unruly eyebrows. And he saw my father, too, disgusting Taro, no doubt. His expression revealed nothing and his eyes were impassive.

He pushed the pastry plate at me and I took one. "I have decided that this is not your fault. Especially your young one." He bowed his whole upper body. "I apologize for my outburst."

I frowned. "Why couldn't you have given Mom a chance thirty or forty years ago?"

His face darkened again. "Some things are not easy to forgive. For instance, what your country did to us. How could I embrace a man from our enemy country as my brother-in-law?" Taro pointed his finger into the air. "It's all about karma. Your mother's karma is bad, unfortunately. Perhaps this is why her heart is now failing. The United States has bad karma from using the A-bombs. This is why you were attacked by terrorists." He took a bite of cold egg. "But, by forgiving her now, I am improving my own karma, and perhaps hers."

Anger built in my gut. Must everything have a payback, a reward or punishment? I knew I should accept that he wanted to give us a chance, however unreasonable his logic, but I couldn't help myself. "What about those sarin gas attacks on Tokyo subways? Those were terrorist acts by your own people. What is that repayment for? The

Rape of Nanking?"

"Fictional propaganda," he said flatly.

"If my mother's heart is her karma, then what about your other sister, Suki? What did she ever do?"

He shut his eyes ever so briefly. "My little sister. Who knows? Perhaps it is karma for our whole family." His face paled and his hands shook a little as he took a sip of tea.

"Shoko left because she was in love with my father, Uncle Taro, not to hurt you."

His voice rose and his color returned. "Your mother left to get what she could out of your father, because she could not stay here. She only hurt herself."

"She's had a better life than she would have in Japan." But for a moment I doubted that. Would she not have been better off here, with her siblings who raised singers and teachers and sports champions?

Taro put his arms on his head and chuckled. "You are like your mother. Never give up. Your face looks exactly like hers when she got mad." He touched my cheek. "I thought you would be an ugly *gaijin*. But I can see her face in yours." He dropped his hand. "I would not be telling the truth if I said I had closed my heart to Shoko-chan. Every day" — his voice choked — "every day I have remembered her."

Sumiko appeared. "Ojīchan! Thank you for feeding our guest. I am glad you are back."

He acknowledged her with a wave. "If you will excuse me, it is my day at the temple." He left the room.

"He is not always so gruff," Sumiko said. "He is a very kind man. But in this one way, it seems he is stuck, you see?" She smiled. "We go to church this morning. It is Mitama service. You would like to come?"

A few people mingled outside Taro's church, waiting for services to begin. Sumiko got her son out of the car. "Do what I do, if you are comfortable."

We washed our hands in a basin near the door. One wall was covered with notes — prayer requests. I looked up at the dark wood beams of the roof. A platform spanned the entire front of the church. There were three altar areas; the one to the left had photos of people in white priests' robes and offerings of fruits and vegetables on pillars in front of it; the middle looked like a larger version of Mom's miniature altar; and on the right was a windowed booth, where a man in white robes sat with his face in profile to them.

Helena grew quiet. She wore the one dress

she had brought with her, a long flowered one that looked like she stole it from her grandma Kate's wardrobe. She reached for my hand and squeezed. "How come you never take me to church?"

I felt a guilty stab. "I didn't know you wanted to go."

The only church I'd had limited access to as a child was my dad's Mormon one; Mom made clear her feelings about that. There was no Konko church in San Diego. The closest one was in L.A. I prayed with Mom often, but Dad never prayed at home, perhaps because my mother objected to it so strenuously and because my father did not like to fight.

The few times I did go to Dad's church — to see a baptism or a film about its founder — I came with a healthy dose of skepticism, drilled into me by my mother. I watched a woman getting dunked, or Joseph Smith spoken to by God, and I simply didn't believe it.

Sumiko whispered, "The middle is the Tenchi Kane no Kami altar." It had a framed scroll with lettering on it, and more edible offerings. A stack of papers sat on one side, and on the other, a big bag of salt. Sumiko went to the main altar, knelt, bowed once, and clapped four times. Taro-chan did the same. Then they bowed their heads.

We copied them. Instead of praying, I watched people discreetly, trying on this religion for size but feeling no profound connection, no shooting light from above. I stood when Sumiko did. The others had already gone to a pew, and the man in the white robe was coming out.

It was Taro. He held a tapering piece of wood, which he stuck into the fold of his robe. He wore a cap with a long plume coming out the back and curving skyward. It wasn't a feather; it might have been carved wood, but I couldn't tell from this distance. He faced the main altar and clapped four times, saying a prayer.

"This is the *mitama* for all the priests who have died. We remember them and pray for their guidance," Sumiko said. Taro-chan held his finger to his lips, silencing her.

The congregation approached the altar. We were offered a tree branch with a piece of white paper attached to its branches. "Put it on the table, and pray to the priest you want," Sumiko instructed quietly.

I looked at the tableau of photos, stopping at a man with a small smile on his face, the expression wrinkling around his mouth and eyes. "That's your great-grandfather," I whispered.

"People are praying to him? Like a god?" Helena peered closely.

"Not exactly," I hedged, though I suspected she was correct.

I settled down and tried to make my mind go blank. What did I want to pray for? World peace sounded like a Miss America contestant. Mom's health was a given, like the health of the rest of my family. I wanted to pray for something I could change. I swallowed. My throat was ash dry. *For guidance. I need guidance in my life.*

Americans have several odd manners you should be aware of. When you eat with others, it is considered impolite to slurp your soup or noodles, though this improves the flavor. If you eat noodles in the company of an American, twirl them on your fork and eat as silently as you can.

Americans are also insulted if you do not finish everything on your plate. They consider it wasteful, though overeating only leads to being fat. Your host may be openly hostile if you leave food, though in Japan, this is only politeness. Take small portions and try to finish it all to signal you are done.

— from the chapter "Turning American,"
How to Be an American Housewife

TEN

After church, Sumiko took us shopping and then to lunch for the best sushi and sashimi I had ever eaten. The fish was pulled straight from the ocean and sliced up, eyes still moving, at a little restaurant overlooking the water.

"What do you want to do for the rest of our time?" Helena dipped deep-red tuna into the sashimi sauce. "We have a week. Are we going to do any more sightseeing? How about the monkeys in the hot spring?"

"Those are in the north." I took a bite of fish that melted in my mouth. "And I still haven't given Taro the letter."

Helena blanched. "Come on. What's the big deal? He'll read it and respond, or not."

"Mom needs an answer, not silence."

"He's not going to change just for you, you know." Helena sounded wiser than I felt. "Will he, Sumiko?"

Sumiko twirled some long noodles into

her son's mouth, a mother bird feeding her baby. The wind picked up and blew her hair off her face. "One never knows with Taro."

"Does he change his mind a lot?" I asked. "How he thinks about things."

"Ah. Never." Sumiko went off to wash Taro's hands.

"See?" Helena nudged me. "Never going to change. Mom, you're the one who said I shouldn't expect people to change. You married Dad expecting him to change and he didn't. Take people for what they are, remember?"

I remembered. "And yet, people do change, Helena."

"But we can't expect it," she prompted.

"Are you going to throw everything I ever said back at me?"

"Yep." Helena grinned. "So let's go see some stuff."

"I thought you didn't like historical sites."

"I do, as long as you're not lecturing me." She leaned back on her black bar stool. "It's nice here."

We looked out at the water. "Less crowded than a San Diego beach."

The only sounds were Helena clicking her chopsticks against the porcelain dish and seabirds cawing as they dove for fish. She swallowed. "Is it funny to feel homesick for a place I've never been before?"

I had been feeling the same way. "No." As much as I called her "my" Helena, she was her own person, by turns introverted and extroverted, coming up with observations it took me years to figure out. "Do you know you've amazed me every day since you were a toddler?"

"Mo-om."

"Of course, sometimes it's sheer amazement at your craziness," I said as Sumiko returned.

Sumiko pulled Taro-chan onto her lap. "Tales of Helena? Tell me."

We lingered over lunch, talking now of our life in America. I watched Helena speak about her grandparents and her plays and her last algebra test, her hands flying around in the air to illustrate her stories, Sumiko covering her mouth as she giggled. Helena and I were not athletes or superstars, we were us. And that was enough.

Taro returned late. Sumiko and I watched the news; Helena had already gone to bed, along with Taro-chan.

Taro acknowledged us with a nod. "How are the *gaijin* this evening?"

"They are family, not foreigners," Sumiko corrected.

"Hmmmph." He clanged in the kitchen, returning to the table with a dish of food and a rice bowl. He wore slacks and a light-brown short-sleeve shirt, buttoned up.

His serenity and dignity at church were completely at odds with the man sitting there, gobbling up rice grains and looking crotchety. "That was a lovely service today."

"Are you Christian?" He ate an unidentifiable piece of fish. It smelled like caramelized soy sauce.

I paused, trying to think of how to explain what I was. I remembered the prayer I had made earlier. "I'm nothing, I guess."

"No one is nothing." Taro drank water. "Is that how my sister raised you?"

"No. She taught me what she could." I braced myself for a join-my-church-it-will-save-you lecture.

Instead he looked at the news, chewing.

Sumiko excused herself.

It was quiet for a while. I watched him. I wanted to give him Mom's letter. No time like now. How can Taro the priest turn down my mother's request?

I went to my bag and got out Mom's letter. I placed it on the dark lacquered table in front of him. "This is from my mother. I don't know what it says, but I do know she wants you to respond."

340

His eyes fell to the paper. Silence.

At last, he rose. "Suiko-chan" — he picked up his rice bowl — "it is very late. I will see you tomorrow." He tucked the letter into his shirt pocket and shuffled off, his pant hems dragging, a very old man suddenly.

When Americans pass on, most choose burial. To Japanese, this is shocking, since being cremated purifies the spirit and gets it ready for the afterlife.

It may be possible to have your spouse or children obey your wishes for cremation. They could also refuse, and you may have to accept that now you are American in every way, even after death.

— from the chapter "Turning American,"
How to Be an American Housewife

ELEVEN

In the morning, Taro had already left, though I woke as soon as first light hit my eyelids. Taro didn't return all morning.

I helped Sumiko clean the house. Was Taro avoiding me on purpose?

"He is at church today," Sumiko explained. "He will return later."

"I'll go see him." After lunch, I left the others watching TV and walked the two miles to the church. The afternoon air was soft, not cool enough for a jacket.

I arrived and immediately saw Taro's silhouette on a bench under the tree in the garden where we had first met Sumiko. I walked up to him, my feet crunching on the crushed-gravel path.

He did not look up, but shifted over to make room for me. "Suiko." He swallowed hard enough for me to hear it. "I am too old to keep up these pretenses. Too old and far too tired.

"I have been thinking about what my parents would wish. I have been praying to hear what they would say."

He shut his eyes. "My sister," he whispered, patting his chest, "no matter what, she is still here." With a soft crinkling, he took the letter out of his shirt pocket and unfolded the tissue-thin stationery. I watched him read, waiting, hoping he would translate it aloud. Nothing. He inhaled noisily, as though the gentle air itself pained him.

"Wait here," he said. Without meeting my eyes, he got up and went into the church. I sat, looking at the birds singing above, making futile attempts at identification. The only ones I knew were the delicate sparrows.

Mom loved birds. She fed them the leftover rice from the pot, soaking it off and pouring it into the yard, sprinkling bread around every day. Until one died of harassment from the family cat, she would keep a canary in a cage, so tame that it would fly out and return every evening.

"Suiko." Taro had a package wrapped in plain white cloth, knotted together at the top. "This, you give to Shoko." He put it on the bench next to me and undid the knot. Inside was a white shirt box, which he opened to reveal white material. He unfolded this to reveal a white kimono, pulling it aloft. White cranes danced across the material, barely discernible. "These are what Japanese dead wear."

I felt the blood drain from my head. Suddenly I was aware of the pressure of the wooden slats of the bench on my thighs, the scratchy tag on my shirt, Taro's crisscrossed crow's-feet embedded in his skin. "But why does she need that?"

I knew why before he spoke. Of course I did.

He tried to use a reassuring tone. "Your mother wants this" — he touched the package — "because someday she will need it. Everyone does, someday. It is blessed by her church."

I stared at the package blankly. But she had asked for this. She thought she was not going to make it through the operation. She expected not to survive.

Taro rewrapped the kimono.

My eyes filled. "She's not going to die." I sounded like a little girl, even to myself.

Taro sat and gripped my shaking hand. "Ah, Suiko. I was tough. Too tough on Shoko." He cleared his throat. "When Suki-chan passed, it was too hard. My wife before her. All of us dying, dying. Ever since the war, we've been dying." He folded his other hand on top of mine, staring hard into the pond. "She told you that I hated Americans."

I nodded.

"That is all?"

"Yes." I took my hand back and wiped at my eyes. "Is there more?"

"If there is, it is not my story to tell." Taro stood and offered me his hand. "Come, Suiko-chan." He helped me up. "I would like to know all about your mother. What has she been up to these past decades?" He laughed and offered me his arm.

"Can you tell me why she likes baseball so much?" I looped my arm through his.

He lit up. "Oh, Shoko and her baseball. You know she was the best player for miles around. Could hit it farther and run faster than any of us boys. I was jealous." We took a loop around the koi pond, then headed home, walking unhurriedly.

The next day, we decided to go see Nagasaki. I had been thinking about it ever since Yasuo mentioned it. Since before that. I had been thinking about Nagasaki my entire life.

In American history classes, the teacher invariably wanted us to debate the effectiveness of the bomb. I always felt torn. Which side should I agree with? "If Americans no do bombs, the Emperor never stop," my mother had told me when I was in high school.

"But it was horrific," I said to her.

She shrugged. "Yes. War is hell, they say."

"Japan was about to pull out at the end," I argued. "It was unnecessary."

My mother looked at me sternly. "Mommy American now, Sue. I got agree with America. Understand? Nobody gonna call me anti-American."

So in class I let the other students argue, shrinking into my desk, waiting for the discussion to be over.

Taro offered to go with us to visit Nagasaki. Rather, he announced that he was coming. "You'll get there easier with me."

We slept overnight on the train. "On the way back, we will stop in Kumamoto. You must see the castle," Taro told us.

"Can we see Yasuo again?" Helena whispered.

"Probably not." I patted her arm.

In the morning, we walked to the Peace Park. It was very clear out, but cool; around us people were walking to work or shopping, dressed in lighter spring clothes and sweaters, hoping the day would warm as promised. I expected there to be no vegetation, but of course it had grown back, the same way it did after fires, after wars. There were kids and dogs running around. It was a normal park to the casual observer.

"On that day" — Taro stopped and breathed heavily — "there was an air-raid alarm in Nagasaki. They turned it off and said it was safe, so everyone was outside."

"Was there an alarm where you and Mom lived?" I asked.

"No. Too far away. Here people thought the B-52s were only doing reconnaissance. You see, the government didn't tell us how bad Hiroshima was. How horrible. They said it was a new kind of bomb, that we would be safe in concrete buildings or in our bomb shelters. And no one thought the Americans would do it again."

We arrived at the main area. There were red brick pavers set in a huge circle with grass growing in between. In the middle was a tall, shiny black granite pillar.

Taro stopped. "This is it. This is where the bomb hit."

One hundred fifty thousand people killed or injured, the inscription said. The bomb exploded five hundred meters above this spot. Everything in the bomb's path was annihilated.

"The toll would have been greater," Taro

said, "if Nagasaki weren't shaped like a bowl. But the poison got many more people than we know." I knew he was thinking of my mother and Aunt Suki.

I inhaled deeply. My lungs felt like razors against my rib cage. People walked by and I felt they were examining me, the American. But it was all in my head. They didn't notice me at all, even as shame rushed up. I stared at the pillar.

Helena took my hand. Her face was more solemn than I had ever seen it. "I don't know, Mommy," she said in a small voice. "I feel like we should say a prayer or something." She sounded embarrassed even to mention it.

"We can pray." Taro took each of our hands.

"Even if we're different religions?" Helena was hopeful. "I mean, I don't even have one."

"We're all here." He closed his eyes and began.

We walked throughout all of the Peace Park. Statues donated by various countries dotted the landscape, all in a promise of "Never again." The most famous one was the Peace Statue. It was a blue-green depiction of a man, designed by a Japanese sculptor, with one hand pointed up and the other horizontal; he looked neither Asian nor European, but both.

"The hand up points to the bomb, the hand to the side means peace," Taro explained.

We stopped at a golden statue of children standing below an adult, who pointed behind to safety. "This way." Taro led us to a stairwell.

We walked through a hallway that brought us to a corridor formed of tall glass mirrored pillars stretched up into a skylight. Above there was water.

"From above, this is a fountain," Taro noted.

We went around a corner. Victims' names were inscribed on a wall. In another room, monitors showed photos of people who had died.

As I looked at this, I couldn't shake how far removed I felt from my comfortable life in San Diego. Or how different my mother's life now was from her childhood.

"I understand why you hated Americans," I whispered to Taro. I had felt the same way in school when we were learning about the torture Japanese performed on American POWs, as though I were somehow responsible in my very DNA. Or learning about the Rape of Nanking. I would never be done doing penance.

He drew himself up straight. "It is good that you bring your little one here," he said simply. "Now let us continue." He climbed the stairs without looking back.

We took the train to Kumamoto City to see the sights. Kumamoto Castle was tall and impressive, looking like three houses, each one smaller than the one below, stacked on top of each other, a Japanese wedding cake. Taro told us it was a reconstruction. "The wooden outbuildings are original," he said.

At its top was a lookout tower, with views to the city and the countryside beyond. "Mom talked about this castle, too," I remarked to no one, leaning against concrete made to look like heavy stones. "Most strong castle in all Japan," she would say, as if she had built it herself, showing me photos she'd taken years ago. "No one can break."

Beside me, Helena broke into a grin. "Look who's here!" She danced forward to someone coming up the stairs.

Yasuo. He looked chagrined as Helena pulled him forward. "I called him from the train," she said proudly. "It's his day off. Isn't this great?"

Taro glanced at him, then strode away to look at another part of the exhibit without a word.

I wanted to chastise her, but restrained myself here in public. Later I would. "Yasuo." I hugged him.

Yasuo sighed. "Helena-chan, I wish you would have given me warning."

"Then it wouldn't have worked at all." Helena took Yasuo's hand. "The view's incredible from up here!"

Taro was reading a photo display of the castle's history. I tapped his shoulder. "I bet you know all of that by heart now."

He grunted. "Go on. I will see you at Sumiko's house."

"No, don't do that." I got into his line of vision. "I'm not saying you have to completely accept Yasuo, but couldn't you tolerate him for a few hours? For Helena's sake?"

Taro glowered. "Two hours, no more."

"And lunch." I smiled, my heart skipping. "Don't forget lunch."

"I must be in a dream world to accept this," Taro grumbled. He held out his arm to me.

Yasuo sat on a bench with Helena. He stood, looking worriedly at our faces. "Uncle." He bowed.

Taro hesitated.

Helena got between them, her arms spread apart as though she were stopping a fight. "If you're going to be mad, be mad at me."

Finally, stiffly, Taro bowed back. "I think they would like to see Suizenji Jojuen Park, don't you?"

Yasuo straightened. "Yes. That is my favorite place in the city. It was built by a feudal lord, Hosokawa Tsunatoshi, on the site of Suizenji Temple. It was made to look like Edo, the route from Kyoto to Tokyo, with a miniature waterway and mountains."

"Most impressive." Taro headed for the stairs. "The original temple was built by Hosokawa Tsunatoshi in 1632."

Late in the evening, we returned to Sumiko's house. Yasuo had walked us all over Kumamoto City. After the gardens, he took us to the art museum, where he bought Helena a black hardbound sketchbook and pens in the gift shop. "So you can practice," he told her.

"She doesn't need practice. She's natural," Taro corrected him.

"Right. How do you know?" Helena rolled her eyes. "You've never seen me draw."

"I see you doodle all the time, even when you do not realize it," Taro told her. "Everyone in our family is an artist. You are no different."

"Even my mother?" Helena looked at me.

"Not for years." I smiled ruefully. "Thank you, Yasuo."

Yasuo bowed, then picked up another sketchbook and put it on the counter to pay. "For you, Cousin."

"No, I couldn't," I protested.

"I insist. To stretch your creative spirit, too." Yasuo presented me with the sketchbook. "To remember our day out."

I hesitated again. Taro tsked. "It's most impolite not to accept a gift," he scolded.

I took it and bowed, feeling awkward. "Thank you."

This side trip had been more exhausting than the flight from America. I stretched out on my futon. Helena lay next to me, sketching away. "This is my sketchbook of Japan," she said. "I'm writing down everything we did and trying to draw pictures, but they look weird."

"Try drawing from life first," I suggested, turning on my side. "It's usually easier."

I closed my eyes. Mom's image danced across my eyelids. I wanted to tell her everything that we had seen.

About her brother. Forgiveness.

Helena had fallen asleep, the sketchbook

splayed across her chest. I asked Sumiko if I could use her phone, then dialed our parents' number.

It was six in the morning there, so by now Dad should have been up, listening to his morning radio and having his hot chocolate. It rang ten times — no answering machine. My parents hated machines in general. Finally Mike picked up.

He sounded funny; there was a delay across the ocean. "Just calling to see how things are going." I did not notice I was balling my pants into my fist. "I have a number now."

"Sue." Mike cleared his throat. "I, uh, have some news. Mom's in the hospital. In the ICU." He sounded calm. Mike always sounded calm, though. "They're looking at doing surgery, but only if they can get her stabilized."

I felt like I had been in a car wreck.

"Sue? Are you there?"

"Can they get her stabilized?"

Mike paused. "It doesn't look good, Sue. I think — I think you may want to come home. Mom won't tell you to, Dad won't tell you to. But I am."

I frowned. Helena appeared, awakened by my voice, her face nakedly concerned. I steeled myself. "Yes. Thanks." I hung up abruptly and sat on the floor.

My whole life, my life spent with a sick mother, I had braced myself for this moment. She had warned us that it would come. But now that it was here, I couldn't move.

"Mommy?" Helena's voice was small, as mine had been earlier. "Mommy, what's wrong?"

Finally I gathered enough air in my diaphragm to breathe, forcing myself to think. "We're going home."

No word in English has the same connotations as the Japanese sayonara, so you can use the term "good-bye." In English, you can say "good-bye" even in casual departure situations as well as in situations where you're unlikely to see the person again. "See you later" is even more casual, and regionalized variations may be acceptable.

— from the chapter "Turning American,"
How to Be an American Housewife

TWELVE

As we packed the next day, Taro stood over me. "Suiko-chan," he said, eating another chocolate croissant, "maybe you come back and visit one day, yeah?"

Taro-chan shoved a fistful of action figures into my bag. I took them out. "I will."

Helena dragged her big backpack into the room. "I didn't buy anything, but I had to sit on it to get it closed."

"I put some stuff in there. Sorry." I zipped my bag closed.

Taro tapped his watch. "Boat time."

"We will always have these memories." Sumiko produced her camera. We went to the edge of their property, the ocean sparkling in the distance. "Stand by Ojīchan. Suiko, you, too." Taro slung his arms over us. He smelled of salt and chocolate and soap.

"Cheese!" Sumiko said gaily, snapping away. Now we would be part of their shoebox photo collection, amid all the other Japanese relatives.

Taro poked us teasingly in the ribs. "You turning Japanese. You're not so butter-*kusai* now."

Helena giggled. "You should talk, with all those croissants."

He grunted. "Good. We match." He held up a hand. "Wait. I have something for you." Taro left, returning with a square gift tied up with a piece of hot-pink silk. I bowed back and accepted it.

"Open it," he said.

I untied the material. Inside was a black lacquered box.

"That was your mother's. She left it," Taro said. "Of course, she threw away all the pictures she had in there when she married your father. These are ours."

I took the lid off. Inside were photographs. Many photographs, all the ones that Sumiko showed me. "I can't take these," I said. "What will you have?"

"It's okay. I have the negatives." Taro crossed his arms. "Take these to your mother. It will lift her spirits." He picked up the top two photos and showed them to me. "These you haven't seen."

In one my grandparents posed in front of their old house with a thatched roof, looking serious, their hands folded in front of them.

The other was of a Japanese toddler in a white Western dress, with puffed sleeves and a huge satin bow at the waist, holding a baby in a white dress in her lap. "That is your mother and me. Take them home to her."

The images were printed on card stock like the one Mom had of her old boyfriend. The one of my grandparents was high-contrast, their faces so white they had lost all definition. In Mom's, a crack ran through her face. I gingerly put them down on the stack.

I turned to him. Mom's face flickered across his. In the strong light, every wrinkle was cast into high relief. How much time had passed without us knowing him, and this family. "I guess it's time to say good-bye, Uncle. Or *sayonara*."

"We don't say *sayonara*." He inclined his head. "*Sayonara* means good-bye forever. We say *dewa mata*. See you later."

"Yes. *Dewa mata*." I hugged him.

He held me tight, then patted me strongly on the back.

"I'm glad you didn't throw us out, Uncle." I stepped back and bowed.

"I never threw anybody out. Sometimes

they leave because of what I say." He smiled ruefully, then bowed back. "Say hello to Shoko for me. I will see her soon."

I did not know if he was talking about here on earth or in the afterlife. "I'll tell her you say hi, Uncle."

$$\bullet \ \bullet \ \bullet \ \bullet$$

PART THREE:
TOKIDOKI

$$\bullet \ \bullet \ \bullet \ \bullet$$

It is difficult to keep one's figure with all the rich foods being eaten in the States. Americans like fried food and rich sweets. The Japanese woman, who stays naturally thin with her regular Japanese diet, may be constantly challenged. But she must keep her figure to keep her dignity.

The best way to control your figure is through having small portions. Avoid potatoes if you can.

— from the chapter
"Cooking Western-Style,"
How to Be an American Housewife

SUE

Dad's thousand-yard stare was trained on the TV in the hospital waiting room. Mom was still in the operating room, where she had been for the past ten hours. I had come straight from the airport, leaving Helena at her other grandparents' house.

I had not told my father anything about Japan. It was as if I had come to the hospital from my home, and not another country. Somehow, I wanted to save it all for Mom. This trip belonged to her.

I yawned loudly.

Dad never took his eyes off the television. Out of nowhere, he said, "Mommy didn't breast-feed you kids."

I shifted in my seat. "I know. She said she didn't have enough milk."

"She did." Dad tsked softly. "She didn't want her breasts to sag." Finally he looked at me, his eyes intensifying into aquamarine. "I wanted her to. It would have been better for you." He stared at his hands. "I wanted you to go to church, too, meet other kids, do activities. She wouldn't hear of it." He spread his arms, then crossed them. "She did the best she could, though. I should have done more."

"It doesn't matter now." I gave him my best cheerful smile. "I turned out fine."

He smiled back. "Are you happy, Sue?"

"Of course," I said automatically. "I have a steady job and a great daughter. What else do I need?"

"If you wait for happiness to find you, you may be waiting a long time." He reached over and patted my hand.

"Now you sound like a fortune cookie. Go home and get some sleep." I didn't want advice from Dad. Not now. "Mom won't be ready to see anyone for hours."

He leaned back. "I can sleep sitting up, you know. Haven't you ever seen me watch TV in the evenings?" My father continued to sit there, stubborn as ever, content to suffer through the hours until Mom awoke. He finally drifted off halfway through a soap opera. A kind nurse put a blanket over him.

A figure entered the room and I looked up, expecting, dreading: Mom's surgeon. But it was Mike, bearing two cups of vending-machine coffee. His wild hair was neatly tied back and his eyes were clear. I blinked. "Hi," I said in a small voice.

He nodded, sitting down with the coffee. "I accidentally got one with sugar. Want it?"

"Thanks." You couldn't pick Mike out of a crowd as my brother. He was a stranger off the street. I had never run out to the tree on Christmas morning with Mike, to see what Santa had left us.

But Mike was there when we needed him to be. Once, when I was six, a wildfire burned up the mountain behind Jacaranda Street, and we were evacuated.

"It's only a precaution," the firefighters told us. "Go across the street." The fire wouldn't jump the street, they said; it wouldn't even come close.

Dad was still at work, but he called and told my mother to grab a few clothes. She did not comply. Mom ran around, crazed, throwing stuff into boxes. Mike came home to help.

"Take this next," she barked at him. He moved everything to a neighbor's yard — all my mother's Japanese possessions, suitcases, some food, my garbage bag full of stuffed animals. The neighbors watched benignly.

The last load consisted of only a Japanese-English dictionary. Mike took my hand and walked me across to where the neighbors had set up lawn chairs to watch the fire's progress, amid all of our stuff.

A TV news reporter and cameraman caught up with him. "Here we have someone escaping with only the few possessions he could grab," the reporter intoned, thrusting the microphone into my brother's face. "What do you have there, sir?"

Mike hefted aloft the book. "A dictionary."

The reporter looked startled. "And what will you do if your house burns down?"

Mike shrugged. "Rebuild. We're insured. Maybe it'll be two stories this time."

"Oh," the reporter said, turning back to the camera.

Even I was old enough to giggle at the absurdity, us standing in the middle of the street holding a dictionary while a fire raged on the mountain.

I looked at Mike, the mystery, here once again when family was required. "Do you like your new job?" I ventured.

"It's all right." He nodded. "Except for people buying reptiles and not knowing how to take care of them. Idiots." He shook his head. "How was Japan?"

I listened for jealousy, but heard mild curiosity. "We saw Taro."

He nodded again. "The uncle who hated Mom? She told me that's why you went."

"Yup." I smiled. "Has it been crazy here?"

"A little. But it'll be all right." He sounded convinced. "Mom's too stubborn to give up, you know?" He slurped down half his coffee in a gulp.

"I know."

Dr. Su appeared, wearing pale blue scrubs and paper shoe covers making whispery rustling noises.

Dad was alert immediately, his eyes bright.

"It was successful." Dr. Su sat next to Dad. He went on about recovery and infection and how she wasn't out of the woods yet. "She's in the recovery room." He put his hand on Dad's shoulder. "You can go in and look at her if you like. She's not awake."

"I'll go see her." Dad got up and limped down the hallway. We followed, overtaking him. Mike and I slowed our pace so Dad wasn't walking behind us. Whenever we went anywhere as a family, Mom would creep along, and Dad would walk quickly in front of her, saying, "Hurry up, Mommy!" as though she were a dawdling toddler.

"Go ahead, I'll catch up." Dad was embarrassed, exactly as Mom had been.

"No hurry, Dad." I smiled at him. "You're going in first."

A few days later, Mom became more alert. She had oxygen tubes up her nose and wires everywhere. Monitors showed her heart beating at a steady, reassuring rate. I settled into a chair and pulled a blanket over my legs. A nurse asked if I needed anything.

"Sue?" Mom's voice came hoarsely.

I bent over her. She opened one eye, her pupil trying to focus. "I'm here."

"You see Taro?"

I nodded. It felt hard for me to speak, too. "He gave me what you asked for."

Mom's hands reached for mine, her rounded nails stripped of coral polish. Our hands were alike, with long, straight fingers. A surgeon's hands, or an artist's, she would tell me. Not the knobby short fingers of my father. "Only for just in case. No worry."

I nodded again. I reached into my big tote bag, touching the smooth lacquered box. "Taro sent this to you." I showed it to her.

Her eyebrows went up. "I thought thrown away! Where find?"

"I don't know how he had it." I set the box on the bed and took out the photos, holding each one up. "These are pictures he sent you."

"Who all these people?"

"Family." I tried to name them all. "Here's Suki and her son, Yasuo."

She closed her eyes again. "Taro tell story of Ronin?"

I couldn't think of who that was. "Is that a cousin?"

"No. Not cousin." Her voice came more forceful. She opened her eyes. "Big story." She reached for my hand again. "Mike don't know either. No tell, okay? This only for you, Suiko."

I smoothed her hair, alarmed. "Rest, Mom, don't talk."

She gestured to the water pitcher on the side table and I gave her water out of a straw and cup. "First," she said slowly, licking her dry lips, "I very proud you. Thank you for go Japan."

"You're welcome." I sat.

She pointed to me. "You are beautiful. Smart. Now be happy. Okay?"

"Okay." I looked at her monitors. Her heart had sped up a little bit. "Please, Mom, get some rest."

"No. I need talk. I fine. Look me." She cleared her throat. "What I want tell now is hard. Long, long time ago, I had another boyfriend. Before Daddy. Another I no mention. Ronin. The real, real reason Taro hate me."

"He doesn't hate you, Mom, not anymore. You can rest easy." I moved my chair close to her. "Go back to sleep, now. You're still tired."

"I no can wait. One thing I know, I no change anything. But you no can tell Mike. He no can handle. Daddy no even want me tell you." Haltingly, she began the story.

"Once, a long long time ago, there a young woman who wanted good life. New life. So this what she did."

Mom shut her eyes, but she would not cease speaking. She talked for an hour, until I was back in Japan with her, with Ronin, until the whole story had spilled, hidden, gritty pearls out of an oyster. When at last she had finished, she opened her eyes again to look into mine.

I put my forehead on the edge of her bed. My brother was my half brother. What an enormous burden for my mother to carry all these decades. I looked at her. "Is that the only reason you married Dad? Because you were pregnant?"

"I love Daddy," Mom said quietly. "Not then. I do now. Love can grow." She touched my head. "No time in this life think 'What if?' Just got do. Okay?"

I wiped at my eyes. "Do you wish you had

left with Ronin?"

She did not pause. "Not possible."

I gazed at her, thinking about my brother and his biological father. "Does Dad know?"

She nodded. "Special kind man. He love Mike no matter what." Her eyes clouded with tears.

I grasped her hand. "But Mike doesn't know."

"No." Her voice creaked.

"Mom, you need to tell him."

"How? He break."

I thought of him showing up at the hospital, at the fire. "Mom, he's not a little boy. He can handle it."

She sighed. "Maybe you right, Suiko." She shifted her weight. "I so lucky. You such good girl. Never thought I would have daughter. First thought daughter was no good, but you . . ."

I kept my gaze on her blankets. "Do you really feel that way, Mom? You're not saying that because of the drugs?"

"No. Not 'cause drugs. Don't be crazy, Sue."

I inhaled, daring to ask one more question now, while she was open. "It's just that it seems like you were so ashamed of me. Because of Craig. Because I can't be everything you wanted me to be."

Mom snorted. "Me? 'Shamed you? How can be? Don't you listen what I did before you?" She hit her bed lightly with her hand. "You 'member, Suiko. You good, good girl. Things no work out way want, yeah?"

"I know." I thought about my daughter, of how I was different and the same from my mother, of how Helena would be different and the same as me.

Mom looked out the window. In the distance, a pale moon was appearing. "Full moon come up."

A giant, silvery moon. I was struck with a memory from my childhood. "Remember when you told me the story of the moon princess whenever there was a full moon, or if I couldn't sleep?"

"Little bit." She moved her legs around.

When I was a child, I was an insomniac, waking and sleeping in fits. My parents' room was catty-corner to mine, and we always slept with our doors open. If going back to sleep took me an especially long time, I'd whimper and Mom would materialize beside my bed, smelling of cold cream and White Shoulders perfume. "What wrong?" she would ask. "Sick?"

"Tell me the story about the princess," I'd whisper.

Mom would sit on my bed and tell me

about the princess who came down from the moon. She would go on and on, rubbing my back, until I fell asleep. I was not like my mother in every way, but when Helena was little, I remembered what my mother had done for me. I never yelled at Helena for waking me up.

I leaned closer to my mother in her hospital bed.

"An old bamboo cutter found a beautiful baby girl in the bamboo," I said. "He took her home to raise her as his own, and in three months she was full grown and beautiful. She shone light in the house, even in the night. Word of her beauty got out and suitors came to call. Her father set forth five knights to get impossible items. They all failed. Then the Emperor himself came and begged her to come live in the palace with him. She said, 'If I have to live in the palace, I will become a shadow.' She got homesick and the Moon People came to get her. She didn't want to leave, but she couldn't survive where she was."

"And she left potion that make live forever with Emperor. He burn on Mount Fuji. That why smoke go up." Mom smiled. "All I ever want is you be happy. Don't forget, you hear?"

A knock-knock-knock sounded. "Come

in!" Mom called. It was Dr. Cunningham. Mom grinned. "Dr. Cunningham! This my daughter, Sue."

I felt shy. He was exactly as my mother had described. Handsome, with kind eyes. "Hello. I thought you worked at Balboa."

"I do. I always come see my patients if they go elsewhere." He smiled. "Nice to finally meet you. I'm Dr. Cunningham. You can call me Seth." He shook my hand warmly, then felt Mom's ankle for puffiness. "Dr. Su's the best," he said. "I want to make sure your recovery goes as well as your surgery."

"Much better now you here, Doctor," Mom purred. I laughed.

He glanced at me, one black eyebrow raised. "I would guess she's on the mend."

"Another minute with you in here and she'll be doing the samba."

He laughed, patting Mom's leg, then checked all her vitals. "Looking good, Mrs. Morgan. I'll see you at my office in a month for a follow-up." He took a card out of his pocket and handed it to me. "Let me give you my card. Call me if you have any questions."

I watched him leave.

Mom did, too. "Now you see what I talk 'bout?"

I put my head down by hers. "Mom, when you get out of the hospital, can we write down how you cook your pizza? And spaghetti?"

"Pinch of this, little bit of that, hard to write down. But I show." She patted my head. "You strong girl. You can do whatever you want." Her arm gestured around the room.

I smiled, surprised. "You think so?"

"I know it. All the time I am proud of you, Suiko-chan. All the time. You much more better mommy than me. Patient. No like me." She paused. The machines whirred mechanically. "Maybe videotape my cooking? I always want be movie star, you know that?"

"I know." I smiled at her.

She wiped away the mascara smudges from under my eyes. "If doctor like you like that, he like you no matter what. You better fix face before see him 'gain, huh?"

I nodded. "I will, Mom."

The concept of shame (*haji*) is unheard of in America. This is why Americans often don't understand Japanese. Americans feel guilt rather than shame.

During samurai times, public shame was as good as death. Americans cannot comprehend this. There are very few things that bring about shame in America. Americans usually do what they want. This is both good — Americans marry Japanese women, providing them with better lives — and bad. Americans may not feel shame for committing crimes or failing their parents, among many other things.

— from the chapter "Turning American," *How to Be an American Housewife*

SHOKO

A week and a half passed, or so Charlie said. I didn't bother keeping track. As I dozed in my hospital bed, I dreamed about my brother and me, hiding in our darkened house. I was kneeling, my head on a blanket so my bottom was in the air like a stinkbug. My parents held Suki close by. Taro got next to me. "Little big sister," he crooned, his cheek pressed to mine, "all will be well."

"How do you know?" I asked, opening an eye. All I could see was the shiny white of his eye, glowing in the near total blackness. A plane roared, deafening, overhead; the house rattled with a not-so-far-off explosion. Suki whimpered, and my mother nursed her to quiet her. I prayed.

"We are together, princess." Then he belched directly onto my nose, his breath fish-stinky, laughing, and I shoved him away.

The room brightened. I opened my eyes and was not in Japan at all, but in my hospital room, an oxygen tank helping me breathe. My heart beat strong in my chest; I pictured the stitches healing magically.

"Shoko-chan?" A male voice. It's so familiar, but I can't place it. Not Charlie or Mike or a doctor.

Then a face wove into view. My baby brother, hair gray, face wrinkled, but the same broad nose and big-toothed grin. My Taro. "I am not dead?" I said in Japanese, surprising myself.

"Too stubborn, like me." Taro laughed. I took his arm and pinched it — not hard, because I was weak. He squealed all the same. He was real.

We spoke of many things. Sue had called after the surgery, and he had decided to come, just like that.

My Japanese flowed through rusty old pipes at first, but then came strong and clear. We talked of our children and grandchildren, but not one word of what drove us apart. It no longer mattered. I took his hand in mine, stuck through with tubes. "Look at us, two old farts," I said, patting his liver spots.

"Only the shell is old." Taro's eyes twinkled as I remembered. My baby sister flashed before me, her lilting laugh, her pigtails flying with her jump rope. Oh, if only I could have seen Suki, too! "If Shoko can't come to Japan, Japan comes to Shoko," Taro said, showing me photos of Sumiko and Taro-chan.

I smiled. "I will come. You'll see."

We have heard Housewives complain of boredom, especially after their children are older.

If you find yourself bored or discontented, try this: Give your house a thorough cleaning. Get rid of everything you have no need for. Make your American house as uncluttered as a Japanese house. There is no better cure for the doldrums.

— from the chapter
"American Housekeeping,"
How to Be an American Housewife

SUE

At last, when I had exhausted excuses to stay away, I was forced back to work the following week. Helena returned to school. Everything was back to normal, yet nothing for me was normal any longer.

Mom was getting stronger, still in the hospital. Taro's visit had jolted life back into her. In a few weeks, she would be moved to another floor. Once she could do a slow lap around the floor, she would be able to go home.

Weeks passed. Taro returned to Japan. Mom got out of the hospital. I talked to Dr. Cunningham — Seth — on the phone a few times, even going out for coffee once, a dinner next. And still I whiled my time away at the office, doing as much work as necessary to keep me employed, running home to attend to Helena, daydreaming about Japan.

How could I miss Japan already? I carried the stone from my family's land in my pocket, turning it over and over in my fingers, its presence a comfort during traffic jams and long meetings. My little house felt odd to me now. I ran into corners, I put spoons in the wrong drawers. I had to think about which freeway to take to work. San Diego had become a foreign nation. Perhaps I needed more time to readjust.

Or perhaps I needed a change. Nothing held me back. My mother had said I could do whatever I wanted. She was right. I could be doing so much more. Look at what my Japanese cousins had achieved. I applied for jobs in other departments, even at a few other companies. A new challenge to keep me occupied. Anything.

One night, while Helena worked on homework at the dining table, I looked up teaching programs on the computer. I made notes of a few programs, what they required to get in. And then, on a whim, I typed in "Teaching in Japan."

It was absolutely ridiculous. To think of me, a woman with responsibilities, going to a teaching-abroad program like a college kid with a backpack. But I took out Toshiro's card anyway, the man we had met on the plane, and looked up his company.

A list of opportunities popped open. One was near Sumiko and Taro on Shikoku. I glanced stealthily at my daughter, sure she could hear my heart rate change, moving my shoulders so she would not be able to see the screen and ask what I was doing. I wasn't ready to answer yet.

I read the salary. Housing was included. It wouldn't be so bad. I allowed myself to imagine this new life, packing up this house, flying back to Japan, training, working.

I took the stone out of my pocket and tossed it on the desk. It clattered and turned like a top, black with purple undertones I had not seen before. I spun it again. I couldn't uproot Helena to Japan. I put my hand over the stone, stopping its momentum.

"Mom?" Helena's voice near my head came low. "What are you doing?"

"Nothing." I made to close the computer window, but she put her hand over mine.

"Japan? Are you serious?"

"Of course not. It's silly. I was only curious."

" 'Teaching in Japan.' " Helena was silent, staring at me.

"I know." I shook my head. "I'm just restless." I smiled at her, touched her chin. "I'll get over it. Don't worry, honey."

"No, Mom." Helena wedged a chair in beside me. "It's not silly at all. I think" —

she took the mouse — "it's one of the greatest ideas you've ever had."

"But finding you a school — you don't
know Japanese — there are so many vari-
ables. No. It's too hard." I watched her face.

There was no hesitation on it. "I would be
learning a new language and culture. Think
of the college essay I could write!" Helena
grinned. "Besides, you could talk to Yasuo.
Do some fact-finding about schools. There's
nothing wrong with that, is there?"

"I guess not." I could rent out this house
for more than the mortgage payment. It
would be two years, tops. I would see if I
really liked teaching. My hands got cold,
my cheeks hot.

Helena pointed to the screen. "Let's see
what the housing is like."

She scrolled down until an ad caught my
eye. "Stop here!" I said. The rent was fifteen
hundred a month, exactly the housing allowance's limit. *For Rent,* it read. *One
solitary house of yearning, in hills of Uwajima.
Three bedrooms, one bathroom.*

The hairs on my neck stood up. I rubbed
my hands together and kept my voice calm.
"It'll be gone by the time we're ready to
rent it."

"It won't be. We can make it work."
Helena turned to me, grinning hugely. She

put her face right next to mine. "Promise me you'll do this. Promise me you'll try."

I nodded, then smiled back. "I will." I would. For the first time in forever, I spun around in my office chair, laughing like a little kid at a carnival ride. Then Helena sat on my lap and we spun together.

■ ■ ■ ■

EPILOGUE:
THE SOLITARY
HOUSE OF YEARNING

■ ■ ■ ■

If you must return home to live in Japan, expect to find re-assimilation very difficult. Children are resilient, but you have become accustomed to the soft American lifestyle.

Remember in Japan not to act too "American" to avoid offense to other Japanese. Your children should behave as Japanese children and not American, as well.

If this book teaches you one thing, let it teach you this. Do not protest against life's strains, but let them unfold and carry you through wherever they may.

— from the chapter "Turning American,"
How to Be an American Housewife

SUE

I stuck my head out the back door, a light mist of rain hitting my face. "Time to come in."

Taro-chan looked up from his mud pie. His face and body were completely covered in the stuff. I groaned. *"Hai."* Taro-chan ran full throttle at me.

Sumiko blocked him. "Clean up first." She held him in front of her like a wet puppy. We marched him into the bathroom, plopped him under the shower to rinse off the muck, then carried him into the *ofuro* for a good scrubbing.

It had only been a couple of months since I arrived, but my "solitary house of yearning" already felt more like home than my old house. Of course, by the time I had gotten here the original "solitary house" had been rented, but the name had stuck. This home, only a few roads over from Sumiko's, was cozy and small, set in a copse of

391

trees, as picturesque as a woodblock print. It had a sloping roof and *shoji*-screen dividers, so even though it was as small as the house back in the States, it felt larger.

Sumiko smiled coyly as we rubbed soap across Taro-chan's back. "You hear from nice doctor man?"

I smiled. "Sometimes." Seth and I had been e-mailing each other, and he had promised to visit as soon as he got time off.

Teaching was enough, for now. *"Sensei,"* the students called out all day. It took me a while to get used to the title. I taught teens in the daytime, and adult classes two evenings a week. They asked about everything, from American celebrities to how to salute the flag.

I wondered why I hadn't changed careers before. I knew why — too complacent at my old job — I chastised myself for the lost years, until I realized that chastisement and what-ifs got me nowhere.

I left Sumiko attending to Taro-chan and went into the main room. Helena sprawled on the floor, chatting on the phone with one of her new Japanese friends. I grinned. Some things knew no cultural boundaries. "Hey" — I patted her leg — "you better be talking to the Emperor if you haven't done your homework."

"In a minute." She rolled over. As the sole American at her school, classmates congregated around her, wanting to know if she knew any celebrities, touching her hair, asking her to help them with their English. She loved being the center of attention. Diving headfirst into Japanese wasn't easy, but her teachers were understanding.

Yasuo invited Helena to an art class he taught on Saturdays, and she'd gotten into anime. We had already been to Tokyo a couple of times, where she made it her mission to try to outdress the funkiest Japanese teenagers, which meant she looked like an anime character herself. Her hair was now dyed purple at the tips. At least she'd return to the States with plenty of pink vinyl jackets.

I had worried that the relatives would be upset at our leaving, but Helena's grandparents on both sides had been unexpectedly supportive of our move. Mom especially. "Big adventure," Mom had said at the airport as she saw us off. "Good luck."

Helena hung up the phone with her friend. "When's dinner, Mama-chan?"

"Soon." I picked some blocks off the floor and threw them into the toy box.

"You should make Taro-chan do that," a deep voice boomed from the door. Taro held a black umbrella over his head. He snapped it closed. "Never too early to teach responsibility."

Taro, telling a boy to clean up? He must be softening in his old age.

"Hi, Uncle Taro." Helena bounded over to give Taro a peck on the cheek.

He smiled. "Helena-chan, did Taro-chan dress you today?" He pointed to her hot-pink pleated skirt and her swirled black-and-white tights, worn with red Converse hightops.

"Very funny." She ran off.

"They still wear uniforms, right?" Taro said worriedly.

"No, they require pink hair at her middle school." I grinned. "I'm just kidding. Come in and sit down."

He knelt near the dining table. "Ah, you are going to make me fat and butter-*kusai*." He sniffed the air. "Is that beef I smell?"

"Sukiyaki."

Sumiko returned from her bathtub foray, wiping her hands on a towel. The front of her shirt was completely soaked. "Suiko, have you clean shirt?"

"In my closet." I went into the kitchen to get the bowls and chopsticks.

"What day is your mother coming?" Taro took the rice bowls and filled each with steaming white sticky rice.

"Next month, the third. They're flying into Kyushu."

"I will pick them up," Taro said. "You still might get lost, you know?"

"We'll go together." I put the sukiyaki pot on the burner in the middle of the table, then turned it on.

Taro-chan clambered up and reached for the pot. "No, no! Hot!" Sumiko said, grabbing his hand.

Helena picked up some vegetables with her chopsticks. Taro had already dug in. Sumiko wiped a stain off Taro-chan's lemon-yellow Pokémon shirt.

I put my chin on my hand and stared, still not quite believing where I was. My American life seemed like it had happened to someone else. Only Helena was proof of its existence.

"Mom?" Helena said, her face abruptly in front of mine. Her mascaraed lashes blinked rapidly. "You all right? You're doing that thing Ojīchan does: staring at us."

"Sorry." I shook my head. "Just lost in thought." I put a hand on Helena's cheek. "I'm going to have to confiscate that makeup bag."

My daughter smiled guiltily. "I thought you wouldn't be able to tell." She held her white porcelain rice bowl up and scooped a wad toward her Cupid's-bow mouth.

"I can always tell, my dear," I said. "When you're a mother, you'll understand."

It is true that the Marriage is a difficult path for some people to stay on. As years pass, however, the proposition becomes easier. The husband grows accustomed to the company of his Wife, and vice versa. This is how families attain the permanence to which we all aspire.

— from the chapter "A Map to Husbands,"
How to Be an American Housewife

"I need sunblock," I said. Charlie handed me the pink bottle. I took off my Cubs cap to slather some onto my face, then poured it into my hand. "Did you get top of your head?"

Charlie took off his Padres cap. I patted it onto his nose and scalp. He wrinkled his face. "This stuff feels greasy."

A cheer went up from the crowd. I stood up from the plastic seat. "What happen?"

"Home run." Charlie pointed to the Padres player running the bases and grinned. "Looks like the Cubs are going to lose, Shoko."

"Only third inning. Plenty of time." I sat back down. We were sitting in the middle section of Petco Park, near the redbrick Western Metal Supply Company building, which served as the left-field foul pole, watching the Cubs and Padres play. I thought I'd never been in such a beautiful place. I could see the entire field better than on television. Beyond, I caught glimpses of the harbor, shining like a nickel in the sun. A breeze from the water hit my face. Charlie didn't really care for baseball, but he took me anyway, even though he hated driving downtown. Those one-way streets confused him.

This being outdoors, doing things, was new to me. Charlie and I had also been walking from time to time. I wanted to get in good shape for my Japan trip, to visit Sue as well as Taro and the rest of my family. My mended heart, with the wedge cut out of it to make it smaller, was doing well. The doctors thought it would add five or more years to my life. I hoped for longer. I told Charlie, "I'm not gonna sit around waiting no more. We got to *do* stuff."

Finally, Charlie had agreed. He would go with me to Japan. We took out a reverse mortgage on our home, one of those old-people loans that paid you the equity of your home until you died, and now we had enough to go.

Mike would look after the house for the three weeks we were gone. He was getting more hours at the pet store, showing up to work on time, keeping his uniform neat and clean. At last, getting more responsible. I had left him stamped envelopes and checks to pay the bills. "Don't forget," I warned him at least four times.

"I won't," he promised, and crossed his heart.

For the first time, I believed he would follow through. He had been changing too, little by little, ever since I had told him about Ronin. After I had told Sue the story in the hospital, I spoke to Mike that very evening. While I still had my courage.

Mike had stared down, rubbing his hands nervously over his hair as I talked. He gulped. "Why didn't you ever tell me?"

"No need for. Daddy and me, we love you." I watched him anxiously, echoing what Charlie had said so many years ago. "Past is past, Mike."

He closed his eyes. "I can't take this." He got up and left, me staring after him. There was nothing to do but hope he came back.

An hour passed. Charlie came in. "Where's Mike? Isn't he supposed to be here?"

"I did something." My voice was faint. "I tell him."

Charlie was silent for a moment. Then he said, "What for?"

"He need to know." I looked at my husband for understanding. His lips were pressed thin. "Please, Charlie. Go home. Talk with him."

Charlie softened. "I can't promise anything, Shoko." He kissed my forehead and left.

Mike returned to me the next morning. He looked tired. He said nothing, just sat down beside me as he always did, refilling my water cup from the pitcher at the bedside table. I wondered if he would even bring up the subject again.

I spoke first. "I do what I think best." I spoke slowly. "I sorry, Mike."

He cleared his throat once, then again. "It explains a lot."

I wanted to ask what Charlie had said to him, but decided not to. That would be between him and Mike, not for me to know. All that mattered was Mike's being there. I touched his hand with mine, tubes trailing, my voice rising. "I no want hurt you, Mike."

"I know, Mom." He smiled briefly, and his eyes met mine. Ronin all over again. "But I don't want to keep talking about it, all right?"

It sounded like something Charlie would say. Mike and my husband were similar in so many ways. And both were more like the Japanese than they knew. A Japanese person was happy to not analyze every problem to death. Sometimes letting go brought more peace than holding on, I realized, though it was harder to do. I pulled the sheets up to my neck and smiled. "Okay."

Mike had not broken, as I had feared. And my secret, uselessly burdening me for so many years, floated away.

A cheer went up from the baseball crowd. I cheered, too, not caring what we were yelling for. It just felt good.

I remembered something else. "I need new suitcase," I said aloud. "We better go store after this." I watched the Cubs pitcher strike out the home team. "Yes!" I stood up and waved my Cubs hat around.

Charlie sighed, holding out his hand to steady me. "There's plenty of time."

I realized he was right. I smiled. "I hungry," I said. "How 'bout hot dog?"

Charlie waved to the vendor with the big box strapped to his front, holding up one finger.

"Five bucks," the vendor said.

Five dollars! Robbery. "That okay. I not that hungry."

Charlie took out his wallet. "How often do we come here?"

I smiled. "Probably only time. But still *takai.*"

Charlie handed me the hot dog. "There

you go."

I took a bite. Watching baseball while eating a hot dog. Now I felt like an American.

Our picture flashed on the JumboTron screen. "Charlie!" I shouted. "Look, there we are!"

We waved frantically, until they went to someone else.

"Wait until Sue hear 'bout this. Maybe we be on the news, too." I polished off the meal, licking mustard off my fingertips.

"Don't bet on it, Shoko-chan."

A breeze blew up and I put on my jacket. Charlie put his arm around me.

I checked the scoreboard: Padres 1, Cubs 2. "Look that! We beat you good, Charlie."

Charlie shrugged. "Like you said, it's early in the game. Let's see what happens."

"Fine." I relaxed against him. "Time for another hot dog. Maybe I have beer, too." I was joking, but Charlie looked horrified. I laughed.

AUTHOR'S NOTE

My mother, Suiko O'Brien, always told me her life would make a great book.

As I was growing up, she regaled me with stories of what had happened to her during her youth in World War II–era Japan. At last, when I was in college and her health had left her bedridden, I asked her to do one last thing for me: record her stories on tape. She obliged, giving me a rambling account of her life.

Several of these stories are incorporated into this novel, including those about how she got shot at by American pilots, how her father picked her new husband from among photographs, and how her extreme beauty caused men to lose their minds over her. I made up all the other stories.

The language Shoko uses in the book was particularly challenging for me. When I studied Japanese, I discovered that some of the words my mother had used when I was growing up were her own personal usages and not grammatically correct Japanese. Since I wanted to preserve the flavor of her speech, I decided to use the same words my mother would have used. Some Japanese speakers might find errors in some of the word choices or spellings, but it's true to how my mother spoke, and how I imagined Shoko speaking. My mother died of an enlarged heart when I was twenty. She was only sixty-one. We never knew what caused the enlarged heart; her doctors speculated it could have been scarlet fever or radiation. There are many new treatment options available since my mother died, including the one that Shoko undergoes in the book, called "left ventricular remodeling." In this, a wedge is removed from the too-large heart. That is an oversimplification, and possibly there's a cardiologist out there who will take me to task, but this is fiction.

The postwar handbook quoted within this book, also titled *How to Be an American Housewife*, is, likewise, fiction, but with a nonfiction inspiration. About twelve years ago, I was going through some cookbooks at my parents' home and found a book entitled *The American Way of Housekeeping*. Written in Japanese and English, it told of how to keep house "the American way" in order not to offend Western sensibilities. I asked my father about it. "I got that for your mother. I thought it was a book for housewives," he told me. "But it was a book for maids." It appeared to have been barely cracked open.

I put the book down and didn't think of it again for a decade. Of course, my father had given it away by then. I finally found a copy after I had written the novel. Written "by the Women of the Occupation" (several officers' wives groups), the book details how to report to "your mistress" and contains recipes as well as cleaning instructions. Though the book was written for maids, another Internet search revealed two references to Japanese brides using it for assimilation. It seems that this book for maids was the best option available at the time.

For the novel, I created my own version of this book, keeping in mind how my mother might have viewed the world back then, through her unique cultural lens.

ACKNOWLEDGMENTS

Thanks to my husband, Keith, for his support and encouragement of my writing and blocking our children from door-pounding at crucial times. Thank you to my children, Elyse, Ethan, and Kaiya, for understanding that Mommy gets cranky when she can't write.

Thank you, Bill and Sharon Dilloway, my parents-in-law, for providing moral support and babysitting services as often as I needed. Thanks to my own family for never telling me I couldn't be a writer when I was little.

Thanks also to several crucial teachers who encouraged me from a young age: Gayle Bean; Norma Garcia; and Carleen Hemrich, who promised to have me back as an author for the Pershing Junior High Book Fair.

To my early readers, Denise Armijo, Hedy Levine, and Barbara Ryan, from the Scripps

College Book Club, who helped rein in a huge blob of a work, thank you. Thanks also to my two later readers, Elizabeth Eberle and Adriane Fleming, for their quick turnaround and moral support.

A big thank-you to Jane Cavolina, freelance book editor and my champion, who would not let me give up.

Thank you to my agent, Elaine Markson, who gave me the greatest early-morning call ever. Thanks also to Gary Johnson, for answering my questions with good humor and alacrity.

And thank you to Peternelle van Arsdale, my editor, who saw the potential in the book and helped me change it in the very best ways possible. She is gracious and generous, a true writer's editor.

ABOUT THE AUTHOR

Margaret Dilloway was inspired by her Japanese mother's experiences when she wrote this novel, and especially by a book her father had given to her mother called *The American Way of Housekeeping.* Dilloway lives in Hawaii with her husband and their three young children. She is at work on her second novel, and also writes a blog, American Housewife.

The employees of Thorndike Press hope you have enjoyed this Large Print book. All our Thorndike, Wheeler, and Kennebec Large Print titles are designed for easy reading, and all our books are made to last. Other Thorndike Press Large Print books are available at your library, through selected bookstores, or directly from us.

For information about titles, please call:
(800) 223-1244

or visit our Web site at:
http://gale.cengage.com/thorndike

To share your comments, please write:

Publisher
Thorndike Press
295 Kennedy Memorial Drive
Waterville, ME 04901